Our Season in Grasmere

Part II of The Grasmere Saga

Adapted from a Story By
Nellie Cohen Wright

Written By
Chuck Goode

First Edition

Printed in the United States of America

ISBN: 978-0-9912166-3-5

Goode God Publishing

Introduction

In the research leading to the publishing of "Prepare for Us a Season", Part 1 of The Grasmere Saga, we knew that there was far more to this history than could be contained in one volume. So "Our Season in Grasmere" was written sequentially to follow George and Theresa into their new lives, in Glastonbury, CT.

We will get to live the experiences of George and Theresa as they live out the stories our grandmother told of the wonderful life she and our grandfather had lived in Glastonbury, on the acres they called Grasmere, before treachery ripped it from them.

Though not burdened by the crushing weight of the Jim Crow laws they left behind in Georgia, Theresa and George found that they could never escape the malicious intentions of those whose diminished spirits were advocates for its effects. That being said, it could not deter their faith or diminish their effort to pursue the dreams and the genius that drove George Cohen to great success in his business. Along the way, he and Theresa met some marvelous friends of all colors, and proved themselves worthy friends as well.

In the midst of the industrial revolution and World War I, the farmers in central Connecticut prospered as they gained the reputation of being the finest cigar wrapper leaf tobacco growers in the world. It is in that environment that the saga progresses and the love story continues to grow; because, after all, that's what this is all about; a celebration of the love affair between the woman we affectionately call "Pank", and the man she called "Son".

Acknowledgements

To Nellie Cohen Wright: Who took the written and verbal history of her mother and father and put them together into the outline of the story that forms the basis of this novel. Her drive and enthusiasm and perseverance were instrumental in bringing this project into being.

To her sisters: Lucy Elizabeth Green, Lillian Polite, and Yvonne Goode Satterfield, for their tremendous help in filling in so many of the blanks and adding so much to the flavor of this novel.

To their children and grandchildren: Thank you for your dedicated efforts to uncover the truth about our family. This group worked for years in digging through archives of information to bring credibility to the history of our grandparents that had previously only been folklore. Their dedication and perseverance was key to the creation of the story, especially during the time George and Theresa lived in Connecticut.

To Wynter Cuthbert, our cousin who did a monumental job of uncovering documents for almost all the descendants of my grandmother's grandmother, Martha Williams. Wynter has written her own historical novel, dedicated to the brave women in her branch of our family: Eliza's Dream.

Above all I give honor to God for His input, for there are creative inputs in this novel that exceed my capabilities. May our Lord and savior, Jesus Christ, be glorified in the results of our joint efforts.

A Tribute to My Grandfather

George W. Cohen

None of my generation ever met him. He was taken from his family before some of his children were old enough to formulate memories, but we knew him from the loving memories that Gram shared about her "Son". Shortly after it became apparent that the legacy George Cohen had intended for his family was more than romanticized memories of a heartbroken woman, but a real estate that was stolen from our family, many of us felt an urgency to place that legacy back into the hands of his descendents. Before the first words of this novel were penned, I was awakened out of my sleep, and like many experiences before, the Lord gave me words that I simply had to write as fast as my hands could put them to paper. The Holy Spirit wrote the dedication to our grandfather

Dear Grandpa,

The Holy Spirit woke me to tell me to write this letter to you. He told me to let you know that your prayers have been answered.

Your children and their children and their children have not forgotten you, nor are they untouched by the sacrifices you made for their provision. The Lord is poised to restore that which the locust and the cankerworm have eaten. The wealth you built for your children was so cruelly snatched by evildoers, but the riches you stored in safe places have sustained us; the seed of faith, the ray of hope, the touch of decency that have transcended the generations through rejoicing and tears continue to blossom within us, and lift us to seek the highest of your hopes.

Gram spoke of you with reverence. Her loving recollections of you are the only windows through which we are able to see you. Gram loved you very much, and because we so loved her, it was easy for us to embrace you in love as well. Your prayers for her were answered. Although she was defrauded, she was never devoid of that which was most valuable; the love you had one for the other, and the love of your children. We rejoiced in gathering together in her presence. We learned at her knee, laughed at her stories, marveled at her vigor, and cared for her until the day she died. She was never alone, never unloved, never unprotected.

Because of her, in honor of you, we bear your name with pride. Cohen: our Sinai connection. Our tie to the twelve tribes of Israel; mixed with the seeds from the motherland; united with the fruit of the maiden native of America. We stand as the symphony of your love song; a melody of strength. A family knit evermore by the harmonies of love that blend common notes in different keys into one beautiful song.

I am proud to be your grandson. Rest in peace. Rest until we come, one by one, to dance with you in the morning dew that kisses the grass beneath our feet in the meadows of Grasmere.

Chapter One

As she listenend to the clackedy clack of the train wheels against the iron tracks, Theresa's mind was dancing somewhere between dreams and conscious remembrances. She recalled the day that she had met the man next to her; the man that she did not even know six months ago; the man that she had vowed to love and cherish all the days of her life; the man she was following to a life built on nothing more than their love, their hopes and faith, and his friendship with a man he hardly knew. She recalled that Saturday on the way to the annual picnic. The sky was deep and wide and blue and clear, and the sun was warm and bright, the air was light and crisp, and the breeze seemed like a thousand soothing hands to administer their effects. The music of the birds seemed symphonic as they harmonized with the melodic laughter of the growing crowds as they greeted each other as they merged onto the main road from every direction flowing to a single destination.

She thought about the special dresses she and Mary had worn on that day, and how they both knew they were looking fine. She remembered how Mary had pointed out the handsome stranger standing with their old friend Felix. She remembered how the only words that would come out of her mouth that day were "Oh, my!". She chuckled to herself.

And now, here they were, together, racing through the dark night towards Savannah; towards a life that, by all accounts, would exceed any vision she had of her life birthed in Bradley Quarters.

She recalled her father's powerful prayer over his family, especially his Reesie, and Geoerge. She knew it was difficult for him to remain strong, since he knew that this would be his good-bye embrace. After he had declared, "Dese an all thangs I ast in de mighty name of Jesus, Amen.", he broke from the "circle" and held her close, his arms encircling her shoulders; her hands cupping his shoulder blades. He gave her one final squeeze, kissed her forehead, shook Georges hand, and turned and silently walked into the empty parlor. Silence fell on the excited gathering as they heard the baleful wailing of his harmonica coming from that room, carrying the melody of "This May Be the Last Time". Everyone quietly walked out of the house.

On the porch, Theresa hugged her brothers and sisters, one by one. Alice and Amy were crying; Gabe and Mary had smiles and words of encouragement, as did John, but he had misty eyes. She then turned and embraced her mother again. They were calm; they had cried their last cry earlier. Sara softly whispered in her daughter's ear, "In yo' crown, there are many stars." With that she stepped back, and bravely smiled as she approvingly surveyed her daughter again.

Little Kay was crying because he sensed the gravity of the situation more so than fully grasped the impact. Everyone was crying because they knew that the woman he had come to know as Momma was going away, and away must be a bad thing if it was making everyone cry. "You gonna stay wit gramma Sara fo a time, an then ya gonna come stay wit me an Poppa George." She had never really settled on a name for Kay to call George. They would work that out later. He was crying uncontrollably; runny nose and all. "Always remembah I loves you!" As she stood, he grabbed her and hugged her and called her name again and again until Mary led him back into the house.

Theresa could see the tears welling up in her mother's eyes, and could feel herself losing control, so she quickly pulled her mother back against her, hugged her ever so briefly, and said "Momma, I love you!" she turned and walked off the porch.

John Hale nervously cleared his throat as he brought them out of their reverie. He had startled them and they quickly corrected their seating arrangements. "I'm sorry to disturb you, but there is something on my mind. I've dreaded this conversation. I am personally embarrassed by the situation." Hale took a seat across from them and offered minimal eye contact.

George could feel his heart pounding as Hale spoke those ominous words. "What's wrong Mr. Hale?"

He glanced at George momentarily, then looked away as he began speaking. "The ship we're taking to New York is owned by the Ocean Steamship Company of Savannah. Under the laws of this country, an ocean going vessel can exercise the Civil Rights of its charter state to determine how race issues are handled on the ship. Georgia law allows these companies to do whatever they want; from excluding colored people, to providing separate accommodations. Damn it! Pardon me Theresa. I worked as hard as I could; I threatened; I called in favors. The best I could do was to get you a place in the section they have for servants travelling with their employers. There were no boats registered in the north making this run. I'm sorry, George. I wanted better for you. I wanted better for your wife. I'm sorry." He was sincere; George had seen him in action before, remembering the incident in the rail yards in Eufaula when they first met, but he still felt the anger welling up in him.

"I know you're sorry Mr. Hale, but if I had known I would have to expose my wife to this...."

"Son, we'll be okay. It only gonna be a couple of days; right Mr. Hale?"

"Yes, Theresa. But George, believe me I understand. The reason I didn't tell you before was that I was working even until we met this afternoon to get you a regular room, but these damn, racist, redneck bastards; pardon me again Theresa; can't do anything but peddle hatred based on the color of a man's skin. Pardon me again Theresa, but I will find a way to make these bastards pay. They'll learn who John Hale really is. You two were too happy when I saw you so I was waiting for a good moment. There really couldn't be any, so here we are." Hale was desperately trying to get George to understand that he despised the situation as much as he did.

"Mr. Hale, I appreciate your efforts, but I will not have my wife exposed to that kind of treatment. I hear stories that there are all kinds of foul intentioned riff-raff thrown in with decent folks, and they all share one big room with cots, like in an army barracks. We can just turn around here and go back home. I'll meet you there later." George was finding it hard to control his anger, though he did not feel anger toward Hale, just the circumstances.

"I admit this is bad, but it's not that kind of bad. I've heard stories too. This company, for what it's worth, is one of the better companies. They have modern ships. Big plush ships, so the people they service pay more money; and those people wouldn't want to get on board with that class of people; white or colored. No George, this ship has separate servants' facilities. Everyone has their own rooms except where arrangements were made to have people share. They are rooms like most of the other rooms except they are not as fancy, and they are the rooms nobody else wants because of where they are on the ship; on the lower deck, and close to where the rudder and propellers are, so they can be noisier and they are usually harder to keep cool when it's hot out. The crew usually gets the worst rooms, next to the engines and directly over the power plant. I was told that your room would be the quietest and the most comfortable available. I am told the cabins are more than tolerable. The City of Montgomery, that's the name of the ship, is just over a year old, so everything is still nice and fresh. The part I have the most problem with is just the idea that they have a completely different set-up for coloreds and whites."

George examined Theresa's reaction to what Hale had just said, but could not get a read on her emotions. She didn't have the same high expectations he had of being thrust into a world where she would be treated as an equal. "Son, if it ain't okay when we get on the boat, we can always get off, but there ain't nothing better waitin' for us in Stewart County. I'll be okay for a couple of days!"

"You're right. It is as it is. Hopefully we can make a mark in this world so our children and their children won't have the same burdens. I understand Mr. Hale. And I know if it was up to you, there wouldn't be any of this mess, but it's out of all of our hands. Let's just get to Connecticut." George realized that he had set his expectations too high. It was naïve to think that a system so ingrained in hatred would change to accommodate his wistful hopes.

As they approached the dock area, Theresa was unable to stifle a gasp as the ships came into view. She was expecting the ships to be larger than the ferries she had been used to seeing on the Chattahoochee, but these ships were gigantic by comparison.

"They're amazing aren't they!" Hale said, seeing the amazement in Theresa's eyes. "That one with the big stack and the two masts; that's our ship, The City of Montgomery."

"Oh my God! That boat is huge!" Theresa didn't know if she was frightened or excited by the prospect of cruising out in the ocean on something that large.

George, still in somewhat of a bad mood, had to smile himself when he saw the "City of Montgomery". Built in early 1910, the vessel was 404 feet long and about 50 feet wide. It was designed as a combination cargo and passenger ship, and could accommodate about 225 passengers. Along with its sister ships, they were a primary link between the southern markets, shipping from Savannah, to New York and Boston. The hull of the long sleek looking ship was black, and the cabin area was white. The sides were lined with lifeboats, and there were two wooden masts at either end of the boat. These were actually the cranes that were used to load the fore and aft storage areas. The deck was about twenty five feet above the dock, and right around the middle of the ship, the huge smoke stack extended about thirty feet above the top deck, to carry the residual smoke coming from the coal burning furnaces that fueled the mighty steam engines.

There were about twenty people who had traveled on the same train who were headed to the same destination. The crew was expecting this group. They were the last of the passengers to arrive. They expertly handled the group and soon had everyone headed to their cabins, where they would spend the next two days plus a few hours. There were lounge chairs on the deck as the group moved toward the hatch that would take them into the interior corridor that would lead them to their cabins. George and Theresa were held to the end of the line, and Hale waited to walk with them. As they walked the long hall to the rear of the ship, people peeled off of the group as they arrived at their cabins. Soon, it was only the steward, Theresa, George, and Hale walking to the end of the hall. As they approached another hatchway, the steward turned to Hale.

"Sir, we must have passed your cabin. What is your cabin number?" he asked.

"I know where my cabin is! I just wanted to make sure my people are comfortable!" Hale responded, somewhat short tempered. He quickly realized he was barking at the wrong man, because the steward had no more power over the situation than he did.

"Very well sir, then just follow me, I will take these good people to their accommodations." The steward responded.

Once through the hatchway, they were confronted with two flights of stairs; one headed up, and on headed down. The stewards lead the way to the down staircase and they clanked their way down the metal stairs.

"This area is what we call steerage accommodations. The cabins are not quite as large as those in first class, and there is a bit more drive noise down here, but actually, our cleaning crew takes pride in keeping these accommodations pristine so that those not fortunate enough to travel first class will still have a pleasant experience with us."

They walked about halfway down the hall, and they stopped in front of door 17C. The steward stepped aside as George fit the key to the lock and opened the door. He could barely get his foot in the door before Hale had half stepped into the room to see what it was like. Having been on this same vessel coming to Georgia back in April, he was familiar with the layout of the first-class cabins. He was happy to see that it was neat and clean, and well appointed; not lavish like the first-class accommodations, but certainly not shoddy. It was considerably smaller than first-class, but not unusual for a steamship cabin. Hale looked at George, who he still blocked from entering. "What do you think? Is this okay?"

"It looks fine. What do you think Baby?" He and Hale stepped out of the door to give her a full view of the room.

Theresa smiled. "It's nice, Son. We'll be fine." She had been prepared for a lot worse, and compared to the lifestyle she was accustomed to, it was actually an up-grade in her eyes.

Hale turned to the steward. "And where are the facilities?"

"I was getting to that, Sir. The colored facilities are across the hall at that third door. The colored dining facilities are through the last set of doors down the fore corridor. They are comfortable and right at the kitchen, so service is prompt. Breakfast is served from 6AM until 10AM, lunch from 11 until 3PM, and dinner from 5 until 9PM. The porthole in your cabin is not functional. Cooling pipes run through the walls, and you have a vent for some air flow. If you need anything, any uniformed staff will be glad to accommodate you. The porter will be along shortly with your luggage. Have a good night. We sail promptly at 6AM."

"Well George, now that we've got you situated, I'm going to get along too. I wish it could have been better, but this is still Georgia. It will be better in Connecticut. I promise. Oh, by the way, I'm in cabin 3A if you need me. I would expect you two want to continue your honeymoon, so don't feel obligated to catch up with me, or linger when you see me, unless you want to."

"Thanks, Mr. Hale. Sounds like a plan. See you in New York!" With that George guided Theresa through the cabin door.

Theresa was saying, "Night, Mr. Hale!" as the door slammed shut. They embraced as soon as the door was closed behind them, and both began to giggle like school children throwing spitballs at the teacher's back. George picked her up and spun once and they landed on the bed. It was soft and bouncy and squeaked slightly. George kissed her and bounced on the bed to make the springs squeak.

"I don't think our neighbors are gonna get much sleep tonight!" George said, continuing to make the bed squeak.

"Stop it, Son! What the porter gonna think when he bring our stuff?"

"Well if he has half a brain, he won't stop. He'll take those bags right back and come back at a better time." Still bouncing to make the bed springs squeak, he pulled Theresa to him, and still giggling, he tried to kiss her.

She was laughing too, but she pushed him away and said, "Son, now stop, we gonna need our clothes an stuff!"

Pulling his head back away from hers so he could focus on her face, he said, "Baby, we don't need no clothes! And I got all the stuff you need!"

Theresa gasped in mock insult, and playfully slapped him on his head. "Why Mr. Cohen, I do believe you are a rogue! Oh, how sweet it is!" With that she pulled him to her and kissed him passionately. He stopped giggling.

The knock at the door interrupted their interlude. "Porter" they heard the voice behind the door announcing.

George quickly responded, "Be right there!" He jumped up, straightened himself, and headed to the door. He turned to make sure that Theresa had proper time to adjust herself as well, and he opened the door. George was a bit taken aback as he opened the door; he was confronted by the whitest smile, surrounded by the biggest pinkest lips, engulfed in the blackest face he had ever seen. The smile reached almost to his ears, and caused his jowls to ride his cheekbones almost to the point that they were level with his eyes.

"Evenin', suh! My name is Jefferson an I have yo luggage. Would ya be needin' me ta set them inside fo ya?"

Still somewhat distracted, George said, "No. No that's okay. I can get 'em. Thank you!" The more he looked at him, the more he was amazed at his perfectly white teeth and the smoothness of his jet black skin. Snapping back out of it, George reached into his pocket and found a quarter to give the porter.

"Thank you, suh. We heard y'all was honeymoonin' so we set y'all up wit the best cabin. We ain't full this trip, so we made sho they won't no folks on either side of y'all. These beds squeak somethin' fierce!" he and George giggled like conspiring school boys.

"Yeah, we know!" George turned and winked at his wife.

"Well, we put extra bedpans an wash basins an pillows in heah fo y'all. We heard yo boss, da peach king, tole our boss's boss dat if we didn't take special care of y'all, all hell was gonna break loose. From what we hears, our big boss own da railroad too, an dat da peach king is one of his biggest customers, so he ain't lookin ta

11

lose dat money! You know how white folks love dat money!" Jefferson chuckled at his statement. "So, anything y'all need, jes let me know. We right down yondah in da kitchen!" What happened next made them all break out in laughter. Jefferson began speaking in a very deep and formal voice. "Sir, Madam! It is indeed an honor to have two such distinguished guests on our modest vessel, and we place ourselves totally at your service. If there is nothing more for which I may be at your service for the moment, I wish you both a pleasant evening. We sail promptly at 6AM!" He winked, tipped his hat, and turned and strutted back towards the kitchen area.

George was still laughing when he locked the door behind him. "Can you believe that? I wonder what all that was about! That Mr. Hale is something else, isn't he?"

"Yeah he is. He got these folks steppin! I bet he's been trained to speak like that around white folks, an was jes lettin' himself relax with us!" Theresa paused, and then started chuckling. "Kinda like me round yo momma! I mean somewhat similar to me being in the presence of your mother!" Theresa couldn't resist the temptation. She had so much of her father's humor in her! "Phew! That was the blackest man I ever seen in my life, an I seen some sun-baked Negroes out in them cotton fields! His people must be the darkest tribe in Africa, and he ain't mixed with nothin'! But you know what they say! 'The blacker the berry, the sweeter the juice!' "

Displaying his hands up and down his body in mock anger, "So what are you saying about me?"

"Oh, Mr. Cohen, you almost got me convinced last night that that ain't true, but I need just a wee bit more convincin'! How sweet is your juice, Mr. Cohen?" Theresa asked coquettishly.

George grabbed her and kissed her and then said, "I can show ya better than I can tell ya!" And they found peace in each other's arms after their first full day as man and wife.

The deep whistle of the City of Montgomery startled them both from their deep sleep. "What in the world was that, Son?" Before he could answer the ship lurched, and she was aware that they were leaving the dock. It must be 6AM, she thought.

"That was the signal horn..."

"Yeah, I know. I was just a bit woozy at first. I know we're leavin!" Then, quickly changing subjects, she added. "I'm starvin'! You hungry, Son?"

"I can see it's gonna take some money to feed you!" He ducked as she smacked him on his head. "Just joking! I thought you'd never ask! You wanna get up now and eat and then get some sleep; because I need some energy and I need some rest!"

"You complainin, Mr. Cohen? I don't remember puttin' no gun ta yo head!" Theresa teased back.

"Baby, you won't ever need a gun ta get me close to you. In fact, if we get me some food and give me a couple of hours sleep, you just might need that gun to get me away from you!" he said, ducking again, expecting a smack to his head, which was Theresa's preferred show of appreciation for his attempts at being the comedian at her expense.

Breakfast was very good, and very filling. They ate like they never expected to see food again. The kitchen staff, all black, were aware of who they were and that they were celebrating, and they could not have been more gracious. They invited them to a crew party that night. It would just be a few of the black crew members and the black guests, getting together listening to music and dancing, and having a few drinks. The whites had a fancy dinner club with a band and a singer. The crew offered this, once each trip, as part of their commitment to help keep things 'separate but equal'.

They slept and laid around most of the day. Later, they dressed up and ventured out to the deck area to see the ocean. They got a lot of stares. By law, they couldn't stare back. They saw Hale and waved. He returned their greeting, but neither made a move toward the other. Hale was engaged in conversation with three men who also acknowledged them by ever so slightly tipping their hats in their direction. George did the same.

George caught a glimpse of a man staring at him intently as his gaze turned away from Hale, but the man turned immediately when he saw the direction of George's attention change. Although he did not get a good look at the person's face, there was something familiar about him that he just couldn't put his finger on. He explained it away in his mind as it being just the look that was familiar. It was probably just another unknown snooty face, framed in hatred, refusing to acknowledge the presence of a black man in their bigoted world. It was probably one of the passengers from the train that he had subconsciously noticed that caused him to find the face familiar.

They didn't stay long. Everyone was so pretentious, standing around having terribly important conversations as they sweltered in the hot August afternoon sun in full dress attire; and the women were just as formally dressed, but most had on bonnets and carried parasols that matched their dresses. Besides, few of the stares were friendly, and it made it quite uncomfortable. Having seen enough, they went back down to their little love nest.

They ate a late dinner. There were more people there now than earlier. Most were servants of passengers travelling to second homes or relocating, but a few had made clandestine arrangements to get passage. One couple was related to an employee of one of the shareholders of the Central Georgia Railway, which owned The Ocean Steamship Company of Savannah, which owned the City of Montgomery. Like George, he had found favor and had been hired to oversee the handling of the tons of cotton shipped to the New York textile companies on board Ocean Steamship vessels. Sally and William Foster were a bit older than Theresa; a bit younger than George. They shared life experiences and current events and discussed some history that lead to the volatile times they found themselves in. Before long, the piano began to play, and a harmonica joined in. One of the maids was a singer, as were two of the porters. One of the waitresses joined in later. The singer announced Theresa and George's recent marriage, and everyone joined in to sing "Let Me Call You Sweetheart". They danced and told stories. There were snacks from the kitchen and someone had some moonshine.

Jefferson stood up and all of the ship's people applauded as if they were expecting great things. He didn't disappoint. He told a few stories about his adventures getting passengers situated, and made jokes about how he played to their expectations of who and what he was. As it turned out he was the son of an African diplomat and he was working the steamships during the summers to absorb the culture, see the country, and get extra money for his education. He was a Harvard student, following the footsteps W.E.B. Du Bois and other notable black scholars. He had plans to return to his parents' home of Ghana and help develop that country's economy. He was born in America, and had made himself a master of dialects. He also considered himself an actor of sorts, and often did one-man shows of famous men. After singing a powerful rendition of "Old Man River" he began speaking in his most formal dialect.

"This is a letter from a freedman to his former owner, who, after the war, wants him to return to work for him for wages. He is dictating this to be written:"

Jefferson takes on a more Southern flavored dialect at this point.

"Dayton, Ohio August 7, 1865, to my old master, Colonel P. H. Anderson, Big Spring, Tennessee.

Sir:

I got your letter, and was glad to find that you had not forgotten Jourdon, and that you wanted me to come back and live with you again, promising to do better for me than anybody else can. I have often felt uneasy about you. I thought the Yankees would have hung you long before this, for harboring Rebs they found at your house. I suppose they never heard about your going to Colonel Martin's to kill the Union soldier that was left by his company in their stable. Although you shot at me twice before I left you, I did not want to hear of your being hurt, and am glad you are still living. It would do me good to go back to the dear old home again, and see Miss Mary and Miss Martha and Allen, Esther, Green, and Lee. Give my love to them all, and tell them I hope we will meet in the better world, if not in this. I would have gone back to see you all when I was working in the Nashville Hospital, but one of the neighbors told me that Henry intended to shoot me if he ever got a chance.

I want to know particularly what the good chance is you propose to give me. I am doing tolerably well here. I get twenty-five dollars a month, with victuals and clothing; have a comfortable home for Mandy,—the folks call her Mrs. Anderson— and the children—Milly, Jane, and Grundy—go to school and are learning well. The teacher says Grundy has a head for a preacher. They go to Sunday school, and Mandy and me attend church regularly. We are kindly treated. Sometimes we overhear others saying, "Them colored people were slaves down in Tennessee". The children feel hurt when they hear such remarks; but I tell them it was no disgrace in Tennessee to belong to Colonel Anderson. Many darkeys would have been proud, as I used to be, to call you master. Now if you will write and say what wages you will give me, I will be better able to decide whether it would be to my advantage to move back again.

As to my freedom, which you say I can have, there is nothing to be gained on that score, as I got my free papers in 1864 from the Provost-Marshal-General of the Department of Nashville. Mandy says she would be afraid to go back without some proof that you were disposed to treat us justly and kindly; and we have concluded to test your sincerity by asking you to send us our wages for the time we served you. This will make us forget and forgive old scores, and rely on your justice and friendship in the future.

I served you faithfully for thirty-two years, and Mandy twenty years. At twenty-five dollars a month for me, and two dollars a

17

week for Mandy, our earnings would amount to eleven thousand six hundred and eighty dollars. Add to this the interest for the time our wages have been kept back, and deduct what you paid for our clothing, and three doctor's visits to me, and pulling a tooth for Mandy, and the balance will show what we are in justice entitled to. Please send the money by Adams's Express, in care of V. Winters, Esq., Dayton, Ohio. If you fail to pay us for faithful labors in the past, we can have little faith in your promises in the future. We trust the good Maker has opened your eyes to the wrongs which you and your fathers have done to me and my fathers, in making us toil for you for generations without recompense. Here I draw my wages every Saturday night; but in Tennessee there was never any pay-day for the Negroes any more than for the horses and cows. Surely there will be a day of reckoning for those who defraud the laborer of his hire.

In answering this letter, please state if there would be any safety for my Milly and Jane, who are now grown up, and both good-looking girls. You know how it was with poor Matilda and Catherine. I would rather stay here and starve—and die, if it come to that—than have my girls brought to shame by the violence and wickedness of their young masters. You will also please state if there has been any schools opened for the colored children in your neighborhood. The great desire of my life now is to give my children an education, and have them form virtuous habits.

Say howdy to George Carter, and thank him for taking the pistol from you when you were shooting at me.

From your old servant,

Jourdon Anderson."

And with that, he literally skipped into the kitchen. He had started speaking with a piece of paper in his hand as if reading a letter, but it quickly became evident that he was reciting what he was saying. His small audience gave him an enthusiastic applause and several cheers amidst laughter. The crowd was abuzz with conversation about the letter he had just recited to them.

After a while, Theresa and George went back to their "honeymoon suite", and honeymooned! The next day, they continued to spend most of their time alone together, but managed to find some time to spend with their new-found friends.

Late Wednesday evening, shortly after they returned from their supper, there was a knock on the door. "Porter" a voice said from the other side. George looked at Theresa quizzically, as if to ask if she had asked for a porter, and she shrugged to suggest that she was as puzzled as he was. He got up from his seat on the side of the bed and walked the few steps to the door.

"What do you need?" George asked the voice behind the door.

"Just making arrangements for your move out tomorrow morning." With that response George opened the door. As soon as the latch was undone there was a sudden burst of pressure that drove George back into the room, as two white men entered. Their faces were not friendly, but one was familiar. It was the face that had troubled him for that fleeting moment the other day, when he and Theresa had gone out to the deck. Now it came back to him in a flash. It was the young broker he had the altercation with in Eufaula. The man Hale had intervened with and sent packing like a wounded pup. He had wondered what had become of him, because he never saw him again until now!

George quickly recovered his momentum and instinctively lunged at the two men. He stopped dead in his tracks when the derringer was stuck in his face. At the end of the derringer was the shorter of the two men, the one George had never seen. He glared into his menacing bloodshot eyes. George could detect the smell of alcohol as the man stood tense and stiff, almost panting with rage or fear or both.

"Now boy, don't be so hasty. My frien' Pup heah is a might nervous bout us comin down heah like this, so ain't no tellin' when he's gonna snap. I jes came heah ta say 'Hi', an ta meet yo bride." With that he turned his attention to Theresa. "Hey, gal, ain't had the pleasure. I'm Gibbs, Johnny Gibbs, but you kin call me 'Suh'; got dat?" To which he laughed until his already flushed face turned a deeper shade of red. By their conduct and the fumes that came from Gibbs' mouth with each word he spoke, George was sure that both men had drunk more liquor than they could handle. Theresa did not respond. She just stared at him. All the disdain she had within her for this brand of red neck came pouring through her eyes.

"Well boy, yo wife seem ta be jes as uppity as yo mongrel ass! That's okay. She's in love. But I come ta show her jes how much a man you ain't. Now that Hale ain't here ta protect yo black ass, you ain't so much, are ya?" George didn't respond. His mind was racing and he was far too busy assessing the situation and figuring a way to at least diffuse the situation until he could figure out how to overcome these two. "Now dat ain't mannerable niggah! I ast you if ya think you a real man without Hale at yo back?" George still didn't answer. This enraged Gibbs. "Why you uppity niggah!", but that wasn't enough to quench his rage. He screamed at the top of his lungs "Niggah! I'll kill you, you mongrel Jew bastard! I'll kill you an' this yella' wench!"

At that moment there were three loud pounds on the thick wooden door. "Hey, y'all alright?" Simultaneously, Theresa screamed "No! Help us! They gonna kill us!" The gunman was startled by the knock and half turned towards the sound, taking the gun out of George's face and turning it towards empty space.

George saw this as the best chance of at least protecting Theresa, so he went for the gunman's wrist that held the gun, and used his momentum as he turned towards the door to turn his body towards Gibbs, as his free forearm wrapped securely under the shorter man's pronounced Adams Apple. Gibbs had responded and was trying to free George's grip from his partner's gun hand. The derringer expelled its lone shot, and Gibbs screamed. George didn't know if he was shot, or if the scream was from the heavy chamber pot that Theresa had just crashed on his head at the same time of the report from the gun. Gibbs didn't say another word as he slid heavily down the wall into a sitting position. Theresa was all over him as he was descending with a barrage of punches, slaps, and kicks.

George had full control of the gunman as he had maneuvered himself directly behind him and was literally hanging the man from his forearm, despite the constant pleas of "I give! I give!" After the man fell unconscious, George let him go and gave him a solid right hook to the side of his head as he fell to the floor.

He immediately turned to Theresa who was standing over Gibbs' now prone body and continuing her onslaught of kicks. All the while her voice was keeping cadence with her heel as it pounded indiscriminately over his upper torso, "I – will - kill - you - you – low - life - crackah - bastard! I – will - kill - you.." He grabbed her by the waist and lifted her and spun her, still kicking, away from the now motionless body.

The door suddenly flew open and Jefferson and three other black men from the ship's crew barged into the room, looking as if they had come ready for a fight. Two had bully clubs and one, a chef, had a meat cleaver. Their rage turned to amusement as soon as they assessed the situation. George was still holding Theresa off the ground, as she was still struggling to free herself to release the rest of her rage on Gibbs. The two assailants were lying unconscious on the floor. The spent derringer was lying in the middle of the floor towards the other side of the room. Jefferson was the first to break the silence. "I thought you asked for help, Miss Theresa!" They all laughed except Theresa, who was still enraged, even after George had let her go.

"Thanks for coming, but things fell to pieces just about the time you all knocked on the door."

"That was me. I was coming down the hall and I saw these two white men outside your door talking. I ducked back in a hallway to keep my eyes on 'em. Don't many white folks come down these halls voluntarily unless there's a lady doing some business down here, if you know what I mean. Well they just seemed to be up to some mischief. I heard that one" he said, pointing at Gibbs, "saying some pretty nasty things about Mr. Hale the other day, so I figured he didn't mean y'all any good."

"Yeah, there's some history there. I'll tell you about it later."

"That's okay. I figured they were up to no good, and then I saw them barge into your room. I came and stood outside the door just to make sure there was nothing bad going on when I hear one of 'em start screaming Nigger, and that he was going to kill you. That's when I banged on the door and Miss Theresa screamed for help."

Hearing this, and having regained some of her composure and a taste of her humor, Theresa asked, "Is that really what you heard? Or did you hear me sayin' 'help us keep from killin these dumb crackahs'?"

The man with the cleaver kiddingly handed it to Theresa as he and the others were laughing at her statement, and said, "Nex' time use dis. It cost a lot less dan dat bedpan you smashed on dat crackah's head!" He was struggling to get the words out as he laughed and directed the others to look at Gibbs, still stone cold, lying with chunks and shards of the broken bedpan scattered all around him.

Jefferson was the first to bring the situation back in focus. "This is serious. We got two white men lying unconscious, with six black folks standing around them. We have a problem. First let's see if these boys are still breathing." George checked the gunman. He shook him a bit and he moaned, although he didn't wake up. One of the other men checked Gibbs. They shook him, but he didn't respond. "Go get some ammonia on a rag. Let's see if that will wake these boys up." Jefferson gave his direction to no one in particular, but Mr. Meat Cleaver hurriedly opened the door and sped away towards the kitchen.

George also grasped the severity of the situation. "We don't have any witnesses but us, and a black man can't testify against a white

23

man in Georgia. They'll charge us for attempted murder, or worse if we can't bring these guys back. What are we going to do?"

One of the bully club bearers answered. "Seem ta me dese boys needs ta go swimmin'. Ain't nobody but us gonna know, an ain't none of us gonna tell!"

Jefferson beat George to the response. "No! We can't even think along those lines..."

"You're right!" George added before he could finish.

"..unless we have to." Jefferson finished.

"I wouldn't trust these men to keep their word, even if they promise not to bring charges." George did not mean to verbalize his thought, because he had not figured out an alternative course of action to stop them from bringing charges.

"What you talkin' 'bout. Them bring charges? What about them bustin' they way into our room and threatenin' ta kill us! Why can't we bring charges against them?" Theresa asked, still emboldened by her anger.

"You're right Baby, but we still can't testify against them. The only way we could successfully bring charges against them would be if we had a white witness to the situation. These men would just as soon see us do life on the chain gang as to look at us..." his voice trailed off as he continued almost to himself, "...but we can't let that happen."

"What about Mr. Hale? Do you think he would help us?" Jefferson asked, including himself in the dilemma.

"How can he help us? He couldn't change the law that kept us from having to sit on the 'colored' car on the train, unless he used his own rail car, and he couldn't get us a room anywhere on this boat except for in the colored section. So, how is he gonna get us a position with the law except for in the colored section?" George deducted as he responded to Jefferson.

There was a knock on the door and they let Mr. Meat Cleaver back in, without his weapon of choice, but with a white hand towel wet on one end with ammonia. "Good. Now wave it under their noses real slow, but don't block the flow of air. They need to be able to breathe deep." Jefferson directed. "That's Peter," Jefferson said apologetically having never introduced the three would be rescuers to George and Theresa. Then turning his head to the other two standing by, "and that's Frederick and Isaiah."

"Thanks for coming to the rescue." George said as Peter was waving the ammonia rag under the gunman's nose. He responded immediately, coughing and snorting and swiping at his nose. As he gained consciousness, his eyes widened as he understood his predicament; he was surrounded by five black men in a very compromising position. He tried to jump up, but Frederick quickly stepped to him as Peter moved to check on Gibbs. "Ya bes be stayin' put til we decides ya kin move! Y'understan?" He only nodded his response, as he stared over to where Gibbs was lying motionless.

Peter was frantically waving the towel under Gibbs' nose, but there was no reaction. "His breathing is too shallow for him to really suck up much of the ammonia. Put your hand over his mouth and nose until I tell you to stop, and then put the rag under his nose while you're holding your hand over his mouth." Peter followed his instructions, and then, after about thirty seconds, Jefferson said, "Now!"

Gibbs gasped as he inhaled the ammonia gas, and immediately began snorting and coughing, but his eye never opened. He just rolled his head ever so slightly. "Do it again!" Jefferson directed Peter. Just as he was about to restart his ministrations, a flood of water hit Gibbs square in his face.

"There, maybe dat will help his sorry butt!" Theresa said as she held the large pitcher over his head. It did have some effect as the shock of the relatively cool water poured against his hot head, caused him to open his mouth as he gasped at the sudden invasion of his senses.

He immediately began to moan as he clutched both hands to his head. "Oh my head! My head! Help me! My head!" he repeated over and over. After a while, he too surveyed his surroundings, and his mean spirit returned. "You niggahs best be gittin me to a doctor! What am I doin heah?"

Out of nowhere a deep African dialect filled the room, as Jefferson took on a more threatening character. "In my tribe, we slice the necks of our captives, reach down their throats and pull out their hearts, take a bite from it and show it to them before life slips from them! Do you want such a moment to cherish, white man?" He had pulled a very threatening looking knife from somewhere on his person and was waving it under Gibbs' nose as he spoke.

Gibbs answered with a weak and sheepish "No."

"Good! Now shut up your face and stand up! You too!" he shouted as he turned from Gibbs to the gunman. Both struggled to get to their feet, but Gibbs needed help to stand and to remain standing.

Jefferson turned away from the two men and smiled and winked at George and Theresa, before continuing in his African dialect. "We will take them away until you decide if you will show them mercy or if we should feed them to the fish!" Still with his back to the two men, Jefferson silently mouthed, "I will be right back." Then turning back to the rest of the men, he directed at no one in particular, "Grab them and we will take them to the bowels of the ship!" Peter and Isaiah held on to Gibbs with more force, and Frederick, who was at least half again as big as the gunman in size, handled him by himself. Then looking sternly into the faces of the two white men, Jefferson said, in the most threatening voice he could muster, "You should pray that this man has mercy on you, and that this is not your last walk. But be certain of this one thing; if you so much as sneeze once we leave this cabin, I will cut out your tongue regardless of whether or not he chooses to be merciful. Do you understand?"

Almost simultaneously, both men nodded their heads in agreement with a soft "Uh huh". Gibbs winced. Even that slight movement of his head recharged his pain, but he dared not cry out. As they were gathering to exit the cabin, Gibbs figured he had nothing to lose. "Mr. Cohen, I didn't mean no harm. Me an my frien Pup heah, was jes funnin'. We was drankin an I got all upset lookin at Hale paradin around on da deck, an him jes lookin right through me like he don't even know who I was. Dat man destroyed my business, an he don't even recognize me! I was gittin' back at him through you. I was jes gonna fun wit you an yo misses fo a bit. We wasn't gonna hurt y'all!"

"You put a gun in my face and you called my wife a wench! What kind of fun was that? I should have let my wife stomp your sorry crackah' ass to death while she was doin' it! What did you expect me to do, just let you come in here and have your way? Somebody had ta get hurt and we did our best ta make sure it wasn't us! Now

27

what do you expect me ta do? Let you go so you can turn me in so my wife and me can go to the chain gang the rest of our lives? You caused yourself this problem, and I don't see how this is gonna end without somebody's life being destroyed!" George was getting more agitated as he spoke, then he suddenly added "Go on and dump 'em. I ain't goin ta jail just because this man is hateful!" He commanded as he turned to Jefferson.

Gibbs was suddenly almost in tears. "Oh please, suh! Please. I swear ta God I ain't gonna turn y'all in! I ain't. What kin I do ta convince ya suh? I ain't gonna do y'all no harm!" He was looking imploringly at George. Then turning to Theresa, "Please ma'am! Please tell yo husband ta let us go. We won't tell nobody. I promise!"

Unflinching and staring straight into Gibbs' eyes Theresa said, "Fish food!"

George added in "I can't see any other way!"

Jefferson was quite amused, as he was trying to figure out where George was taking this. "If you speak one more word, or make one more sound, I will keep my promise. I will take you away from him and give him time to think, but he holds your fate. We go now!"

Peter opened the door and looked and listened for the tell tale sound of footsteps on the metal plate floors. It looked clear so he continued out the door, pulling Gibbs along with him. Pup, who was openly weeping, walked along with Frederick like a repentant child. Jefferson was the last one out of the door and he turned back and smiled and said "I'll be right back."

No sooner had the door closed than Theresa was all over him. "What in the Sam hill was all that 'bout? Is that the man you an..."

"Yes! That's him. Why he's here? I don't know. Did he follow us? Doubt it! Probably just a coincidence that led to mischief. I thought I caught somebody staring at me the other day on the deck that I just couldn't place. Now I know. It was him."

"So, what now? Son, what we gonna do? We can't throw those men overboard!"

"I know Baby! I'm just getting into their heads. I don't know how this is gonna end but..." He was interrupted by three sharp raps on the door. "Who is it?"

"It's me!" came Jefferson's now distinctive deep voice. George barely got the door opened before Jefferson scooted past him, closed it quickly behind him and asked, "So, what in the world are we doing?"

"I was telling Theresa that, right now, I don't know what the end plan is, but I just know that the only way ta let everybody walk away from this in one piece is ta scare him so bad he wouldn't dare tell anyone!" Jefferson gave him one of those 'You gotta be kiddin' me!' looks, but he continued. "I know it's dangerous ta trust him, but that's the only way, unless...."

"Unless we get some white man that would be willing to be a false witness in case things go bad. Now I wonder who that could be, oh chosen one?" Jefferson said, in a mocking tone.

"I don't want to go there. I can't keep running up under Mr. Hale's wings every time I have a problem with white people. I think...."

"Son, this ain't no time ta be prideful. Our lives is on the line! You don't need to prove nothin' ta me, and I know Mr. Hale would take great pleasure in settlin up with this red neck fool! And besides, up north you'll be able ta hold your own with white folks, by the law. It just that right now, we still on Georgia property, and that Georgia crackah can ruin yo life just by tellin a lie nobody could believe except they wants ta!"

"Mr. Hale sounds to be a very just man. Why would he not want to see justice done? This man invaded your cabin, held you and your wife at gunpoint, and threatened to do you harm. Why would a just man not want to protect an innocent man from injustice for simply exercising a right that every man is given; what America's founders call certain inalienable rights; the right to life, liberty, and the pursuit of happiness? What I call the right to keep from getting killed without putting up a fight!" Jefferson paused and placed a hand on George's shoulder. "I know you are a good man, and a strong man, and yes, it's okay, to even be a proud man, but prove yourself a wise man as well. Choose your spots to exercise your independence. God created man a social creature so he could have comrades to help him through circumstances that are beyond what he can handle alone. Know when you need help. That does not make you needy. It just confirms your wisdom."

George knew he was right, but he hated the thought of getting Hale involved. "Okay, I'll let Mr. Hale help me, but I'll have ta do it my way." He half smiled at Jefferson and patted his bicep and then looked directly into Theresa's eyes. "I've got a lifetime to share with my beautiful bodyguard! I won't let anything stand in the way of that." He walked over to Theresa who was now sitting on the far side of the bed and kissed her gently. "I'll be back soon. Don't worry about me. Just take care of you 'til I get back."

As soon as they left the cabin George told Jefferson to take him to the two men.

"I thought you said we were going to get Hale down here to help us!"

"I didn't say that. I said I would let him help me. I didn't say I would get him involved at this point. Listen, I've got a plan that I know will work. See, this is how......." George disclosed his plan as they walked.

"Alright, it's time to make your peace. Your evil will cost you your lives this very night!" Jefferson boomed in his convincing African dialect. Above the pleas from the two men, Jefferson continued, "I will not give you the comfort of seeing a friendly face as your eyes turn to smoke. Take the little one away. Since he is the one that put a weapon of death in your face, and who called your bride a foul name, you can take him. Take him away. Go with my friend!" He turned to Frederick, "Take him to the coal bins."

Frederick had no problem dragging Pup away above his struggles and shouts of protest. George followed them as Frederick dragged Pup through several compartments until they stopped in a tool bin where the shovels and other tools were stored. George nodded to Frederick and he let his grip on the man slacken.

"Sit down!"

"What ya plannin ta do ta me? It won't my fault. He made me come wit him! It won't my fault!" Pup continued begging.

"If you say one more word, you'll prove yourself a liar, and your convincing me I can trust you is the only hope you've got." George turned to Frederick, "I'll be okay. Can you fetch us two bottles of moonshine? I need something ta settle me down." Frederick nodded with a perplexed look on his face, but he obeyed.

After he left, George went right to work at Pup. "I really don't want ta do this, but I got no choice. The way you folks have things

31

worked out, even though you committed a crime against me, I'll pay a dear price simply because I had ta protect me and my wife. So, tell me, what choice do I have?" George didn't give him time to answer as he continued. "It's not just me I have ta think about, but it's my wife, and now these other men, who just came ta help me and my wife when we were in trouble. I know they would just as soon throw your sorry ass in the furnace as look at ya at this point. Why should they risk their lives ta save your sorry hide?"

Pup immediately began promising and begging, but really could not come up with a compelling reason why he should be spared. "I'm not convinced yet. Keep talkin'" Pup continued with his inane rhetoric until Frederick returned with the two bottles of moonshine.

"You gonna like dis. If dis can't settle yo ass down, nothin' can!" He reared back and bellowed out a hearty laugh that, under different circumstances, George would have found infectious.

George gave it a weak smile but kept his concentration on Pup. "I'm gonna take a couple of sips of this. I ain't a drinking man, but I got it for you. I know you like strong drink, and this might make it easier for ya to face what's coming! Ya see, some folks have compassion for other people, even if circumstances say they don't have ta. Do you want some of this? Here!"

Pup all but yanked the bottle out of his hand, and put the bottle directly to his mouth. He took one big gulp and then snorted as the extra proof drink burned his nasal passage and then even seemed to be burning the backs of his eyeballs and even the inner workings of his ears. Some of the liquor came out through his nostrils as he snorted.

Frederick laughed again. "I tole ya dat was some mean juice. It ain't like dat fairy piss y'all white boys be drinkin! Bet ya take anothah swig like dat an' yo eyeballs'll pop right on out! Go on, take s'more!"

Pup didn't have to be forced. He was taken by surprise, but he was willing to meet the challenge. He took two more gulps, but neither was as robust as the first.

George took the bottle from him and wiped the rim of the bottle and tipped it to his mouth as he turned towards Frederick, feigning a big gulp. "Whoa! You're right. That's got a kick! Why don't you take the other bottle down to our other friends? I'll be OK with this little weasel." George handed the bottle back to Pup, and let him take a couple of more short swigs before he took the bottle away from him. He could tell he was getting tipsy again, and felt this was his now or never chance. He wondered how Jefferson was getting along with Gibbs.

"There's only one way you don't get used for fuel tonight, and that's for me to convince the others that you can't do them any harm. I'm gonna need some help. I know I can get Mr. Hale ta say he was with me tonight going over his business. He would do everything in his power ta keep Gibbs from getting the upper hand on him. So even if ya decide ta try and turn us in for protecting ourselves against you and your low life friend, no one will believe ya; especially against the word of a man like Mr. Hale. Just ta be sure, we colored folk have a way of keeping our eyes on you white folk."

George tapped Pup's drinking arm and he acted like a conditioned dog and raised the bottle to his mouth again. He was mesmerized by what George was spinning. "We have ta know where y'all are, just for our own protection. I know these boys, and they'll kill ya before they let ya do them, no, any of us, any harm. Do you understand what I'm saying?" George took the bottle from Pup as he was finishing his question because he saw that the moonshine was beginning to get the better of him.

"Yes. Yes suh' I understans perfect. I swear. I know we was wrong. I jes wanna git outta here. I ain't lookin' ta keep dis goin. I promise. I jes wanna git outta here!"

"We're gonna be scattering like the four winds when tonight is over. I'll be legally protected from your hatred where I'm going, plus I will have a strong alibi ta prove you are nothing but a hateful little crackah! By the time you get to me, if you ever could, I'll have time ta let the others know. They'll hunt ya down and serve ya to the hogs in little pieces before ya can enjoy any of the evil you send my way. Do you hear me?"

"Oh yes suh. I know y'all gonna git me if'n I ever cause y'all any trouble. I ain't. I promise."

"Your promise doesn't carry any weight with me. I just need you to understand the truth and hope you aren't dumb enough to ignore it."

Sensing hope, Pup was at his agreeable best. "I know. Like I said, I jes want dis ovah! Dats all. An I sho don't want ta be in dis situation agin'. I promise it's ovah." He began to openly sob, and George handed him the bottle to shut him up. Pup took it and took a quick series of short swigs.

Changing his tone, George spoke in a friendlier voice. "What's your real name Pup?"

"Brian. Brian Wilson." Pup's words were noticeably slurring at this point.

"So Brian, where ya from?"

"Macon. Me an my folks got a little spread in Macon."

"What ya doin' here?"

"My mothahs brothah is a cotton broker in New York. He's gittin' sickly, an dey wants me ta learn from him so I kin take his place."

George stifled a chuckle. This buffoon would certainly bring a just climax to his family's decades of taking advantage of the frailties of the oppressed. "I see. So, how do ya know Gibbs?"

"We jes met tha othah day! I jes met him when he saw you on tha deck tha othah day!"

After hearing that, George was curious. "So how did Gibbs convince ya to come down ta my cabin and do harm ta me and my wife?"

"Me an Gibbs was drinkin' buddies, an he kept talkin 'bout how this Hale fellah had ruined his life cause of some trouble he had wit'chou over in Eufaula. He convinced me ta help him scare ya an make ya look bad in front of yo wife. He swore we wasn't gonna do ya no harm." Pup had stopped his blubbering until the last sentence. George waved his hand in an encouraging gesture and Pup interpreted it to mean take another swig and he did.

"Well Pup, here's the deal. You're gonna finish the rest of that bottle, and you're gonna pass out. When you wake up, you'll either be dead or you'll be wishing you were. If you wake up, you'll still be drunk, and we'll all be long gone. That's if they don't decide ta be safe and have ya vanish. I'm gonna try and convince 'em you won't be a problem."

"Oh no suh! I tole ya I jes wanna walk away from dis nightmare!"

"You don't have ta convince me. I have ta convince them!" George's mind suddenly went to Theresa and his heart began to pound as he suddenly worried about how she was taking the uncertainty of not knowing what was going on or where their lives stood because of the situation they were in. He had to end this and get back to his wife. "We'll be long gone but we will still have eyes on you. If they see you make one move towards Gibbs or anyone in authority, they'll wait and pick the next best opportunity. Do you remember how the African said they would do it?" George mimicked his best sorry imitation of an African dialect and said, "We will slit your throat and reach down and pull out your heart and eat it before you close your eyes in death!" Then, turning back to his most intimidating voice he commanded, "Now, drink. Drink it all!"

Even for Pup, it was getting to be difficult, but he did as he was commanded; for as long as he could.

Theresa ran to his arms as soon as he entered the cabin. She wasn't as much crying as she was whimpering; almost like a frightened puppy that was trying to calm down after it found safety in its master's presence. They just held each other as her spasmodic shudders fed by the tears and fear she had endured, for what seemed like endless hours, subsided. George was silent. He was calm. He felt at peace. He had done all he could to prevent the wild circumstances of the past two hours from snatching the hope out of the promise of their new lives.

After a long while he felt her loosen her embrace and lean back and look up at him. Her smile was weak; flavored by a sense of fear accented by a hint of trust. Her nostrils were flaring as she fought back the tears. She fought hard because she had endured so many shudders fueled by her tears that her stomach muscles ached. Keeping that ache subdued was worth all of her effort to avoid their return. She gathered herself and as calmly as she could, she simply asked, "So, what happened?"

"It's gonna be alright, baby. I promise."

Her melancholy smile lifted her cheeks a bit more as she did her best to let her faith in him project from the depths of her soul, in her best attempt at a smile. "I know, Son. I know you did the right thing, but what happened?"

He gently extracted himself from her embrace and sat on the edge of the bed. He suddenly felt drained. Perhaps the thought of having to revisit all of the insanity of the past few hours was more than he could handle at the moment. He reached for her hand and guided her to sit next to him. As she sat, she scooted up to the head of the bed, behind him. She seated herself at the head of the bed with her back leaning against the metal headboard and gently pulled him back so his head rested in her lap. He laid there silently for a while, blindly staring at the ceiling, as she softly stroked his forehead. Whenever she did that, he would go to a place so peaceful that it blocked out the world, and the only thing he felt was the love radiating through the warmth of her hand.

"Son?"

Her voice called him back to the task at hand. "Sorry Baby, it was just so peaceful where your hands just took me that I was drifting away." He paused a moment before changing gears. He told her how he and Jefferson had concocted a scheme to intimidate the two men, and to strip them of confidence that they could ever escape revenge if they went to the authorities. It had taken a good amount of convincing to keep Jefferson from simply dumping them at sea. Neither wanted blood on their hands, but both agreed that unless they were convinced the incident wouldn't cost their own lives, they would be left with little choice. They decided to keep the men separated, to magnify the fear factor. Gibbs was in worse physical condition of the two. He was having severe headaches and vomiting. Jefferson had made him drink the moonshine anyway. That was an important part of the plan. The men from the ship had been around enough drunks to know that a man who drank past the point of waking up after he has been shaken, will stay out for many hours; sometimes a day. And perhaps the biggest benefit of their drunken stupor was that it would buy time for all parties involved to be far away when the two men came to their senses. They also knew that men coming out of that condition were at a distinct disadvantage. They would be physically miserable and could not focus on much more than that miserable condition, for as long as another day. They would awake with hangovers that would make them question the value of being alive. They would be disoriented and have a hard time sorting through what was real and what was imagined. Place them in a strange environment and that would really freak them out. The other thing they were hoping to achieve was to diminish their credibility if they did try to go to the authorities. The initial response to them would be that they were raving drunks in the middle of a drunken rant. This would be especially true if they were perceived to be vagrants without identification or visible means of support. Extra steps would be taken to make sure this was the case.

"Do ya really think that will stop them? What if..."

He cut her off in mid sentence. "If they convince someone they had a problem on the ship, it would be too hard for the police to find anybody. None of them will be in New York and none of them will still be on the ship. They all have plans to make a life for themselves and their families in the north, but none of 'em planned on being in New York. This was just their way of working their passage north. If they come looking for me, I have them convinced that Mr. Hale will let them know that he was with us all the time, and that they were just two vicious racists." He went on to explain that the plan called for the stewards that attended the cabins in the main compartment of the ship would clear out all of Gibb's possessions as if he had packed and left with everyone else when the ship docked in the morning. He would be taken off the ship in a trunk and dumped somewhere in an alley or something near the docks. No possessions. No identification. Just his vomit drenched clothes and Pup's hat, bloodied with blood donated by a self inflicted wound from Frederick. It was done as a final intimidator. The thought was that it would be one of the first things he found, and both had been warned that their good fortune in being spared might not be shared by their partner if the partner gave them any problems. The hope was that he would deduct that his partner's fate wasn't the same as his. Pup, the least likely to cause a problem, would be roused by the stewards when they made their final cabin checks. He would be escorted off of the ship, probably still too drunk to walk on his own. It would be witnessed by the white senior crew that he was obviously hung over from a drunken binge the night before, and therefore unlikely to have an accurate memory of that night. When out of earshot of the senior crew, he would be told that his friend had vanished, and then asked if he had any idea what happened to him. He'd be given a bloodied handkerchief and then taken somewhere along the dock to sleep off the rest of his stupor. It was suspected that the hobos that lived in the area would pick him clean, so he would have a problem navigating for a while. Whatever fate befell the men at that point wasn't a big concern. Whatever it might be, it was well deserved. The most important thing to George was that he could walk away from the situation with his and Theresa's lives secure, and yet not having another man's blood on his hands to secure it. "I'm gonna let Mr. Hale know, so he can cover me if anything ever came of it."

"Do you trust him that much?"

"Our being here is a sign of how much I trust him. Yes. Yes I trust him." He drifted off to sleep with her still stroking his forehead. The fatigue, which travels with stress, rowed him languidly down the river of slumber to the shore of peace.

They were both nervous as they walked down the ramp towards Hale, who was standing near a pile of luggage that included theirs and his. He had sent a porter down earlier than scheduled so they wouldn't have to wait until the ship was cleared of passengers and their freight before their luggage would be retrieved.

"Good morning George! Theresa! I hope you had a pleasant trip. Welcome to New York. We're just a few hours from your new home!"

"Good morning Mr. Hale! Yeah we're okay." George did his best to cover his nervousness. Theresa forced a smile, and simply nodded in Hale's direction in response to his cheerful greeting.

George was looking around to see if there was any unusual activity on the ship's deck, but all seemed calm. People were scurrying around connecting with their luggage and their travel partners. Greetings were being made. Handshakes and farewells were exchanged among newly discovered friends. As he looked back towards the deck, his heart jumped, as he made eye contact with Jefferson. He was standing near the senior crew as they oversaw the departure process. George couldn't read his face at first, so he was nervous as to whether his being there at that moment held any significance to the events of the previous night. It was only when that silky deep coffee orb was intruded by the whiteness of that now familiar smile that he relaxed a bit. Jefferson tried to take the smile off of his face, but was having a hard time not breaking out into laughter as he turned his head towards the docks to George's right and gave one firm definitive nod as his eyes flashed as if to shout, "Look!" George turned his gaze in that direction and his view was blocked by a pair of men standing there boasting about getting back home to their wives. He had to step back and lean a bit to get enough of a view to see a man about 50 yards away slowly walking away pushing a small luggage wagon with one large trunk on it. George understood immediately and felt the beginnings of a genuine smile, borne as much out of amusement at the situation as relief. He turned himself back in the direction of his friend, Jefferson, but he wasn't there. He searched the deck for a sight of him between making small talk with Hale, but he never saw him again. He thought to himself how sad it was how people flow in and out of our lives. They could even hold a position of great importance in your life for a season, and then they go away; by acts of omission or commission, they fade into the banks of our memories.

"Here's our ri.." Hale paused in mid sentence as he realized that the wagon he had hired to carry them and their luggage to the train was being drawn by two Percherons. He instinctively looked to George, as did Theresa. She was looking at him expectantly to determine his reaction.

As George let the moment sink in, all he could muster was a soft, almost disconnected "Wow". He smiled, and the more he smiled, the brighter it got. He felt so much joy in seeing two animals that looked like his Buck. It was almost as if he had been sent a special welcome to a new life, by one of those friends that, by an act of commission, would someday fade into a memory. He soon found himself fighting an urge to shout for joy at the potency of the moment. Neither was as well conformed as Buck, but both were big boys. One was much more speckled, and thus appeared a darker gray. The other was the opposite, and a bit stockier than Buck. Their conformation was typical of horses used primarily as draft animals. They used their strength muscles but hardly ever opened up and sprinted. This made them rounder in appearance. Buck, used both as a draft horse and as a mount, had more fluid lines; kind of like the difference between a 230 pound weight lifter and a 230 pound sprinter. "What beautiful boys! They remind me of mine! They're beautiful!" All thoughts of the previous night fled from the center of his consciousness, as he walked to a point between the two horses and wrapped his arms around their muzzles and tenderly massaged behind their throat latches. He stood there smiling and feeling somewhat silly for his strange reaction, but he couldn't help himself. Theresa came up behind him and embraced him.

"He just had to leave one of the finest examples of horse flesh I've ever seen. A big Percheron that looks like he's built for war! He's just feeling a bit melancholy!" Hale felt the need to explain George's behavior to the coachman.

The coachman smiled and nodded towards George. "Take your time fellah'. I understand."

George looked up at the coachman and smiled and said "Thanks.", but he almost immediately turned away from the horses and hugged Theresa and said, "Buck is gonna' be fine. We're gonna be fine."

She hugged him back. "I know."

Chapter Two

The morning had passed quickly and by 11AM on Thursday, they were leaving the Ninth Street Pier in New York. It had taken them 52 hours, and they would remember every minute; some for discovering the beauty of each other; some for exposing the treachery of the bigotry they hoped they were leaving behind; and some for revealing their power as individuals and as a team;

They took a train from New York to Hartford. They were both amazed as they saw the northeastern industrial complex for the first time; from the sprawling landscape of New York to the concentrated pockets of industry they passed as they traveled through Connecticut, it was unlike anything they had ever seen. They were surprised that Hartford was as large as it was, and they were impressed with the golden domed capital building as they approached the station. There were tree lined streets and flower gardens interspersed everywhere between the massive brownstone buildings. Close to the train station, they caught a trolley that took them into Glastonbury.

Hale had been acting as a tour guide the whole way, but as they were rattling the last few miles to Glastonbury, he unfolded a copy of the Hartford Courant to catch up on the latest local news so he could have some sense of what was going on. As he reached into his pocket, he felt an envelope, and he remembered that he had been asked to give it to George. He handed it to George, who seemed to be deep in thought as he looked over the gently flowing countryside as it unfolded.

"Oh George, I'm sorry. One of the porters handed this to me as he was unloading a trunk off the ship this morning, and asked me to give it to you. I hope it's nothing that required an immediate response. I'm sorry. I'm starting to forget so many things!"

"That's okay Mr. Hale. If it was that important, whoever it is would have come to me with it!" George's quip belied the pounding that lodged in his ear drums as he felt his heart thumping like a bass drum beaten with a two-inch mallet. What could this be? He hoped it wasn't instruction to something he should have taken care of in New York. The front of the envelope simply read; George.

Theresa looked at him quizzically. She too felt the pangs of anxiety, and could see the nervousness in her husband's normally cool demeanor, as he opened the letter.

George's eyes slit almost shut as he began reading. His face was grim at first, but quickly relaxed as he leaned back and silently read the message.

My Dear Friend George,

We have said our goodbyes and wished each other well, but I just want you to know that everything will be alright. You are a very special man; one who I have come to greatly admire in a very short time.

As we travel down the roads of life, sometimes, along the way, we are blessed to find companions to share these trying miles. After we have shared the distances for a season, however brief it may be, the journey must eventually end. It is often not until then that we can appreciate that the rhythm of our companions' feet has met the cadence of our own and that we have walked in unity. Even after the road has forked, and the sounds of those familiar footsteps grow faint down the road of time, those companions fill a place of friendship nurtured by common bonds, and travel forever on the hallowed paths of our wandering memories. From that place, neither time nor space can erase the remembrance of that too brief season we shared.

From time to time, there come precious moments that lodge themselves indelibly in our memories. When we recall them, we can reclaim them, and bring them forth for our pleasure. Like a fine wine is fermented in charred kegs, so are our memories sealed in the charred kegs of our hearts, to be poured out and shared at times when their recollection brings us comfort. A mere sip from that fluted glass can refresh our very souls; but unlike fine wine, our memories can be shared and sipped upon frequently, without ever fearing that the bottle will run dry.

Of such are the memories I carry back to my home, of the brief time we shared. I rejoice in meeting you, and pray that we will meet yet again. Until we do, but even if the answer to my prayer is contrary, we can go to the wine cellar and select from the vintage we trod together, and sip, and taste those precious moments once again.

You may walk away from this time assured that your interests have been well protected, and that the flower that was planted will not rise up as weeds.

May the Lord bless your life in all the most important ways. May He protect and nurture you all the days of your life; and if He allows that we meet again, let us remember when we walked

that common ground, and know that a common heartbeat
transcends the distances between us.

Give my best to your lovely bride.

Be at peace. Stay encouraged!

Your Friend,

Jefferson

He smiled at Theresa and nodded and tapped the letter to his heart."Just a nice farewell from our friend Jefferson." He handed the letter to her to read.

She hastily scanned over it. It was hard for her to focus with all that was going on around her, but one passage jumped off of the page at her: "You may walk away from this time assured that your interests have been well protected, and that the flower that was planted will not rise up as weeds." She didn't quite know how to take that passage, and she felt it would be better left ambiguous. As she looked out of the trolley, she could see the blue gray waters of the wide Connecticut flowing slowly southward in the near distance. Every so often she would catch a glimpse of something flashing at the surface of the water. She couldn't tell if it was a fish breaking the surface or just the sun kissing the tip of a wave. Whatever it was seemed to speak of life in that big river. It's so much bigger than the Chattahoochee, she thought. The clear blue sky stained the river and framed the stately Cottonwoods that lined endlessly along its banks as they waved a languid emerald green salute in rhythm with the soft summer breeze.

She felt a sense of awe that she was now looking at the land that her grandmother is supposed to have come from over seventy years before. She had heard her mother tell the story many times of the last time her grandmother and her sister had seen their father, the chief. She recalled the lore of the day of their last goodbye.

The morning sun rose too soon that day, for it was called to kiss the teary faces of his family as it chased the chill left by night and broken hearts. He embraced them one by one, and felt them convulse against him. He dared not look in their eyes, but his heart painted their picture of sorrow much deeper than eyes would ever dare. He put strong hands on the shoulders of the three warriors he sent to guide them, and silently, once more, prayed their strength. They mounted and he saluted them with a raised open hand, and they turned with the morning sun kissing their left cheeks. When they reached the top of the rise, Sarah, then Martha, then the men, one by one, turned to see their village from a distance. Then they turned as if one, kicked their mounts, and vanished into the horizon. Feeling a hunger to extend the moment, he and their brothers ran to the top of the rise and watched until they faded into the woods on the trail that led them from the land of the Mohegan.

As she surveyed the horizon, she wondered which hill the chief had ascended as he watched his daughters vanish from his view. A smile came over her face as the beauty of the Connecticut River Valley laid out its welcome mat, almost as if to say welcome back home.

George had been watching her and got the feeling that the letter had the same reassuring effect on her as it had on him. When her eyes looked up at him, his were there to greet her. "Be at peace."

"I am."

"This is our new home. This is our new life. This will be wonderful."

"As long as you're by my side."

George smiled. "Til the cows come home!"

Hale's son, Stancliffe, had been waiting at the trolley station. He was driving a surrey, hitched to two beautiful chestnut mares.

"Hello Father!" His son seemed genuinely excited to see his father.

"Son!"

They walked quickly to each other and grabbed each other on the upper arm as they shook hands. Both were all smiles, with the older Hale being very animated in his head movements, as he seemed to be filled with joy at the fact that his son was standing before him. Both men were about the same height, with the younger being very fit. He was a younger, more chiseled version of his father in the face, with a full head of black hair pulled severely back from his broad forehead. He was the closest of their children; not just in distance but also in the nurture of the bond that existed between them. He lived right next door, renting the house his uncle George owned.

"How are Ida and my grandchildren?"

"They're fine Father. Catherine is a handful. It's really true what they say about the terrible two's!" Stancliffe said, as his attention turned to Theresa and George.

"Son, this is George Cohen and his new bride, Theresa! George, Theresa, this is my son Stancliffe. We call him Stan."

Stancliffe immediately looked directly at George and offered his hand. "Pleased to meet you, George. My father speaks highly of you." Then, turning to Theresa, he bowed politely. "Pleased to meet you Mrs. Cohen. I hear you have had an exciting couple of weeks."

First George, then Theresa returned his greeting, and after some small talk, they turned to the surrey. Hale had bounced ahead, anxious to greet his beloved mares. They were purebred Oldenburgs, a German breed that was bred for riding and carriage. Hale had been offered them five years ago in a business dealing with one of his export customers. They look like a more delicate version of the Clydesdale, the Budweiser carriage horse. He had named them Olga and Gretel. They seemed excited to see him, their heads were bobbing up and down, and they were almost prancing in place. He walked to them and simultaneously put his head between theirs and pulled them close on either side. He stood back and smiled. "Did you ladies miss Daddy? He sure missed you!" he said as he squeezed them to him once again. "George, meet my girls. Now you see why I won't buy a car. That would be insulting my girls!"

George was impressed with their size, conformation, and beauty. "They are magnificent Mr. Hale. I wish Buck could have met them, he'd be one happy horse!" George took a chance at humor.

Hale responded well. "That brute would scare 'em off! Stan, you should see George's horse. He's a Percheron, he's built like these Oldies, but taller and more heavily muscled. Now that's a magnificent creature!" Hale collected himself, "Let's get on home. We got a lot of people I'm dying to see."

"Hi Frank! Bring the bags to the house. You know mine. Take theirs to Luigi's. They're moving into his place next to you. George this is Frank, Frank, George. You guys will be working together, and you'll be neighbors." The men did not move from the seats they had in their respective vehicles, but managed to give each other a respectful, if not overly friendly, nod.

Theresa marveled at the beauty of the Connecticut River basin. She could see rolling hills in the distance. Everything was so lush and green. She was surprised at the heat and humidity. She had a much cooler climate in her mind.

It was a relatively short ride to the Hale's home. As they approached the house, they were awestruck by its design and beauty. The Second Empire style house was unlike any either of them had seen in Georgia. It looked to be five sections connected and decorated with ornately carved white trim. It was most impressive.

As they were getting out of the carriage, Hale seemed to be excited well beyond what he had shown up to this time. The fact that he hadn't seen his family since early April, was becoming a heavier burden the closer he got to the end of his season without them. He had been doing this for many years now, and it was getting harder each year to stay separated from his family. The door swung open as they stopped and a wisp of woman in a flowered day dress burst into their view with a smile that seemed almost too big for her face. "John!" she shrieked like a schoolgirl as she hurried to close the distance between her and Hale.

"Hey Addie! How's my sweetest peach?" He responded as he closed ranks and pulled her tightly to him and kissed her on her upturned lips. "Gee it's good to be home! You're lookin' great!" He said, just before turning to Theresa and George. "Addie, this is George and Theresa Cohen. This is the nice couple I spoke with you about! Theresa, George, this is my wife Addie Hale!"

Addie almost pounced on them with aggressive hand shakes for both. "Well, John has told me so much about you. I am so pleased to meet you; Theresa and George." Her wide toothy smile crinkled the flesh around her eyes and gave them the appearance of refreshing gray pools peering through the branches of willows dancing in the breeze.

"Please to meet you Mrs. Hale." George said as he bowed slightly to her as she was shaking his hand.

As she released George and turned her attention to Theresa, Theresa said, "And I'm pleased to meet you too, Mrs. Hale."

"Welcome to both of you! I had the house in back cleaned and spruced up so that you two newlyweds would be comfortable. You must be starving!" Not waiting for an answer, she continued, "I've got some ham sandwiches and nice macaroni salad that Rosa made. She's our housekeeper and cook. John said that George met her husband, Luigi, down at his momma's house. She's leaving next week to go be with Luigi in Pleasant Valley, so there's a job open if you want it! John says that you are a fabulous cook! I bet you want to freshen up some before we sit down and eat. Follow me! I've got some clean towels and all out for you in the guest room!"

"Whoa woman! Take a breath! My Addie can say more in one minute than anyone I ever met in my life!"

"I'm just excited, John. Now stop being silly and let's get these nice folks something to eat! Oh look, here comes Ida and Katie."

Theresa looked to see a very attractive woman, in a light blue summer dress desperately trying to keep up with an auburn haired two-year-old in full charge mode. "Pop Pop! Grammy! Pop Pop!" She shrieked as she ran that meandering trot that youngsters use as they compensate for legs that still have not mastered the art of rapid mobility.

"What a pretty little girl!" Theresa blurted before realizing she had spoken her thoughts. As if awakened from a frenzied trance, the little girl stopped short of the group and began walking as if on a tightrope to her father. She was just a little older than Kay. She made her realize how much she missed him. She reminded herself to have a picture made and sent to him so he would remember her.

"Hey princess! Give Pop Pop a big hug" Stancliffe said as he picked her up and handed her to his father. Even though his father was only 57, Stancliffe always had the fear of his father not coming back from his Georgia excursions, so being able to hand his daughter to him verged on being a religious experience. As if connected to the same psyche, he received his granddaughter with the same reverence. She was barely walking when he saw her last, although she had begun talking shortly after her first birthday. His son made it a point to show Katie pictures of her Pop Pop so that she would not forget him. It had paid off.

"Well look who Pop Pop has here!" he said as he buried his face in her belly as he lifted her supine body to his lips. He blew air on her, making a farting sound, which made her laugh hysterically. He realized how he had missed the simple pleasure of hearing his innocent grand-daughter's reaction as he did silly things to make her laugh. He soon lifted her to a sitting position on his forearm as he held her close.

By this time Ida had walked up to him and embraced him around his mid section and given him a kiss on his cheek. "Hi, Dad. It's sure good to see you home!" He kissed her forehead as she looked up at him. Before he could say anything she had moved the conversation on. "This must be George and Theresa. You're a striking couple! I understand that congratulations are in order!"

"Very pleased to meet you, ma'am."

Picking up on George's disadvantage, Hale stepped in. "This is Stan's wife, Ida! George, Theresa."

"Very pleased to meet you Mrs. Hale." George said, correcting himself.

"No need to stand on formality with me, unless you prefer I call you Mr. Umm."

Realizing she did not recall their last name, her husband came to her rescue. "It's Cohen, honey, but you're right, no need to stand on formality. Just call us Stan and Ida."

Theresa was having a problem with the jealousy she felt as this very pretty, sophisticated strawberry blond acted so familiarly with her husband. She did not understand her feelings. As she was struggling to keep the smile on her face, Ida turned to her and said, "And that goes for you too Theresa. Ida and Stan will do just fine."

"Yes ma'am. I mean Ida. It's good meeting you." Old habits die hard. It was totally foreign ground for her to speak in such a familiar manner to a white adult. Though still very pretty, Theresa could tell that she was considerably older than her and a bit older than George. To shake her discomfort, Theresa turned her attention to Katie. As she reached her hand out to the little girl, Katie turned away and buried her face in her grandfather's chest. "That's okay Katie, you and me are gonna get to be friends. You just wait and see!" Katie peeked out from the protection of her grandfather's chest and smiled.

Lunch was accompanied by a meandering stream of conversations. There was a lot of catching up to do, and a lot of discovery as well, as everyone being anxious to bring everyone else up to the minute on their personal life history. They didn't accept George and Theresa as strangers, nor did George feel like one. This was still too far removed from who and what Theresa had been to be comfortable for her right away. At lunch Addie did more than her share of the talking, but today, it was interesting. She had filled Theresa and George in on the fact that Stan and Ida had lived with them when they first married, eleven years ago; and how, when Hale's brother, George, who owns the property right next door, had built this beautiful estate just south of here, he had rented the old place to Stan and Ida. They got a lesson in the genealogy of the Hale family. They had their first, Stancliffe, shortly after they married, then came Mosely, their other son, who is married and living in Massachusetts; then Emily, or Emma as she was known, who is married and living in northwest Connecticut, with her husband Francis, and their baby, Dorothy, who is a few months younger than Katie. Francis is a minister. Marion, 19, is eight years younger than Emma, and was a bit of a surprise. Laura, who is only 12, was a complete shock! Addie was 44 years old when Laura was born! They would meet the two girls later. Marion was taking some summer courses at Trinity college, over in Hartford, and Laura, along with Stan's children, Mary, 10; John, 8; and Larry, 6, were all guests at Camp Courant, a new camping area in the Avon Mountain overlooking Hartford, designed to give the young people in Hartford a place to enjoy the summer. A family friend was a counselor, and had offered to take the children with him, so they could enjoy the outdoors. Addie and Ida both agreed that the social exchange in being with children of other ethnic and economic groups would be a boost to their children's development.

They talked about Glastonbury being a melting pot, with a lot of Europeans and southern blacks coming to work on the farms. Through Luigi recruiting family and friends, they had quite a population of Italians working for them, but most would be going to Georgia, shortly after harvest, to rejoin Luigi.

John and Stan had a two minute window to talk about the business before Addie slammed it by saying that George and Theresa had no interest in that, since they were on their honeymoon.

Theresa and Katie were playing a running game of peek-a-boo during much of the conversation, and Katie was welcoming the attention. It wasn't long before Katie pulled away from her grandfather when Theresa held out her arms. That was the beginning of a love affair. She helped soothe the pain of being without Kay. It was also a comfortable place for Theresa to hide from the discomfort she felt with Ida. She knew it had to be her mind playing tricks, but she felt that Ida and George were exchanging far too many glances, and way too many smiles. No one else appeared to take offense, or even notice.

"Well, I don't know about you two, but I'm dog tired, and I think Addie and I should take a little nap before the girls get home!" The look that passed between him and Addie made it clear to the two younger couples that the older Hales had some catching up to do of another sort. After inviting everyone back to dinner, Hale asked Stan to show George and Theresa to the house out back that would be their new home.

Stan and Ida walked with them out the back door, and led them down a stony path that was lined with trees and curved just enough so that they walked about fifty yards before they came to the clearing where the duplex was situated. Stan simply pointed at the simple, large two story white Cape Cod house with two walkways; one leading to each side of the house. He put his hand on George's shoulder and said, "The left side is all yours. We tried to make it cozy, but let us know if there is anything else you need. Dinner won't be for a few hours. They'll probably have Rosa come and announce. Well, it's been nice meeting you. Welcome to Hale land." He extended his hand to George and nodded at Theresa.

Ida smiled and nodded at both, and then said, "May I have my child back?" She kidded with Theresa, who was still holding Katie. Katie reluctantly left Theresa to go to her mother, and was peering over her mother's shoulder and smiling as they walked through the opening in the neat row of Spruce trees that led to their house.

Before they were out of sight, George turned to Theresa and simply said, "Mrs. Cohen", as he bowed and scooped her up in his arms. With her securely in his arms, he turned the brass knob, and he carried his bride over the threshold, into their first home.

Theresa gasped when she entered. It was beautiful. More than she had expected. "Son! Look! Look at this!" They had walked into a tiny foyer, with a door on the left that led into a bright yellow painted kitchen that seemed to be bouncing rays of sun from its walls. On the right was a wider open portal that opened into a large living room with a sofa and two well-cushioned side chairs. The room had been papered in pink and white flowers on a pale green background. Between the two was a flight of stairs that led to the upstairs bedroom. She stood there for a moment, as if entranced, admiring her living room. Her living room. The thought resonated. It was her first place; a place where she was the woman in charge. The gravity of the responsibility and the elation of the realization tickled her to her core. She walked down the short hallway and noticed that both the living room and the kitchen had second openings on the far side of the rooms. Just past these openings were doors on either side; the one behind the living room led to a bedroom; the one behind the kitchen led to a small room that had two doors. One led to the basement stairs. The other led outside. There was a wash tub there, and the walls were lined with shelves. "How convenient!" she thought. "Son we have everything I hoped we would have." Theresa had visions of those shelves being filled with mason jars full of canned goods and plenty of all the other staples she would need to make sure her man ate well every day!

George had come up behind her and pulled her back against him. She smiled and looked back over her shoulder at him. He made her feel vulnerable and protected at the same time. "So, Mr. Cohen, what's on your mind?"

"Well, I was just thinkin'" he cooed with his lips pressed tightly against her soft black hair.

"Oh yeah? What was you thinkin?" she asked as she pressed herself tighter against his strong body.

"I was thinkin' that we need ta explore the cellar, since it's right here, but then I thought better of it."

"Oh really? So what could be better than explorin' our new cellar?" she teased.

"I'm just too tired ta climb all them stairs. Besides, the bedroom is just around the corner, and I figured we needed ta get a better look at that. Wouldn't you agree?" he continued, speaking softly into her hair.

"Well, since you the man of the house, I 'spose I best do what ya say."

He turned her gently around to face him. "You best face the situation; you're here with a strong young man, just a few feet from a bedroom. I think you might have a problem."

She pressed herself hard against him and looked him squarely in his eyes. "Oh no Mr. Cohen, it's you who got the problem. It's gonna be a while before dinner!"

George smiled down at her. "I know." He said as he led her around the corner to their first embrace in their new home.

That next morning George met Hale for a tour of the farm and a fuller explanation of what his responsibilities were. Hale explained to George that he needed him to oversee the processes that were being employed in growing everything on his farm. His job was to increase the quality and yield of his crops. Of particular interest were his fruit trees; peaches and apples.

There was also a growing market for tobacco, and Hale was looking to become a bigger player in that arena as well. Tobacco was already in its second priming; the process of collecting the most mature leaves from the plants, so Hale just wanted George to observe the processes and make assessments of them and perhaps develop better ones for the next season. He also wanted George to lead his move from Maryland Broadleaf tobacco to Sumatran Shade Grown tobacco.

The rich glacial silt, a leftover from The Ice Age, which formed most of the sediment of the Connecticut River Valley, supplied a unique soil that yields some of the world's most sought after cigar wrapping tobacco. The broadleaf imported into the area from Maryland in 1833 is used as a cigar wrapping tobacco, but is too course and aromatic to be used for the finest cigars. Many of the best wrapping strains were being bought from Sumatra or Cuba. This affected the Connecticut broadleaf growers, as more cigar producers found better revenue streams by producing the finer cigars wrapped with the more delicate imported leaves. Around 1900, it was discovered that the climate that helped keep the tropically grown leaves more delicate, more supple, and their flavor less robust (this was preferred because the star of the show in a cigar should be the taste of the filler blend), could be duplicated by growing the crop under shaded tents. The introduction was met with several setbacks during the first few years, as the product and the process evolved. The great news was that the advantages of the Connecticut River Valley soil made Connecticut shade grown tobacco far superior to any other wrapping leaves in the world. By 1904 Connecticut farmers were producing very highly regarded wrapper leaves. The demand for these leaves was growing rapidly, with no end in sight. Most of the tobacco grown in the Connecticut area was still the coarser broadleaf types, grown using traditional methods, but the number of farmers who had been sitting on the sidelines waiting for the right time, deciding to make the switch to the shade technique, was growing rapidly.

The benefit of shade tobacco is that it yields such high rewards, but it is also burdened with tremendous expense and risk when compared to more traditional methods. Hale wanted George to learn everything he could about growing shade tobacco. Hale explained that there was a local industry support program called the Connecticut Agricultural Experiment Station that was at the forefront in developing growing and harvesting techniques. He wanted him to take a trip up to Windsor Locks, just a few miles upriver, to learn as much as he could from the experts there. He said he would arrange for George to spend a few days there in a few weeks, after the peaches were harvested, but before the apples were brought in. He even had several books and articles on the subject that he lent to George to help him become, what Hale called, "a master Tobacconist".

Theresa had stayed around the house, getting things situated, and getting ahead on the laundry she and George had accumulated on their trip. As she was doing her chores, her mind took her many places; she wondered about her mother and father and her sisters and brothers. She felt somewhat guilty because she didn't miss them as much as she had anticipated. "Truth be told," she mused, "I ain't had time to really miss 'em." The honeymoon kept her busy, and the excitement of travel hoarded her sensibilities. And now, here she was starting a whole new life with so much to do. She missed them, but she knew the time would come when she would miss them so much more. She made a mental note to write her mother as soon as she was settled in. She made a promise that she would write her often, and to write Ma Nellie as well.

Dinner last night had been very pleasant. Theresa found the Hales to be very entertaining and truly caring people. This applied to Stan and Ida as well, although Theresa still found it a bit difficult to feel completely comfortable around her. She couldn't put her finger on it, but it had something to do with her feeling that this woman might try to tantalize her George. After all, she was a very comely woman in the prime of her womanhood. Maybe it was the fact that she exposed far more cleavage than Theresa felt comfortable with, and that she didn't seem the least bit self conscious. Theresa figured it was all in her head, because Ida actually seemed to go out of her way to be pleasant and inclusive; nor did Ida seem jealous of the fact that little Katie had fallen madly in love with Theresa and wouldn't sit anywhere but on or next to her. In fact, she joked in an unassuming way about the fact that Theresa had just come to town and already stolen her little girl's heart away. Theresa figured she would one day get over it or one day figure it out, but in the meantime, she tried her best to keep the malice in her heart undetected.

Mrs. Hale had repeated that she had heard about Theresa being a cook at the Bradley's, and that a position in the kitchen was opening in the next few days when Rosa left to join Luigi in Georgia. She asked Theresa if she would be interested in the position. She would be willing to pay Theresa 40¢ an hour (that would be about $9.30 in today's money value). She would need her about six hours a day. That was $2.40 a day, or $12 a week, or $14.40 if she had to work a Saturday. She was only making $8 a week at the Bradley's when she left, and she was working eight hours a day! She and George had decided to keep Sundays Sabbath, and to spend that time together, unless there was a real emergency on the farm. Theresa was excited to accept the offer. She and George had discussed it, and they both agreed that she would work for the Hales if the expected offer came. This would give her something to do and bring extra money into the household. Their plan was to use her earnings as their guaranteed savings, and bank as much of his money as they could so they could eventually buy their own farm. Once she had a baby, they agreed that she would stay home and care for it. Her duties were to prepare all meals for the Hale household, but she did not serve them. She was also charged with maintaining the food stores for the house.

They were both excited when George came home that night. They chatted all through dinner about the Hales and what a wonderful family they seemed to be. Theresa told George she was excited about the job offer from Addie Hale, and they agreed it would be great for them to be able to bank her earnings. They talked about the fact that their rent was part of the compensation package for George, and that they had access to inexpensive food there on the farm. In fact, as it turned out, there were enough culls from the harvests that they were getting their produce and fruit free. George said he had a lot to talk about his job too, but that he would save it for after dinner. Theresa cleaned the kitchen while George pulled the weeds from around their modest porch. He was done before she was, so he went back in to see if he could help her.

"Naw Son, I'm fine an' besides ya waited 'til I'm most done before you asked!" she joked. She continued teasing him. "Besides, ya don't want Frank tellin' the fellahs round here that you're hen pecked do ya'?"

She was referring to Frank Saglio, their neighbor and Hale's foreman under Luigi. Though it was never discussed with the two men, the fact that George was brought in to replace Luigi meant that Frank now was to eventually report to George. The Saglio Family shared the duplex with George and Theresa. They occupied the right side of the house with their three children, Charlie who was 6, Johnny, almost 5, and 19 month old Hazel. There was some unspoken tension between George and Frank that comes with the territory anytime two alpha males share overlapping boundaries, so they danced that macho dance that men so often dance before they yield to mutual acceptance or friendship. That type of machismo was strong in Frank's Italian culture. He hadn't come to the country until about ten years ago, so it was deeply imbedded. His English was still very broken, and at this stage in his life, it probably never was going to change. Frank looked to be in his early forties, but his wife looked to be a lot younger. Jo-Anna was pleasant enough, and her pretty plump face was quick to smile, though Theresa caught her looking troubled whenever she didn't know she was looking.

"Shoot I don't care what people say about me, as long as you don't pay attention to their foolishness. Why don't we go sit out on the porch and I'll tell you about my day. It's way too hot in the house right now."

The myths that southerners held about it always being nice and cool in the north were quickly debunked for Theresa and George. Not only was the temperature in the nineties, but the humidity that settled in the Connecticut River Valley made the night as hot and steamy as any could have been in Georgia.

"Alright. You take a couple of chairs out there an' I'll go get some fans to keep the mosquitoes away." Another disappointment. The Georgia mosquitoes followed them to Glastonbury! After the sun began to set, the local mosquitoes became very pesky unless you actively fought them off.

"Good idea!" George yelled over his shoulder as he moved the chairs out to the porch. He heard voices out in the front yard, but he couldn't see anyone. He heard a man speaking with an Italian accent. He realized that Frank and someone else were talking in the front of house. They were speaking in normal tones, but the fact that they were around the corner subdued the sound enough that he could not distinguish words. The other voice was a female so he assumed it was Jo-Anna.

Theresa handed George a fan and a sprig of some sort of weed. He looked at her quizzically. "It's Rosemary. Jo-Anna gave it to me. She says it's an old family remedy for keepin' the mosquitoes at bay. Seems they don't like the smell."

"I ain't so sure I like it either!" George kidded as they both laughed.

"That you Theresa?" Jo-Anna yelled before she appeared around the corner. She stayed at the front of the house; about fifteen feet away from the little porch. Before she could answer, Jo-Anna continued. "You got your Rosemary? These mosquitoes are on the prowl tonight, girl."

"Yep! I sure do. I got my fan and some Rosemary. Thank you. I hope it works, 'cause mosquitoes seem right partial to me."

"That's 'cause you're so sweet!" George intervened in a tone he knew only she could hear.

Theresa reached out and squeezed his hand and smiled at him in appreciation of his continuous flattery. It was good to see that the honeymoon wasn't over, and her hopes were that it never would be.

Almost simultaneously, Jo-Anna yelled back. "You know that's the truth. These little beasts are just like men. Always tryin' to get a bite of us ladies."

Still holding onto George's arm, and looking at him almost apologetically, she quipped back. "They ain't like my man, My man is picky about who he bites." she said, as George rolled his eyes and smiled.

"Sounds like you got you a honey bee, but there's a whole lotta mosquitoes round here!" Jo-Anna chuckled.

"She talkin' 'bout you Frank?" George yelled, assuming that Frank was lurking around the corner just out of sight, and that he was a silent pawn in the conversation just like he was.

Frank suddenly appeared behind Jo-Anna and answered in his broken English. "Bah! Not a me. Frank, he a bumble a bee. When a he sting a, you a know a you no gotta stinga by no a mosquito!" That was the most George had heard Frank say since they met. They all laughed at his machismo.

"Well with that, I'm gonna round up the kids before the stingin' starts." Jo-Anna quipped. "Goodnight y'all." She said, mocking Theresa and George's decidedly southern flavor. They watched her turn and walk out of sight. Frank gave a slight smile in their direction and nodded almost imperceptibly as he turned to follow his wife. They were gone before they could respond. They heard the porch door slam, followed closely by Frank yelling something at the boys from the back of the house.

"Ahhh! The sound of peace and quiet." There was no response to his remark except the song of the crickets as they called out in their never-ending pursuit of a mate.

Theresa broke the silence. "They're nice people, Son. They're just a bit different. It was good ta break the ice. After all, they are our neighbors. She's been sweet, and it seems that Frank is loosening up."

"Yeah, that was alright, although I wish we had more privacy. I don't mind people, but it always seems like they butt in on your time when ya have something else you wanna do or talk about. Tonight, I just wanted a little time with just me and you, so we can kind of catch our breath. Everything has been movin' so fast. Are you okay, Baby?"

"I'm fine, Son. Everybody has been really nice and the house is nice too. I got everything a po' woman needs!" she joked.

"You, my dear, are far from po'!" he quipped, as he threw her own slang back at her. "Remember, you are a child of The King, and you are married to a prince. There is great wealth in your Father's house. The Earth is His and the fullness thereof, and they that dwell in it. The cattle on a thousand hills are His, and I plan on claiming my inheritance in this place!"

"Tell it preachah'!" Theresa mocked as she grinned ear to ear. That was one of the things she loved the most about George; his deep faith. She knew he meant every word.

"Baby, I ain't playin'. This is the land our Father has given us to prosper in, and if I keep my hand to the plow and my head to the sky, He will give us more than we have the nerve to ask for." He took her hands and enveloped them in his. He looked into those eyes that melted his heart, and he felt an inexplicable lump in his throat. "And you are the woman He has given me as my wife. Flesh of my flesh, bone of my bone. The weaker vessel. I remember Reverend Grubbs saying that you weren't some clay cup but a delicate crystal glass. I think about that a lot. I think about all of the delicate things a wife is called to do in the background so that the family can stay strong and whole. I love you…"

"Oh, and I love you too, Son." She interrupted him mid-sentence.

He squeezed her hand, smiled, and nodded as he continued. "I love you so much and I want to keep every promise I ever made to ya and to your family about the life I would work ta provide, with

God's help. You trusted in me when you accepted my proposal and moved so far away from your family and home. I will not betray it. I truly want everything we ever hoped for."

"And so do I. You ain't the only one that got blessed when we got married. I trust you 'cause every step of the way you have proved yourself worthy of my trust, and my admiration, and my love. I know The Lord will bless our family, and I know that you are the one ta lead. Wherever that might be, or whatever it brings, Son, know this; I stand behind ya." She was beginning to tear, so she withdrew her hand and stemmed the flow before it started.

George noticed and tried to liven things up a bit. "Oh I know that Baby. I bet that fellah' that got that bedpan upside his head knows it too!"

She pushed him away as they both laughed. "See, that's what I'm talkin' 'bout!" Her smile faded almost as fast as it had appeared. "I wonder what happened to them men."

"Well they have intruded in my life about all I'm gonna let them. I'm not worried about 'em. I ain't even thinkin' about 'em. I expect God has them wherever He wants 'em, and I'm trusting that He will not let them do any more harm in our lives!" George pulled her back close. "Besides, this is a conversation about our future, so let the past alone. Every day is a challenge unto itself. We'll do good to handle the todays as they come."

"I ain't worryin' either, Son. I was just thinkin', but I agree with you. It ain't worth another thought. Now, tell me 'bout my tomorrows." She said as she pulled his hands to her lips and gently kissed them.

"Well, Mr. Hale and I had a great day. He showed me things around the farm, and took me out to the orchards. For the next couple of weeks things will be pretty hectic preparing for the peach harvest and getting ready for the apple harvest. He has apple and peach trees as far as the eye can see. He surprised me though. He needs me ta help with that right now, but he also stressed that it was real important for me ta learn as much as I can about tobacco farming."

"Tobacco? I didn't even know they grew tobacco up north." Theresa queried.

"Exactly. Neither did I, but it seems it's really big up here, and apparently it's getting to be the biggest cash crop around these parts. They use the tobacco from here to wrap cigars with. The biggest thing right now though, is the shade tobacco. It seems they actually grow the tobacco under these tent like things. They have been doing it for a few years further upriver, but the farmers in these parts are starting to catch the bug. It seems there is a premium paid for the quality of that tobacco, but that it is real expensive ta get into, and that there are a lot of risks involved. But the rewards seem ta be big enough that a lot of folks are willing ta take the risk. Mr. Hale thinks that my scientific approach to farming would be a big help ta him in making the transition. You know him. He wants ta be the tobacco king!" They laughed, but they knew it was the truth, and that his drive to be the best could very well catapult George to the top of the industry as well. "He wants me to observe the harvest and other techniques that his men employ so I can make recommendations to improve whatever I think can be done better. He also wants ta send me upriver to Windsor for as couple of days. They actually have a research place that is available to the farmers in the area ta help them learn the best ways ta raise and harvest tobacco. He even gave me a couple of books ta study."

"That sounds like it could be a real chance ta make it."

"It is a chance ta make it!" George said, emphasizing the "is". He knew that this would open many doors when it proved successful. He wasn't thinking about anything in the conditional tense. "I can make a lot of money here, and we don't have ta spend much. We can save all your money until the babies start coming, and we can save a lot of mine. The better the crops yield, the better I get paid. The more money the farm makes, the bigger my bonus when we go to market! My hope is that, after a few years, we can buy our own place. There's still plenty of farm land ta be had around here, but I think that the land will be going pretty fast if this shade tobacco thing really catches on!"

"Then that sounds like a plan. We'll work our butts off for a few years and save as much as we can so we can buy our own farm and then, you can work your magic ta make money for us, and not somebody else. Not that I begrudge Mr. Hale any benefit he gets from you workin' for him, but you know what I mean. Right, Son?"

"I know exactly what ya mean, and agree. I don't want to be a borrower but a lender. I want ta leave my grandchildren an inheritance, just like it says in the Bible. I want us to have a house full of beautiful children who have everything they need, and who will have every opportunity ta make more out of their lives than we ever hoped of making out of ours. I want you to never have ta worry about there being enough of anything in our house. I want you to have all the best that money can buy." Then, thinking about the impact of his last statement, he added, "...within reason." They chuckled. They were on the same page. "Most of all, I don't want any of that ta be the most wonderful part about our lives together. If anybody ever sees fit ta write a story about our lives, I wanna make sure my life speaks the most about three things: number one is that I am the covering in a family that loves Jesus, and that trusts in Him, and relies on Him, and seeks to glorify Him by how we treat each other and our children, our family, and our friends and everybody we touch. Next, is that I love me some 'Reesie', and that she loves her some Son, and that we stood shoulder to shoulder and back to back to make a wonderful life for our children and their children comin' behind them. I will work my fingers to the bone to give you everything I ever promised you. And..."

"You don't need no money ta make me happy, Son. As long as we are together, trustin' God and doin' our best to honor him and each other, then that will be enough for me. Whether that means wealth or fame doesn't matter ta me. It'll be good if it comes, but I just want life ta deal with us using a fair measure."

"Tell it preachah'!" George quipped back.

"You crazy. You know that? But I love ya anyway."

"I didn't finish. The last is that I used all I was blessed with ta keep my promises to you and our children and their children behind them." George just looked at her and smiled and squeezed her. They both looked out over the short distance between them and the row of spruce trees that lined the back of Stancliffe's property and their little section of the Hale estate, and watched the brilliant dance of the fireflies against the stark blackness of the night. The moonless sky served as a pallet for the myriad of stars that were scattered like diamonds on a black velvet blanket.

"Let's call it a night. We've got mules to catch in the mornin'"

"Sounds like a plan. It should be cooler in the house now that the sun's been down for a while. I'll help ya with the chairs."

"Naw, Baby. That's okay. I have 'em. You just go on in there and turn down the sheets. I'll be right in." George teased.

"Oh, so it's like that, huh?" Theresa snapped back as she stopped short and, with hand on hip, spun around and looked him squarely in his eyes.

Looking directly into her challenging eyes, he kept up the repartee. "It's gonna be like that 'til the cows come home! How else do you expect ta have all those children you been braggin' about filling up our home? You and your Momma did have that little talk, right?"

"Why mister Cohen, you gonna make me blush!"

"That's exactly what I'm talkin'about!"

"Well, come into my parlor, said the spider to the fly."

"Bzzzzzzzz!" George carried both chairs into the house and caught the side of the door with his heel and slammed it shut.

Chapter Three

That year's harvesting went without any unusual problems. A couple of bad storms in August gave them a scare with the tobacco crops, but they turned out to be less than feared and there were no major losses. George was learning the Hale methods but was alo able to give some positive input on the orchards' practices. He gained a good foundational knowledge of the tobacco industry, and he continued his personal quest for knowledge. As he saw it, there was a tremendous benefit for him to become the master tobacconist that Mr. Hale wanted him to become. Frank and George gained a healthy respect for each other, if not a close friendship. They were both excellent at what they did. Frank was more expert with vegetables than anyone in the region. He had a tremendous amount of respect from the farmers in the valley. The Hale crew was doing well, working as a team and sharing their areas of expertise.

Hale's main crop remained his peaches, and it was an impressive sight to see the railcar pulled down the trolley side track and hitched to the late train to New York. It would be there in time for display and sale the first thing in the morning. It was unusual for a car to leave Glastonbury that wasn't already claimed by some broker or merchant. Hale peaches had a worldwide reputation for quality and consistency unparalleled in the industry. His apples were also highly regarded, and they kept the railcar busy well into the Fall harvest. George Hale, John's brother, was partner in some of the orchards, but also had a sizable orchard of his own. He too took advantage of the Hale railcar to get product to the market at the peak of their ripeness and freshness.

Theresa was doing well, and like George, was gaining quite a reputation in the Glastonbury area, as a cook; mostly through word of mouth from the Hale family. Addie Hale raved to everyone who would listen about Theresa's cooking, especially her rolls. She never failed to compliment Theresa and tell her about the feedback she got from her guests. "Your rolls just melt in your mouth. All my guests love them too! I don't know where you got that recipe from, but it's the best roll I've ever had!"

Theresa would always receive the compliments graciously, but never explained where the recipe came from, nor any of its secrets. She knew that her rolls were a key to her personal success. George would often tell her that it was okay to teach, to help someone improve, but never teach them everything, because then they wouldn't need you.

Stancliffe had bought a large house further down Main Street that he converted to an inn. He named it The Hale Tea House, and it was soon renowned for its warm ambiance and for its fine food. One of the key items so highly favored by its clientele were the buttered dinner rolls. Theresa had been recruited by Ida to prepare sheets of rolls each day. Ida would have one of her employees come and pick up the uncooked rolls and bring them back to the inn in a cooler box. The cook at the inn would bake them all during the day as needed. The aroma of the freshly baking rolls wafting throughout the inn was a part of the ambiance that its faithful customers had come to love. She was paid by the dozen and the process kept her busy about two hours a day. Those two hours a day paid her almost as much as she earned in four hours a day working for Mrs. Hale. Ida would supply all the fresh ingredients. Mrs. Hale would allow the use of her kitchen, and the maid cleaned up. She was strictly hired to make rolls. Her misgivings about Ida never proved to be founded on anything of substance. She was a nice person, appeared to be a good wife and mother, and from all reports, she was an excellent business woman. Theresa just chalked it up to jealousy of Ida being such a handsome woman who had the maturity and sophistication that just enhanced her looks. She still thought she showed too much cleavage, and that she seemed way too animated when George was around, but then again, that part could be all in her mind. At any rate, they thrived off each other, and they both loved little Katie. Katie would come to visit her grandmother some days and spend most of her time in the kitchen with Theresa. She had Theresa longing for Kay, or even more, a baby of her own.

She consoled herself by justifying her need to continue to work for as long as she could to help George build the savings they would need to buy their farm. George was determined that when they set foot on the land that it would be theirs free and clear. The land, the house, the animals, the furnishings, the seed, the stores, and the operating capital for one year had to be in the bank before George would make a move. They were counting on her being able to bank her money for a couple of years. It would be a tremendous help. They were pretty sure that by then she would have conceived their first. They were certainly trying hard.

One night after dinner, after they had been on the job for a couple of months, Theresa and George sat down and set up their plan. Based on her work at her two jobs, they could bank almost all her salary until she had a baby. They were not counting on any of the extra she could earn at the Hale House on Saturdays and Holidays and special events when they needed an extra cook, so that would all be plus money for their furniture fund. They figured that it shouldn't cost them any more than a third of what George earned to live on, since they only had to buy a few groceries and a few necessities like coal for the stove and furnace, their clothes, and other incidentals. That meant that George could save most of his salary, plus his harvest bonus. Depending on the success of the harvest season, Hale would pay his foremen one to four weeks pay as an incentive bonus. They didn't count the bonus either. That too went into a special fund. This one was for George to buy a pair of horses to work the farm and serve as carriage horses. He wanted two animals like Buck. George figured that they would need at least $5,000 to buy the property he wanted, and another $3,000 to get them up and running. He figured he would be with Hale until 1918, at the latest. He and Theresa both agreed, however, that their plan could be held off for a while if doing so would hurt Mr. Hale. They both agreed that they wanted to leave him better off for having given them this opportunity.

They settled into a routine and everyone continued to prosper. Theresa kept in touch with their families back home by writing letters almost every Sunday. She was excited every time she got a letter back. Everyone was doing well. The letters, both coming and going, were special times for her and George. They shared those soothing moments, like they did with so many things.

George was an avid newspaper reader. Mr. Hale always brought the paper he read earlier to the morning meetings they had with the men as they discussed goals for the day. He would give the papers to George and he would read them after supper and share major events with Theresa. This kept them abreast of the events that were shaping a rapidly changing world. This was their six o'clock news.

They also took a few minutes a day to read passages from The Bible. This kept their faith strong, and bound them together even more. They also prayed together every night before they said their individual prayers. They rejoiced as they watched their prayers being answered. The prayers that were not answered they received as God's way of saying 'It's not time for that yet!'

The months rapidly moved into the second year. One day in June, George got a letter from his mother. After dinner, he and Theresa sat down to enjoy it as they always did. This one was even more special than most. She was telling them that it was rapidly approaching two years since they were married. It was time for them to prepare for Ben. She had promised to give them two years to get established without the burden of caring for a child, but it was time for Ben to come live with his father and his new mother. Ben was excited, and though she was saddened by the prospect of being without him in her own house, she was excited for both him and George being united. She was letting them know that she planned on bringing him in August, and they had that time to get things ready and to make plans for Ben's going to school.

"I can't wait to see him. He's six years old, and I bet he's grown like a weed!" George was as excited as Theresa had ever seen him.

"That's wonderful, Son. He's gonna' love bein' here with his daddy."

"And his Momma. Don't forget how quickly you and Ben bonded. I'm sure you'll pick up where you left off."

"I know, and I look forward to it, but he loved being around you so much. You loved being together so much that it's just gonna' be good for you two ta be togethah again. I wish Kay's father would let him come, but Momma says things are goin' fine like they are. At least we got one of the boys with us now!"

"Well Baby, don't think this is going to change anything between me and you. I'll never stop loving you the way I do, and we'll never stop being the way we are." George said as he sought to reassure her.

"I ain't worried 'bout no child steppin' between me and you. But it will mean that we should make some changes. You'll have ta make some time for just you two ta be togethah. We'll have ta be a bit more careful about what we say to each other and what we do around the house."

"Oh my goodness, not that!" George blurted out with his right hand across his chest feigning a heart attack.

"Stop cuttin' the fool, Son. You know that's gotta change, but it ain't gonna stop. That's what they got doors for. I just don't want you thinkin' that I'm thinkin' that Ben comin' is gonna shut down our honeymoon. He'll just add to it; another person in the house that we can share our love and God's love with. Don't worry 'bout me. I'm as fine with this as you are. Besides, it's about time ta start raising our family. Ben will just be the start. It'll be like I was pregnant for two years and the baby came out half grown!" she kidded. "They say that if a woman wants ta have a baby, she should bring a child into the house. Well, this could be the start of somethin' big!" she added excitedly.

"Well, Miss Theresa, we'll just have ta work on that!" George pulled her to him as he said it.

"Umph! Sounds like it's gonna be a mighty hot July Mr. Cohen!"

"We'll have ta sow our wild oats before he gets here. Once you have kids in the house, some things will definitely change. I want us ta do something special for our anniversary."

Intrigued by where this was leading, she just looked up at him and said "Okay!" in a tone as much a question as it was encouragement for him to continue.

"Do you still have that dress you wore the first time I saw you at the Church picnic?"

"Yes. Yes I do." Still intrigued, she was eager to hear more.

"Good. I want to take you some place special in Hartford on our anniversary, and I want you ta wear that dress. I'll never forget how beautiful you looked that day. I know I'll probably have ta fight the men off you, but it'll be fun!" He pulled her even closer as his tone became more serious. "You know, you stole my heart that day, and you still have it, Baby! I haven't been the same since. The only thing that I need ta do, besides breathe, is to be with you."

"The same for me. It's been like livin' a dream since the first time I saw you. Sounds like it's gonna be a wonderful night."

"You know it!" he said as he pulled her to him and kissed her.

It was a wonderful night; their second anniversary celebration. It became a precious memory that they would never let fade.

Nellie and Ben were scheduled to arrive at 6:15 on Friday evening. George had gotten off work early to get himself cleaned up to go meet them at the Hartford train station. Mr. Hale offered George his buggy and his "girls" to go pick up his mother and Ben. He had also offered his buggy last weekend for their anniversary night. Ford had finally seduced Hale into adapting to modern transportation, so it helped him keep his horses exercised when George used them for errands and such. Theresa stayed home because they were concerned about the room they would have for her and the luggage.

It was well before 6:00 when he got there. He had time to hitch the buggy and find a bouquet for his mother. He bought one from a vendor just outside the station. He looked around for something for Ben when a display across the street caught his eye. There was a drug store there, and in the window they had little pop-guns. They had corks attached to strings that made a popping sound when they were suddenly forced out of the barrel of the little guns by the air pressure built when you cocked the chamber.

He was standing on the platform when the New York train was announced. There was quite a crowd on the platform and many cars on the train. Rail travel was at its peak during these times, before the dominance of the automobile, and air travel wasn't an alternative.

Though just over six feet, George was tall for his era, and that served him well as he peered over the top of most of the crowd trying to pick out his mother's head in the sea of heads that were streaming from the rail cars. When he saw her his heart leapt. She was two cars down from where he was standing and had already worked her way through the crowd towards the stairs that led from the platform down one story into the cavernous granite lined waiting area. It was crowded there too, but certainly offered more space to maneuver than the platform. George immediately headed to the door closest to him. As he went through the door that led to the stairs, he looked to his right and saw her again. This time there was just enough room to catch a glimpse of Ben holding her hand as he followed closely behind her. It was useless to yell out to her. His voice would have blended into the cacophonous blend of greetings and squeals and hollers and laughter and conversations bubbling over the background of the bullhorns' constant alerts of arriving or departing trains. He pushed his way through the crowd as he moved to the wide bank of stairs that landed in the middle of the hall, as she and Ben were heading down the stairs to his left. He could see her head constantly moving as she scanned her surroundings looking for him. He was moving down the long flight of stairs that connected the platform to the main hall of the station some twenty-five feet below at a faster pace than she or the rest of crowd on either stairway. Perhaps it was this movement out of synch with the rest of the crowd that caught her eye as she caught the first glimpse she had of her son in just over two years. They both broke out into huge grins and waved frantically at each other as if not doing so would make them disappear in the crowd. He reached the bottom well before she did and began to rapidly weave his way through the crowd that was continuously flowing at him like a tidal surge after a passing storm. When she landed at the bottom, she moved diagonally towards the back of building to get away from the flow of the crowd. George adjusted his direction to intersect hers.

"Ma! Oh Ma!" was all he had time to say as he caught her as she flung herself into his open arms.

"George! You look wonderful!" she said as she hugged him as tightly as he could ever remember her hugging him.

"Ma! It's so good to see you. I missed you so much!" he said as he gently pushed her away. "And look at you, Ben. I'm so glad to see you. Man, you sure have grown!" As he had pushed her free of him he immediately had turned to Ben, bent to one knee, and hugged him as he greeted him.

"Hi Poppa!" Ben said somewhat less enthusiastically than how he was greeted. He was glad to see his father but he was a bit shy because it had been so long since he had seen him last.

Ben had a small sack that looked like it might have held some books or other diversions to keep him occupied on the train. His grandmother carried her purse and a small suitcase.

"I know you have more luggage than that. Where is it?"

"Oh, I gave it to a porter to take back to the freight area. It was far too much for Ben and I to handle. I hope it's not too inconvenient."

"That's okay Ma. You did the right thing. Let's get goin'. I know Theresa is dying to see you guys."

"Oh my goodness, in all of the excitement I forgot about Theresa. I mean, I didn't forget about her, it just didn't register that she wasn't here! Why didn't she come?" Nellie asked.

"Well, we just have a four-seater with just a small luggage compartment and we were concerned with there being enough room for everyone plus the luggage. Besides, she's home fixing up a real special supper." George explained.

"Oh, I see. Well let's go. Your father sends his regards, and he also sent you a nice big surprise." As she added that last part she did her best to suppress a grin.

As they rounded the corner to the back of the building, George saw a crowd standing around a very large Percheron stallion. "Look at that big Perch, Ma! He's bigger than Buck." About that time, the horse snapped its head back and spun suddenly. With its ears flicking about at first, and then standing straight up, the horse lunged against the bridle, trying to get away. "Why that is Buck! That's Buck. Buck. Buck!" George yelled as he pulled the surrey to a halt and jumped off and ran like a school boy to the horse. Meanwhile, the horse was spinning and rearing and jerking its head so violently against the reins that it frightened the rather slight young man who was handling him, and he let Buck loose. The big stallion bound the twenty or so feet that remained between them and hit into George so hard that he would have been knocked off his feet if he hadn't hugged him around the throat latch as soon as he could touch him. George was hugging him cheek to cheek and calling his name over and over. Buck was bouncing his head up and down and snorting and whinnying in a sound that came out almost like the whine a dog makes when he's happy to see you.

George turned back to look at his mother, who had also left the surrey and was walking with Ben towards him. "Ma. Ma thank you. Thank you so much. How did you..."

She cut him off. "Your father did it all. He's been wanting to do this for two years. When he heard I was coming up here to bring Ben, he just set things in motion. All I had to do was to hand you this claim ticket. He even called Mr. Hale to make sure that there was someplace you could keep him. Mr. Hale was just as excited as your father. He said he had plenty of room in his barn, and that you could put him up there! He's such a wonderful man."

"Yes he is, and so is my father. I can't wait to thank both of them. Theresa is going to be shocked. I've been saving to buy a pair of Perches when I buy my farm. Now it looks like I only need half as much!" He was smiling and wide eyed when he turned back to Buck. He hugged him again and said, "I can't believe you're really here with me!" Buck nodded his head as if he was agreeing with George.

They tied Buck to the back of the surrey and headed back. George sat Ben on the front seat between him and his mother. None of them were very wide so they could fit snuggly. They needed all the back seat for the trunk they had brought with Ben's things, and the other luggage she had for her short stay. He pointed out different things as they made their way through Hartford to the Hartford bridge, where they crossed the Connecticut to East Hartford and then down the highway to Glastonbury. Nellie was impressed with the buildings and the landscape along their route.

When they got to the Hale property it was getting to be dusk, but George stopped by so his mother could say hello to Mr. Hale and meet Mrs. Hale. He also wanted to thank Mr. Hale for his part in getting him and Buck back together. George and his family were invited to dinner on Sunday afternoon.

Theresa was just as excited as he had been when she saw how big Ben had grown. Nellie was just as pretty as ever, and what a surprise to see Buck again. They all had a lot of catching up to do during dinner. Theresa had fixed a roasted chicken and giblet gravy. She had mashed potatoes and sweet peas and she had kept a dozen rolls from her batter for the Hale House and made a fresh batch of her butter rolls. She made peach pie for dessert.

After dinner, George looked around at everyone sitting with him at the table and said, "This is just so wonderful. I've got my wife here who I love and who just cooked my family a beautiful meal. I have my mother and my son with me who I haven't seen in two years, and my son has come to stay, and I got my horse back. Now, do you know what could make this better?"

By voice or movement they all said "No".

"Some ice cream!" He laughed along with the two Mrs. Cohen's, but it didn't quite strike Ben as funny. Ben's smile only came after his father made the ice cream; a perfect mate for a big slice of peach pie.

Saturday was a busy day for the men around the farm because they were getting prepared for the final priming (harvesting) of the tobacco crop. This year's crop was abundant and healthy, and this last stage of the harvest was crucial to their success, so George had to work even though he wanted to spend every possible moment with his mother and Ben, as if it could make up for the last two years of being without them.

Ben got to meet Johnny and Charlie Saglio. They were all about the same age. Johnny was seven, and Ben and Charlie were both six. Their friendship was almost instantaneous, and they would be inseparable for years.

Theresa and Nellie took the trolley to Hartford. She had told her mother-in-law about the famous G. Fox and Browne-Thomson department stores and she wanted to see them and "pick up a few things". They left Ben with Jo-Anna and the boys because Ben didn't want to do anything but play and explore with his new friends. Jo-Anna was glad to watch out for him, and Theresa saw how well she looked after her sons and was comfortable with her. On the trip back, they stopped at the Hale House, and Nellie met Ida and got a chance to watch people appreciate Theresa's rolls.

Mr. Hale again offered George the use of his team and his surrey so George could take his mother to church. They had visited the

First Congregational Church a couple of times and found them uplifting but lacking the high octane experience they were used to in the Southern Baptist churches they were raised in. They had heard several good things about Shiloh Baptist Church in Hartford. Rev. W. A. Harrod was said to really 'bring The Word'. Coming from a church pastored by a firebrand like Rev. Grubbs, Nellie preferred going to Shiloh. They weren't disappointed.

They went to the Hale's home for dinner. Stancliffe and his family were also there. Everyone got the chance to meet and the conversation was filled with tales of adventure from their very diverse lives. Theresa caught her mother-in-law staring disapprovingly at Ida's well exposed cleavage. She chuckled to herself, knowing that she now had company! George and Mr. Hale got into a discussion about the merits of regular broadleaf tobacco versus shade grown and were soundly reprimanded by both Addie and Nellie.

As they were saying their goodbyes, Nellie thanked everyone for being so welcoming to her son and his wife. "It was hard saying goodbye to George two years ago, and it's going to be harder still on tomorrow. This time, I am not only going to be saying goodbye to my son, but to my grandson as well. It is so comforting to know that I am leaving them with such wonderful people. From his lovely and loving wife to all of you gracious people, I know that George and Ben are in a good place with great people. If my husband were here I know that he would say the same. Thank you so much."

She left that Tuesday morning, and as fate would have it, it would be many years before she returned. As they were riding in, George told his mother about his plans to own his own farm by

1918. She told him that she and his father would be glad to help; that they had some money set aside for him if he ever needed help. George told her that he would let her know if he did.

It was a sad goodbye. He felt more hurt for Ben's sadness than for his own. Ben balled most of the way back and didn't stop until his father stopped and bought him a couple of big lollipops. He'd been with his grandmother since he was just a few months old. Johnny and Charlie were there to meet him and they got his mind off his loss in short order.

George had become a very instrumental part of the Hale Farm and Orchard Company. They had assembled a good team and they were growing more successful as the seasons passed. Stancliffe had taken over a larger part of the business end of the farm and, along with his father and his Uncle George, continued to maneuver the business into one of the most successful agricultural businesses in the state. Frank Saglio had taken the best of what he learned from Mario Paro and from George and had become "the man" when it came to producing quality fruit and vegetables.

George had studied the tobacco industry and specifically the farming aspects of growing shade tobacco. There were a lot of financial considerations in getting involved as well. He had brought all the facts to Mr. Hale and Stancliffe, for them to do the financial analysis. They worked very closely together and decided to put 50 of their 200 acres of tobacco under shade for the 1914 season. Connecticut shade was exploding in popularity in the world markets. Shade farmers were getting three to four times the money for their leaves as the broadleaf farmers were. The Cullmans of Windsor were expanding their holdings rapidly, and were millionaires already because of the high demand for their shade product. Connecticut shade was preferred over the imports, and it was judged superior to Florida shade, which began cultivating using this technique shortly after the Connecticut Valley farmers learned how to simulate the Sumatran growing environment. Some said that the Florida product was just as good, or, at worse, only very slightly less appealing than the Connecticut shade, but the major investments in the Connecticut market by two of the industry's major players made them prefer the Connecticut leaf. American Sumatra Tobacco Company, which claimed to be the "largest growers of shade tobacco in the world", was buying farms, and contracting crops as fast as they could get their hands on them. It was the right time.

The Hale shade tobacco venture had a few hiccups along the way, but the transition went very smoothly during their test year, and they even managed to turn a slight profit on the crop. They learned how to refine their techniques and established systems that better accommodated the complexities of the shade growing process. After World War I broke out abroad, in 1914, the supply of Sumatran and Cuban wrap tobaccos was beginning to decrease, and 1915 promised to bring an even greater demand which would dictate a better price. They increased the acreage under shade to 100 acres.

In May, the luxury liner Lusitania was torpedoed by the Germans and sunk, and the eminent threat of the U.S. joining forces with its allies to fight Germany drove the foreign supply down even further than expected. The crop in 1915 was a bumper crop, delivered into a hungry market.

They had gone all-in for their 1916 crop. All 200 acres of tobacco were under shade. It was a bit more of a struggle than previous years because supplies were not growing as fast as the demand for them, so a lot of the purchased components such as netting for the shading, fertilizers, and even people to work the farm were in short supply. They were able to overcome their obstacles but they definitely had an effect on their stress levels, as they escaped one potential calamity after another.

Theresa was doing well with her work and her little business of selling her rolls to The Hale House. They had been able to stick to their savings plan, and were well ahead of where they wanted to be. It was partly because the money they had not counted in the plan to buy the farm, like her extra work for The Hale House, her pay raises, his harvest bonuses, and his pay raises. The other part was that they figured Theresa would have gotten pregnant before now, and her income would have been cut off or greatly diminished. They weren't in a panic about it because their faith told them to hold on and in due season, The Lord would provide them the desires of their hearts. They took it as a sign that God wanted them to accumulate more and learn more before they set out on their own and begin raising a family. They decided that 1918 still looked like a good target date for them so they kept their eyes on that horizon.

It was September, the tobacco crop was drying in the barns, the peach harvest was finished and shipped off to markets around the country, and the apple crop was rapidly coming into its harvest season. It was Saturday night and George came in dirty as usual, but without his Saturday night smile. Saturday was payday, and they could take off a bit early so they could have some time to enjoy their families. It was always a special time to George because he was able to spend as much time with his wife as he wanted without the specter of having to get up at 5:00 in the morning hanging over his head. On Sundays, they always had a nice leisurely morning; a good breakfast, some time to read the Sunday paper, and then head off to church. There was no joyful anticipation on George's face this evening. He smiled when he walked in the door, and she walked to meet him halfway across their little kitchen drying her hands in her apron and smiling widely, as she approached him. "Hi, Son!" she bubbled as she threw her arms around him and kissed him. She could tell immediately that, despite his effort to appear normal, her Saturday night man was not in the room. "What's wrong?"

"I'm okay. It's just..." and he paused as if choking back his emotions. "You know what, Baby, give me a minute. I just want to wash some of this dirt off me. You and I are okay. It's Mr. Hale. Give me a minute."

Ignoring his plea at first, she responded in alarm. "Mr. Hale? What's wrong with Mr. Hale?" She looked at her husband's blank face and remembered his simple request. "I'm sorry, Son. Take your time. I'm right here."

All he could do is pull her to him and kiss her forehead and turn to the pantry off the kitchen where he knew Theresa would have a tub of warm water and fresh clothes waiting for him. As he pulled off his shirt, she was once again amazed at how pale his back appeared against the deep bronze of his tanned arms and neck. She thought she saw a drop disturb the smooth surface of his bath water as he leaned against the tub for support as he leaned over to remove his socks. She turned away to give him some privacy.

"George, do you have a minute? There's something I want to speak with you about." Hale had asked him as he went to the house to collect his wages. Hale had insisted on his foremen, Stancliffe, Frank, and George collecting their pay from him personally. He usually just handed them their envelope and gave them a few words of gratitude or encouragement. Matters of more substance he usually resolved during an impromptu meeting out in the fields. He had taken to having someone drive him out in his Model"T" on the wagon trails that formed a system of roads that allowed convenient access to just about anywhere on the hundreds of acres of fields and orchards of his vast farm. They were used to seeing him mounted on one of his mares, as that was less restrictive in getting to the few places that were less accessible. Today, he had a look that didn't strike fear of reprimand as much as it appeared a plea for something yet unmentioned.

"Sure, Mr. Hale. Is everything alright?" George had asked.

"I'm not going to honey coat this, George. I'm sick. I'm very sick."

Alarmed at this blunt declaration, George blurted out, "Oh my God! What's wrong?"

"I'm bleeding inside and they can't seem to fix it. I've been getting weaker, and Doctor Rankin suggests bed rest and some kind of medication for a while. At this point, as hard as that might be, I don't feel like I can do anything else." Hale explained.

"And you better behave and do what he tells you to do or I'll help Miss Addie tie you down!" George dug for anything that would lighten the burden of this moment, although he realized there was nothing he could say that would bring light to this dark moment.

"Until I get better, I'm putting Stancliffe in charge. He's my son, and if something happens to me, he is the heir that I trust to take over running my business. My brother George, has his hands full running his own farms in Seymour. We'll get the partnership dissolved so there won't be any complications."

"There's no need to talk like that, Mr. Hale. You just need to relax for a while. You know we've been dancin' on the point of a needle these past few years getting this shade thing going. You just relax and Stan and Frank and I will have everything in good shape when you're feeling better." George spoke with more conviction than he felt in his heart. He knew Mr. Hale would never present him with a petty situation that might cause this degree of alarm.

Hale chuckled. "I pray you're right, but you know me. I know you know me well. I know you well, and that's why I am talking to you now. I respect you far more than to let you hear about this second hand. I care far too much about you than to have you wonder about your future. As long as you choose to, you have a job here, assuming you don't digress into some form of idiocy." Hale said, taking a stab at humor himself. "I'm also asking that you let Stancliffe lead. Give him all the support you can. I know he'll do well, but he'll need you and Frank by his side, just as I have needed you. As long as I am able to draw breath, I want you to feel free to come to me for whatever you might need. I know you're going to start your own farm one of these days. There's a lot I can do to help."

"Oh I know, Mr. Hale, but we'll cross that bridge when we come to it. Right now the important thing is that you get better."

"And I heartily agree, but it doesn't mean that it is the only important thing. In the event I don't get better, I want you and Frank and Stan to be in good positions to take advantage of all the opportunity I see coming in the next few years. Don't worry about me. I'll be fine one way or the other. I serve the same God you serve, and I've never known him to be a liar. This Earthly vessel is of clay and one day soon must crumble, and only He can decide the day. But His promise is that if I believe in His Son, I will have everlasting life, so, like I say, one way or the other, I'll be fine." Hale was surprised how soothing his own words were to his heart that was struggling so mightily to wrestle his faith free from the hands of his fear of the uncertainty that clouded every thought of his tomorrows.

By that following April, Hale was completely housebound. He had been failing steadily to the point where he had no strength left to get up and even occasionally carry on his normal activities. George remembered the day that Hale had come out to where he was preparing the seedling tobacco plants for this year's crop. George had made some insightful deductions as to what kinds of fertilizers and protective coverings to start the seedlings with and his plants looked particularly robust this year. He had told Hale about them when he picked up his check the previous Friday and Hale had promised then that he would come take a look at them.

Hale's voice was weak and somewhat raspy, and his face was ashen and his skin looked dry and lifeless. He was very gaunt about the face and George could see that his body looked frail. It would not have surprised George if he had fallen over right on the spot, so fragile did he appear. John Hale was still a warrior and he would muster all of his strength occasionaly to oversee or celebrate a circumstance of importance. "George, you're right. You've got the Midas touch when it comes to plants. You see, a green thumb is a Midas touch when it's on the hand of a farmer controlling hundreds of acres of prime farm land. They look fantastic." Hale said, trying to exude as much enthusiasm and encouragement as he could muster through the service of his weakened body.

"Well thank you, sir. It's sure nice to see you up and about."

"Well it's sure nice to be here, but I don't feel like hanging around. I just wanted to see your plants. I knew they would be a lift to my spirit. It has not been a good news kind of day. The U.S. declared war on Germany yesterday. That's been coming on since the Lusitania, but it's tough to hear that it's really here. There's gonna' be a draft, but they haven't said who would be included yet. They expect the cut off will be between 18 and 31. There will probably be some exemptions. Farmers are important to keep at home to feed the troops. You're too old for this one, but it sounds like they could stretch the limits as the need arises."

George had to strain to hear everything Hale was saying. He felt worse for Mr. Hale's condition than he did about news about the war. It's not like it was a surprise. Like Hale said, it was just a question of when, ever since the Lusitania was sunk. There had been additional provocations and the United States' staunchest allies were already in combat. No, that wasn't as traumatic as watching this once robust firebrand of a man barely able to stand with the support of a walking stick and looking like death warmed over. "Gee, that's too bad. I expect we'll have to cut back on tobacco at some point to grow additional crops."

Hale smiled at him. "Is that all you're worried about. You better start planning a way to keep your butt home. They won't come for you if you own a farm. That's for dang sure. I've been watching you and Theresa. You certainly should have enough stashed away to get yourselves a place. I know Frank's got his money saved, and he plans on buying a place as soon as possible. I would suggest you do the same."

"Well, if the truth be told, I plan to as soon as you can take my place around here!" George kidded.

"Well, son, I mean George, you might be waiting in vain. Honestly George, you see what's happening here. I'm getting weaker by the minute and they aren't giving me any hope that things are going to get any better. I'm 63 years old and some change. I've lived a good life. I've done some remarkable things. I don't owe anybody anything. I've done well by those I love. I know Jesus Christ is my Savior. Don't make your life changing decisions on my account." Hale's resignation to his mortality was making George uncomfortable, but Hale seemed strong.

"You're going to be alright!" George was still trying to be encouraging.

Almost as fast as he got the words out of his mouth, Hale was coming back at him. "No, I'm not George", as clearly and with as much power as anything he had heard him say in a while. "No, I'm not, and I want to get you situated while I'm in a position to help."

"But you said you needed me and Frank to be here for Stan while you're off your feet. I won't turn my back on him now." George said as he began to choke up as he realized that he and Hale were speaking with certainty of his not being here long.

"George, sometimes circumstances dictate a change of plans. You or Frank will be of no use to Stan or anyone else if you're over in France somewhere with a darn bullet in your ass! Your using your God given talents to provide plenty of food to sustain this country and its troops is far more important than your taking the risk of being sent over there and not being able to make any kind of a difference here; for Stan or otherwise. Stan knows enough to survive. He can call you if he really needs your advice, I'm quite sure." Hale put his hand out to George, as if to seal an agreement.

George took the frail hand and gently squeezed it and shook, not knowing quite what he as agreeing to. "You better believe I'll always be there for you and for your family. I'll never let you down. You've been my back on so many occasions; in so many ways." George was near tears. "I'll never let you down Mr. Hale!" George reiterated.

Mr. Hale cupped him behind his neck and playfully punched him in his stomach. With a twinkle in his eye, he simply said, "I know." And turned back to the car where his driver had been waiting.

True to his word, by mid May, Hale had arranged a land purchase for both Frank and George. Frank paid $3,500 cash for a fifteen acre farm with some fruit trees, but also with vegetable crops. His property was on the west side of town, near the Connecticut River.

George's transaction was bit more complicated. Hale's doctor, Charlie Rankin, had a big plot he had sold to a fellow a few months before. Doc Rankin had taken a deposit and was acting as the mortgage company. The fellow, Delbert Evans, was concerned that he would be drafted, so he had asked Rankin if he would keep his eye open for a buyer, so he could get a smaller place that he could afford. He had a wife and a baby girl that he needed to make certain had a secure home while he was away. About the time they had agreed to sell the place, Hale told him that George was looking for a farm and it sounded like the perfect match. It was agreed that George would buy the farm from Evans, through Rankin.

George agreed to pay $5,000 for 29 acres nearer the center of town, and he would close on the property as soon as Evans closed on another property for his family, but no later than April 1st of 1918. As it turned out, Evans decided he and his family would move in with her parents until he could build a house on a smaller piece of property. George took possession in June.

Neither Frank nor George left the employ of Hale Farms as long as John Hale was alive. However, both did some planting on their own farms and raised as many crops as they could, given the abbreviated time they had left to devote to their own business. That barrier was exacerbated by how late in the year it was when they started planting, but they were dedicated to Hale to the end.

The end came on Saturday, October 13, 1917, the day after the completion of the apple harvest, the last major crop of the year, John Howard Hale died in his home with his family around him. Theresa and George were down in the kitchen, so they could be nearby. Doc Rankin had let the family know yesterday that they should stay close because he only had hours. He passed at 5:00AM.

When Theresa heard Addie yell, "Oh, John", she knew their vigil was over. She had coffee and apple and peach tarts ready. She looked at George and allowed him a moment of silence. She went to the chair where he sat with his head down and cupped in his hands and pulled his face into her midsection. She hugged his head into her for a few seconds and gave him the only reassurance she could think of at the moment. "He's better now George. He'll be pullin' for ya' up in heaven now." He didn't respond, but she felt his body convulse as he finally let his grief find its release.

Chapter Four

Theresa and George sat on their back-porch stairs overlooking the strip of land about 200 yards wide that ran out to a stand of trees that ran about ¼ of a mile across the back of their property. The hills ran down to the edge of this 6-acre peninsula of farmland. The vibrant colors of the October autumn in the Connecticut valley painted a beautiful picture. The late afternoon sky of this Indian summer day was clear except for the gold and grey tint of the cirrus clouds that floated in front of the sun that was swiftly sinking behind the trees at the tops of the hills on the horizon. The soft 70-degree breeze caressed the warm spots on their foreheads where the last rays of the afternoon sun flickered like a dancing butterfly.

"A great poet named William Wordsworth, once described his home in a place in England called Grasmere as being 'the loveliest place on Earth that man has ever found.' What a wonderful place that must be to inspire a man to say something like that. That's how I feel about this place; our place. I can see why they call it Grasmere. Look out there, Baby. This is our Grasmere. This is the place that the Lord has given us. He has prepared us for this land. Our children and their children will dance in these fields. One of these days they'll sit out here on some October afternoon and look out in awe at what the Lord has given them here at our Grasmere."

Theresa looked at him. His face was painted gold by the setting sun. It had only been two weeks since Mr. Hale died. George would not leave the Hale farm as long as Mr. Hale was alive. He wanted to be nearby so that Hale would know he kept his promise and stayed near. He had driven himself hard to put in a crop of hay and corn, along with apples, peaches, blackberries, strawberries and melons at Grasmere that first year. The fruit trees and berry patches came with the land, so they only required maintenance to get through to harvest. He would work his magic, but major changes wouldn't be implemented until next season. The crops he chose to put-in were crops that he could work without too much effort, because he still felt obligated to bring in that one last tobacco crop for Hale. He hired four workers to work the farm and to help him bring in the harvest. He put a lot of miles on Buck that season; getting back and forth between the Hale farm and Grasmere. George finally looked to be at peace. He had kept his promise to someone whose kindnesses he could never repay. Now he could rest. He was finally home.

They used this past week to move into their new house. It was a two story colonial with a large kitchen and living room, and a nice size dining room and a utility room similar to the one at the Hale ranch but much larger. There were four bedrooms upstairs. The master bedroom was large, and two bedrooms were nice sized, and the fourth was rather small. They painted, and repaired, and decorated the house on their evenings and Sundays. The furniture was ready, but Theresa had not wanted it moved into the house until they were ready to move in. Her furniture fund had grown to be a rather substantial amount during the seven years she saved. Their bedroom suit was the most expensive room, and it cost just over $100. They gave Ben the smallest bedroom and let him "help" pick out the furniture. She also furnished one of the other bedrooms for family and guests when they came to visit, as well as the living room, the dining room, and the kitchen. She wanted to save the rest for when the children came.

Theresa continued cooking for Addie Hale for a while, but gradually she began transferring more of her hours to the Hale Tea House. Eventually, Ida just sent food from the Hale House home to her mother-in-law.

Ben was sad that his buddies, Charlie and Johnny, weren't right next door anymore, but they were all in the same school so they got to be together there. They called him Benny, so he wouldn't be the only one in their little gang without a "Y" sound at the end of his name. The name stuck at home, and he would be Benny to his family and friends for the rest of his life. Their homes were about 8 miles apart so they rarely had a chance to play together outside of school and occasionally on the weekends, after harvest season, one of their fathers would bring them to the other's place and they would run themselves ragged. The boys were 10 and 11 now, so they were expected to work on the farm, handling some of the smaller chores like collecting the eggs, feeding the chickens, picking produce, or working in the tobacco fields. In those days, life was their video game. It kept them strong and healthy, but more importantly, it taught them that you had to work for the things you needed, and that you had to work even harder to get the things you wanted.

The year before, while he was working the farm, he met his neighbor. James Hoffman lived on the small farm down the street. He was renting the property, but it was far too small to support his family and pay the rent as well, so he hired himself out to the local tobacco farmers to make ends meet. He and his family had moved up from North Carolina a few years earlier to get away from the discrimination they felt coming their way from both directions; from the whites and the blacks. He was a mulatto, as was his wife. Being a black man in the eyes of the law, he was not respected by white society any more than any other black man, except for the man he cropped for. Rumor had it that he was his father, but no one ever openly talked about who his father was. Because he was shown preferential treatment on the job, and because of his comportment and his skin color, the blacks interpreted that as his feeling he was better than them and decided that his family should be ostracized. He had no money when he stole away to the north. He owed his employer more than he could earn in the perverted slavery called share cropping, so he couldn't just walk away. It took him over a year to work his way to Connecticut, where he heard there were plenty of jobs working in the tobacco farms, which he had been working since he was a little boy in North Carolina. He worked hard and gained favor with the owner of the farm that he lived on before he passed, and his widow offered him to stay on the property and work the land. She would bankroll the crops, and he would pay her back, give her a cut, and pay her rent. It didn't leave him much, but he hustled to save a few dollars here and there. He and his wife Alana shared their modest house with his son John, his daughter Mary, along with his deceased step son's wife Ava, and her two daughters. He owned three cows, an ox, some chickens, a strawberry patch, and a nice plot of vegetables. The owner was only concerned about the 10 acres of tobacco that she financed. It was this crop that funded his savings to someday purchase the land he worked.

During that first full year, James proved to be an invaluable ally. Whenever James was free, he would help George, and in return George would do the same. More than their physical labor, and their ability to manage the direction on projects, they had a wealth of knowledge to share, and they both grew. George hired two men to work with him in getting the fields plowed and planted, and to manage the day laborers they used to work the harvests, especially the tobacco fields. Tobacco was such a labor-intensive crop, yet it required expertise and delicate care. Having someone with expertise in handling this delicate weed was second only to having someone expert in managing the process.

He bought another horse to team with Buck. He was a big chestnut Shire, George had named Ned. He was as tall as Buck, but somewhat short for this massive breed of draft horses. What he lacked in height, he more than made up for in his exceptionally dense muscularity and his wide physique. He looked very powerful, but even his powerful appearance didn't divulge the massive strength of this young gelding. Most of the ground was easily plowed by one horse, and Ned seemed to thrive on the resistance of the plow cutting paths through the rich black soil, almost like an elite athlete in training. Buck was kept for hauling and was still George's preferred form of transportation, but on the occasions when even Ned's incredible power wasn't enough, Buck was teamed with Ned, and they made the ground shake as they proved to be the irresistible force that moved what had been perceived to be an immovable object.

1918 Proved to be a good harvest year for George and for most of the farmers in the area, especially those who were focusing on tobacco. Because of the effects caused by the World War I embargos and blocked shipping lanes, supplies of the exotic cigar wrapper leaves from Sumatra, Cuba, and other exotic tobacco growing areas were reduced to fractions of their normal levels and demand for American tobacco was rapidly growing. That was especially true for Connecticut broadleaf in general, and even more so for Connecticut shade, already considered the best wrapper tobacco on the market, demand was unaffected by cheaper foreign competition. It also meant that the food crops were demanding top dollar as well because so much land was devoted to tobacco crops it reduced supplies.

The factors facing the farming industry that were driving prices up were made worse by the fact that World War I had so drastically reduced the labor pool, either directly or indirectly; directly by the hundreds of thousands of boys who were called out of the farming communities across the country into service; indirectly by those remaining on the farms being lured into the cities to take more lucrative factory jobs to support the war effort.

"There's gonna' be a draft, but they haven't said who would be included yet. They expect the cut off will be between 18 and 31. There will probably be some exemptions. Farmers are important to keep at home to feed the troops. You're too old for this one, but it sounds like they could stretch the limits as the need arises." Hale's conversation with George often replayed in his mind. It was almost prophetic. Between 1917 and 1918, 98% of the adult American male population between the ages of 18 and 45 were registered for service. 24 million men were told to be ready if they were called to leave family and home to go fight and risk their all for their country. The first registration in June of 1917 registered all men between the ages of 21 and 31 who were of age as of that date. The second wave came one year later to incorporate all men who came of age within that year. George would have been disqualified for the draft under either of these two registrations since he was 34 in 1917. The draft that he felt so grateful to Mr. Hale for convincing him to become a farm owner right away to avoid was the registration of September 1918. This was the draft that extended registration to all men between the ages of 18 and 45. Farm ownership gave a man the highest draft exemption. Managing a farm gave a man the next highest exemption. Those who supported the country by continuing to supply food were highly valued. Had Hale not convinced him that this day was imminent, he would have been more exposed to the possibility of being called to serve. It would have been ironic to serve in an army that would have disrespected him more because of the black blood that flowed through his veins, than it would have respected the red blood he may have had to shed in defense of a freedom that some parts of the country so vehemently denied him and his people.

Grasmere was very prosperous for George and Theresa. George would hitch the horses to the wagon and deliver fruit and vegetables to the regional market just across the river in Hartford. The war had driven prices very high because the western European countries had such shortages due to the ravages the war had inflicted on their farm lands. Benny was old enough to deliver eggs and milk to the local families. Theresa continued to cook at the Hale House, but she got up early enough to take care of the things she needed to do to sustain her "men", and returned home in the early afternoon to handle some of the chores before the sun faded over the hills.

In the summer of 1918, Theresa's brother, John, came to Connecticut to find a life better than what was waiting for him back in Florence. Sam had long ago given up on the dream of his being able to ever work himself and his family hard enough to ever buy his freedom from the deadly cycle that hovered menacingly over the life of the sharecropper. Unlike his attitude about young Sammy leaving for a better life, he encouraged his youngest son. He and Gabe and the girls made a living in the fields at Bradley Quarters, and Sara continued her daily walk over to the big house. John had been excited by the letters they received from his sister, and he wanted to taste this wonderful life she described. The others felt the same way, and each resolved to get there in their own time of release. Sam resigned himself to the fact that the land had shackled him to life such as he knew it, but he lived with joy knowing that his children had a means to escape his fate. Sara found her peace in standing strong at the side of her man, regardless of what that fate might be. This was her way. It was the way of her people.

John was a tremendous worker and a joy to have around. He was full of energy and there was never a dull moment with him around. He ate like a horse, and it was harder to keep him out of the berry patches than the rabbits and birds. He never gained weight of any consequence. He inherited that lean sinewy physique from his father.

George made good money that year, and gained respect of the larger farmers in the area. One day in October, Doc Rankin came out to speak with George. He and George had always had a warm cordial relationship, but their relative stations in life, initially, kept them from building a real friendship. They had met shortly after

George came to work for Hale. Doc Rankin was the Hale family physician so they were both an important part of Hale's support system through his illness. Their relationship blossomed after Buck came to town. Rankin was a real horse lover and was immediately captivated by the powerful impression that Buck made as he trotted in the fields under George. As they talked they both recognized a common interest and would often have side discussions about the relative merits of different breeds of horse. It was during one of these discussions that George was convinced that he should buy a Shire for the farm to handle the heavy lifting. He had wanted to get a Belgian like his father's horse Duke, but Rankin convinced him that the merits of the superior lines of the Shire made him a better wagon horse than a Belgian, and George's plan was to use the horse a lot to pull the wagon to market with Buck. That conversation opened the doors to easy conversation between the two. They got a chance to deal with each other from a business perspective when George bought Grasmere from him. During Hale's illness, Rankin often confided in George because he knew of the mutual love the two men had for each other.

"Hey, George! How are things going? Not that I really need to ask."

"Hi Doc! What do you mean by that?" George asked.

"Well you know I'm on the Glastonbury Agricultural Association and The Chamber of Commerce, so I get to hang around all the muckety mucks in Glastonbury. Your name has come up when they start talking about what they hear a man has made on his farm and you made a ton of money off of your place this year."

"Well, I did okay, but it wasn't that much. It sure wouldn't compare to what Bantle and Affleck and your friends in your neighborhood made I'll bet. My place ain't nothin' but a speck when you compare it to those guys." George replied.

"That might be true, but everything is relative. Seems like you put away more money per acre than anybody in these parts has in quite a while. I wish some of my land paid me off as well as yours is paying you." Rankin was rumored to own more real estate than anyone else around town.

"I've got a plan, and I have been working hard. My son, and my wife, and now even my brother-in-law, John, have pitched in. And I have good people working with me. James Hoffman was a big help too. We've been blessed. I believe that as long as I do what The Lord has called me to do, I'll prosper, and my land will be fruitful." Rankin began smiling as he was speaking. "What?"

"Oh I'm not mocking you. You just made me smile because you sound like my father. He was a reverend, and that was the theme to his life. His children were his pasture, and we all did alright. His middle name was George. The right reverend Samuel George Washington Rankin."

Rankin was startled when George broke in. "Wow. You gotta be kidding me. What a coincidence." Then George paused for a moment and then asked, "You wouldn't be kidding me would you?"

"Kidding you? Kidding you about what?" Rankin askcd.

"About your father's name being George Washington Rankin."

"Why would I kid you about that? My father's name was Samuel George Washington Rankin. Why? You're not gonna tell me he's your father too, are you?" Rankin joked.

"Stop playing. It's just that my name is George Washington Cohen. It's just that it seems like such a coincidence."

Rankin was less impressed than George. "Well, George Washington was the father of our country. Hell, I think my great grandfather could have known the man. It's not that uncommon of a name. I'll tell you what. To keep the tradition going, since you're named after my father, then your firstborn should be named after his son, Charles George Rankin. How's that."

George fell right in line with the sarcastic banter. "My firstborn is already named Bennett. My next born, if it's a boy, won't be named after you. He'll be George junior. And if it's a girl, we'll name .."

Rankin interrupted "..her Lucy, after my wife!"

"I don't think so. Besides, on a serious note, I was thinking about me and Theresa coming in to see you. We've been married over seven years now and she's not getting pregnant. We haven't even had any false alarms." George's voice was subdued because of the difficulty of the subject. It was especially hard talking to another man.

"Well I assume you know what you're doing!" Rankin teased but wanted to retrieve his words as soon as he spoke them, sensing George's discomfort more acutely. "I'm sorry, George. Bad joke. Look, just relax. It's not that unusual that some transient factor can affect a woman's ability to conceive. I'm assuming it's not you, because you have already fathered children, as evidenced by little Benny, and you can't deny that little fellah'."

George wondered if he should reinforce the perception of his potency by mentioning that Benny had two sisters as well, but he knew that it would not promote the conversation beyond where it was. "I know. It's just that it's so personal. But, since it's out, is there anything you can do to help?"

"Sure, why don't you let me know when a good time would be after the meeting Monday night?"

"What meeting?"

"Well I'm glad you asked. That's why I stopped by. I don't know if you're aware of it or not, but there is a Glastonbury Agricultural Society, and they hold meetings the first Monday of every business quarter to discuss mutual interests. Stan Hale asked me to ride out and invite you to attend. This meeting is about farming. Seems that Consolidated Cigar is coming in and trying to buy a lot of farm land and setting up shop. There's some concern that they might affect us like General Cigar has affected Windsor and Enfield. We're just trying to figure out what to make of it all. We just want to get as many perspectives as we can and your opinion on things would certainly speak well for the family farmer." Rankin summarized.

"That sounds great. I would love to be involved. It's important that we all work together. I'll be there. When and where?" George asked.

"Seven sharp Monday night at the Williams Memorial Center. Wear your church clothes. It usually lasts 'til after ten, so tell Theresa not to worry."

"Will do. I'll see you then." George said.

When George got back in the house, Theresa was curious as to what brought Doc Rankin out to their home. "He came to invite me to the Glastonbury Agricultural Society meeting. They're gonna be discussing this big tobacco company that's been buying up a lot of farms around these parts and growing shade tobacco."

Theresa was proud that her husband would be invited to sit and meet with such influential people. "Gee, George, that's really somethin'. Just think how special that is. A black man from Georgia being asked to come join a bunch of rich white men and talkin' business." She walked over to him and put her arms around his neck and pulled his face down to hers and gave him a kiss. "I guess that means you're important around here. We sure don't have the kind of money those men have....yet, but I know you're gonna be blessed. Just you wait and see."

George was too preoccupied with his next conversation to give her word of encouragement much more than a weak smile. "I also talked to Doctor Rankin about what we talked about last week." George said, referring to a conversation he and Theresa had about starting a family. They both wanted a large family, and they were both concerned about her inability to conceive. As Theresa had put it, "We certainly been tryin'!"

"Baby, would you mind if we use Doctor Rankin to find out what we can do to get you pregant? He said that we should come see him but I wanted to make sure you would feel okay with a Doctor that we see out and about." George searched her eyes for a reaction. There was no alarming response there, so he believed what she said.

"No, Son. I don't think it would bother me. I mean he is a doctor and that's how I would look at him. Are you sure you won't have a problem with it?" She now read his eyes to measure the sincerity of his response, because if she sensed a problem, she would suggest that they go to a doctor in Hartford to keep things as far from personal as possible.

"No, Baby, I'm okay with it. I feel the same way. So then I'll tell him that we can see him any afternoon next week, after I get back from Hartford." George was still making a few runs a week to deliver apples and some fall crops. By rotating his plantings, as late as August, he had fresh greens and cabbage and other green vegetables to deliver until the temperature dropped under freezing.

They met with Doctor Rankin that following Wednesday afternoon and he gave Theresa a thorough examination and said that he could see nothing physically wrong with her that would stop her from conceiving. He told them that sometimes stress could cause a woman's hormones to get out of whack and cause her to appear infertile. Theresa asked him how she could be stressed for seven years when she has been perfectly happy with her life. Doctor Rankin suggested that perhaps her mind hadn't freed her until they were at the place they had said they wanted to be when they started their family: where they were now, on their own farm. He told her to wait another three months and see if that worked. If not, they would take some additional steps then.

As the days grew greyer and colder and shorter, George noticed a change in Theresa's personality. She wasn't as easy to laugh or to smile as she once was. She loved Christmas and everything that went with it, but she didn't show anywhere near the joy she usually showed during the holiday season. He knew that her not conceiving weighed heavily on her. They went back to Doctor Rankin in January and he gave Theresa some positions to rest in after she and George were together, and told her to keep a chart of her cycle time and explained the best times for them to try and conceive. Then, as they were on the way-out Rankin told them to wait a moment. He had something he wanted Theresa to start taking. He came back with a bottle of dark liquid with a label with the picture of a prissy looking woman on it.

"This is Lydia Pinkham's Vegetable Compound. It isn't medicine but it has gained quite a reputation for helping women through problems. As best I have been able to find out it's a bunch of herb extracts that have been said to help women with their female problems through the ages. She's put some of those and her own herbs together and it has gotten quite a following. It's mostly for helping women who have a hard time with menstrual cramps and other related complications. It seems to work."

Theresa interrupted him. "But I don't have problems like that. My problem is that I don't have a problem with that. It comes every month like clockwork. I don't have a bad time with that like some women do. I just want my baby. I just want to have my baby before I get too old." She was beginning to cry out of frustration.

George put his arm around her and pulled her into his side. "You're still young, Baby. We're still young. 28 isn't too old to start having children. Everything in God's time. Let's just keep trusting Him and believe that He's in control of this. When He wants you to have a baby, you will. Now do you trust God?"

Feeling a bit embarrassed at being emotional, she looked down as she said, "You know I do." Then looking up and smiling, with tears in her eyes, she added, "Lord, nevertheless let Thine will be done."

"And maybe this moment is all He wanted to see, for some reason. In fact, I know that this time next year, we'll be holding our first born." George said more to soothe her than to reflect any divine revelation he'd received.

Rankin stepped back into the conversation. "Anyway you never let me finish telling you about this Lydia Pinkham. It's also said to have a reputation for helping women who have had a hard time conceiving to get pregnant. There's a saying going around that 'there's a baby in every bottle'. Now most doctors don't believe in it, but then again, most doctors don't believe in anything they can't explain. I think it's worth a try. We'll try Lydia and trust God, and I'm sure that between the two of them they can work this out. Now give me a smile, and I'll let you name your firstborn Charles or Lucy."

Theresa smiled and even managed a giggle. She was tickled because George had told her about his previous conversation about naming children.

George chimed in. "I see you're still on that kick. I'll tell you what. If we are standing here this time next year, with a baby, you've got a deal." George chuckled and extended his hand. Rankin smiled and took it.

Then he said, "That'll be seventy five cents for the Pinkham. Watch this stuff though. It's got 14% alcohol. That's more than some good wines."

"Doc, if it's supposed to be that good, I'll buy a case of it!" George said.

"Let's hope you won't need a case!"

They left the office very hopeful. She was very dedicated and took her medicine every day before she ate breakfast. They tried on all the best days to try, and she took all the proper post coital positions to help her conceive, but nothing happened. He saw her getting depressed again and he did everything in his power to keep her happy, and if happy didn't work, he tried keeping her busy. By April she was finishing her third bottle, but he kept her mind too busy to deal with her frustration during the days. There was nothing he could do for the sleepless nights. It was time to start a lot of the seedlings that they would plant in May. He gave her the task of starting the tobacco seeds, which wasn't so much hard as it was tedious to set thousands of seeds in neatly sectioned trays. After two weeks of setting seedlings, he came in the barn early and saw her busy at the bench putting seeds in little mounds of dirt. She was humming a song and smiling. He was glad to see her feeling better.

"Hi Baby! You sure look chipper. It's good to see you smile." He said as he walked over to her and gave her a peck on her forehead.

"Well Son, I'll tell you what, I just planted my one hundred thousandth seed and it just made me happy that I was able ta serve ya so well, my mastah." She said with a glint in her eye and never losing that hint of a smile.

"Well, I see you're in a rare mood. What's gotten into you?" Somewhat amused, but a little concerned.

"Why nothing but you." She quipped.

"What? What does that mean?" he asked.

"It means that it must be you because you're the only thing that's gotten into me!" She was obviously amused at having him at such a disadvantage.

"OK, Theresa! What are you talking about?"

"You're the only thing that's gotten into me so this must be yours!" She was almost to the point of laughing but she kept her face in character.

"Are you alright?" She was beginning to sound disjointed.

"This baby. This baby inside of me. It must be yours. You're the only thing that's gotten into me!" She allowed herself to smile broadly and laugh as the tears began running down her cheeks.

Still not quite sure if she had lost her wits, it took him a few seconds before the substance of what she had said sunk in. "You're pregnant?" he shouted as she danced in place and shook her head yes with her hands against her mouth almost as if to stifle a scream. "You're pregnant?" He asked again as if to verify his first inquiry.

She repeated her response except this time she verbalized. "Yes!" she screamed. "Yes, Lord, yes! Thank you, Lord. Thank You for answering our prayers. Yes, Son. We been blessed! We been blessed!"

By this time, she was openly wailing in joy, like the sisters down at Mt. Moriah used to get 'happy' on Sunday mornings. "How do you know?" he asked, as he tried to hold her in vain. Such was the power in her dance of joy.

"I'm late, Son. I'm two weeks late. I ain't never been late a day in my life. Don't you see that God answered our prayers? It's just like you said. I'm gonna have a baby in January. I already figured it out." She had stopped dancing as she spoke to George, but she was still panting from her frantic activity

Not wanting to rob her of this moment of joy, George was concerned that this could be a letdown if it proved out that she wasn't pregnant. "I'm so happy, Baby! I'm gonna go see Doc Rankin and ask him what we should do!" He was hoping against hope that she was pregnant because he could only imagine how badly she would take this being a false alarm.

She was pregnant. She was back to being her old self. In fact, she was like a spiritual butterfly, deftly floating from place to place yet never having to fight against winds that blew across her path. George was very protective and he would never let her lift anything heavy. She had a case of morning sickness during the early months of her pregnancy, and George took every incident as a sign that there was something wrong. He could not accept that it was a part of the process of preparing the mother's body for the baby growing inside of her. She assured him every time that she was alright and that he needn't worry. She would take good care of herself.

It was a very busy season for him; this his second season as the lord of Grasmere, but he always found time to spend with Theresa at the end of the day, and often during the day. John was a big help, and Benny was handling more. He was strong for an 11-year-old, and very savvy about conducting business around the farm. He practically managed the egg and milk business by himself.

One evening in August, when Theresa was about 4 months pregnant and just beginning to show, they were sitting on the back porch and looking over that stretch of their land they saw on that October afternoon when they agreed that Grasmere was the perfect name for their own personal paradise. The view was quite different now. Everything was deep green and the six acres were structured in lines that ran together in the distance. The golden colors of the autumn horizon were yet weeks from their release but rested in the multi-colored sunset of August. Benny appeared to be a multi-tone grayscale as he groomed big Ned under the broad canopy of the chestnut tree, that only hours before served as an oasis from the evening sun. "We've been blessed, Baby. All of our hard work and our dedication to saving for these days is paying off, and now," he said as he gently reached over and caressed the roundness of her swelling belly that cocooned the child they had prayed for so long, "we can begin our life together for real with all those faces just waiting to come into this world so we can love 'em. God is good, and He is prospering us."

"Yes, He is. I'm so excited about our lives. I wish my mother and father could have had the same hope as we have. We're living a life they didn't dare dream about. I can tell from their letters that they are really cheering you on. They are so happy that I have a man like you in my life. So am I, Son! I love you. I love carrying your baby." She said as she reached out and tenderly put her hand on the hand caressing her belly.

"You know, money on a farm is like the ocean. It comes in waves and it goes in waves, but after all is said and done, you can still see if it's high tide or low tide. We're riding a high tide right now, and we have to go with the flow and take hold of this blessing The Lord has laid before us and ride it for all its worth."

He told her about the recent Glastonbury Agricultural Society meeting he attended. That's the group that Rankin had invited him to meet with in April. During that April meeting Stancliffe was elected president. His position as a member of the Hartford County Farm Bureau, gave him a tremendous insight as to what was happening in Northern Harford County.

George had been well accepted by some of the friends of the Hales and some of Rankin's neighbors, but he sensed that not everyone was thrilled about his being there. He wasn't sure if it was because he didn't have the history in the town as the others, or because he was small potatoes compared to most of the rest of the farmers, or because he was racially different from the rest. He was amused by some of the looks he got, as if they weren't quite sure what he was. Regardless of that, the promise of growth in the tobacco industry in Glastonbury had everyone on the same page, at least on that point.

The center of shade grown tobacco had been along the Connecticut River, north of Hartford to well north of Springfield, Massachusetts. The Cullman Brothers had been pioneers in growing Cuban tobacco under shade in the Connecticut Valley. They bought up hundreds of acres of land, primarily to feed their own tobacco company, United Cigar Manufacturers, who in 1917 changed their name to General Cigar Company. They were busy buying hundreds of regional and cottage cigar companies and were busy consolidating their most popular brands. Everyone was excited about the growth General was bringing to the industry. They introduced White Owl, Van Dycke, Robert Burns, and William Penn, by running commercials on the radio. That was unprecedented in the industry and their brands caught on immediately. It also gave demand for cigars a spike which called for more and more Connecticut shade to feed the hungry beast. American Sumatran Tobacco, the result of the merger of 12 growers in Georgia, who claimed to be the largest shade tobacco producers in the world, conceded that if they were going to be in the game, they had to stop trying to compete with Connecticut shade with their Florida shade. They decided to buy up as many farms and open land as possible. Land was rising in prices as the demand for the tobacco and the land that grew it kept skyrocketing.

More and more tobacco farmers in the Glastonbury area were converting to shade. George had been instrumental in helping Hale make that transition. The cost of entry was high, when you considered the cost of building the large sheds for curing, the poles and tenting to cover the acres of crops, and the high cost of seed and fertilizer. This was compounded by the fact that the cost of land was escalating so fast it was difficult to enter the game once the war started. That was much of the conversation at the April meeting.

Now, a few financial advisors in the group were encouraging local farmers to expand their land ownership and their involvement in the shade industry. They had discovered that those rumors that Consolidated Cigar would come to the Glastonbury region and duplicate what General and American Sumatra had done in Windsor weren't just rumors. Consolidated Cigar was the largest manufacturer of quality cigars. Their flagship brand, Dutch Masters, was the single most popular cigar in the world. They were following General Cigar's lead in taking advantage of radio sponsorships to promote their brand. Their business may have been growing faster than anyone's at the time. Not only were they seeking farm land, but they were also looking for a sight to put a wrapper processing plant. Stan Hale and the others wanted to be sure that the Glastonbury farmers were leveraged to take best advantage of the circumstances as they arose. They also wanted to announce that Stan and a few other investors had formed a bank, The Glastonbury Bank and Trust Company, and that they would be able to sign their letter of incorporation in September. They offered their services as a means for the local farming community to pool their resources and help each other grow their businesses.

"Baby, I'm gonna' start preparing to start growing some shade tobacco next year. I want to start out with about a fifty-fifty mix of shade and broadleaf. If it goes as expected, I'll probably convert to all shade in '21. We have enough to cover everything this year, except for payroll. I'm going to get a short term harvest loan to cover that. That way we can have a little set aside, just in case. You still have almost half of your furniture money set aside, so we really won't have to do anything differently. Does that make sense to you, Baby?"

"Son, you know I leave all that business stuff to you. You know what you're doin' and I don't, so I have to trust you'll see us through."

"What do you mean you have to trust me? Like you don't have a choice!" He feigned that his feelings were hurt.

She smiled and playfully slapped his shoulder. "Oh you know what I mean George Cohen. You know I'm happy to put my trust in you, because I know you put your trust in God. I'll trust you 'til the cows come home."

They laughed. The theme slogan of their relationship took them back many years; back to when they didn't dare dream they could be this happy and secure. "Speaking of cows, I want to buy a couple of more cows and a bull. We can expand our milk deliveries, and we can raise some steers to sell, and we can put the bull out to hire to some of the other farmers around that want to expand the bloodlines of their herds."

"My, ain't you just full of ideas tonight. Well before you go spendin' all our money," she joked, "don't forget you promised to take me to Hartford so I can get the baby's things and we can pick a few things to finish that other bedroom."

They had wanted to wait until she was at least four months before they bought anything for the baby, and he knew she was just counting the days until she could shop for the baby for the first time. In September, they took a trolley into Hartford because

George felt the ride would be smoother for Theresa than hitching the horses and traveling over the bumpy roads. He also wanted to take a train to Springfield to the new fair that had started a few years ago. It was the Eastern States Exposition, a huge agricultural fair sponsored by all six New England states. George had heard so many things about the livestock and the contests for farmers that he just wanted to see what it was like. Rumor had it that it was the best place to get snacks and trinkets.

On the trip back, they leaned against each other on the train ride back to Hartford. He pointed out the huge tobacco fields as they traveled along the Connecticut River track bed. The shade tents were already down in most places, but the vast expanses of cultivated land were an impressive sight. It was after seven o'clock when they arrived at the Hartford station.

"Son, that was a beautiful day. I'm glad I got to share it with you. With the baby coming, it might be a while until I have that kind of freedom again."

"Naw, Baby. We can do that every year. That was fun!"

"This time next year we'll have a nine month old, and our lives will be changed. We won't be able to come and go like we do now. And then, that next year we'll have a nine month old and an eighteen month old. And then the year after..."

He pulled her to him and swayed her gently from side to side, acting as if he was brutalizing her. "Alright. Alright, lady. I get the picture. You're saying that this is the last time you'll let me have this much fun!"

"No! That's not what I'm saying. I'm saying that some of the fun things you want to do, you may have to do without me." She smiled and hugged his arm as they walked towards the trolley that would take them back home.

She had never seen him act so much like an excited little boy as he ate his way from one exhibit to another; hot dogs and chicken and candy apples and popcorn and who knows what George didn't eat. He was mesmerized by the horse pulling contests. There were horses there that were bigger and stronger than Ned or Buck, pulling huge loads on wooden skids until their strength gave out. They would drop almost to their knees and strain against the heavy leather harnesses and gave their all until they could pull no further. The horse or tandem that pulled the heaviest load the furthest, won. They had huge barns filled with show quality horses of many breeds and just as much space devoted to championship cattle raised by 4-H families. George made a note that this might be something he could do with his children some day. He found a breeder that would give him a good price on a bull that had never won in a fair, and that was a little past his show prime, so he was willing to sell him relatively cheap. He was still a fine Holstein specimen, but not up to the standard of the animals his stable had made its reputation for putting up to stud. He was big enough, but he lacked proper conformation for the breed. They arranged for George to come out to their farm, in Bloomfield, that following Saturday.

Theresa was excited when she saw George sitting relaxed in the seat of the wagon as Buck and Ned pulled the load almost effortlessly up Oak Street and into their driveway that led down to their house. The wagon almost filled with the furniture for the baby's room and the guest room. Her eyes darted immediately to the woven wicker top of the baby carriage. "Oh, Son! Oh, Son it's beautiful. What a surprise." That wasn't on their shopping list, since they figured they couldn't use it until April.

"I got a deal. The manager and I got to talking while they loaded up the stuff we bought, and it seems he loves Hale peaches, so I promised him a bushel from our final picking and he gave me the carriage at what it cost him to buy it. I couldn't turn him down."

"It's beautiful. I'm so happy everything is coming together. We're really gonna be a Momma and Poppa!" She threw herself in his arms as he got off the wagon. "Oh my goodness, look at the size of that bull." Theresa squealed, finally paying attention to the beast that was tied by two stout ropes to the back of the wagon that were connected to a big brass ring through its nose.

"Yeah, he sure is big, and he's strong as an ox. It..."

She interrupted him in mid sentence. "I know that ring gotta be hurtin' him."

"Well, it's not gonna hurt him unless he fights against it. That keeps him moving in the direction you want him to go. You can't lead a bull like a horse. Their nature is just too ornery be led gently."

"He's scary lookin'."

"Baby, bulls don't have a reputation for being house pets. Don't ever be anywhere around him unless there is something substantial between you and him!"

Theresa quipped back, "Oh, you ain't gotta worry bout me. In fact, watch this!" She said as she mounted the porch stairs and, with a false sense of urgency, she slammed the door behind her.

George just shook his head and smiled. He connected the six foot ring pole to the nose ring and loosed the ropes and walked Dynamite to his pen.

The months went by like a smooth stone skipping across the mirrored surface of a pond at dawn. Christmas was upon them, and Theresa was in high spirits; a far cry from the depressed state she was in this time last year. She was very heavy with child by Christmas, but that promise of eminent joy took this Christmas to heights of fulfillment she had never experienced before. George and John had gone out and found the perfect tree, right on their own property. They shared warm cider and sang carols as the men and Benny followed her every command so that she could decorate the tree while seated across the room. It was a beautiful holiday. George and Jesus shared birthdates, so Theresa went out of her way to make sure it was an extra special day for him, but it's always tough on Christmas time babies; you never know if you're just getting your other Christmas present in birthday wrapping paper.

Chapter Five

"Son! Son!" George heard her agonized screams from the kitchen and probably only touched three stairs as he rushed upstairs to their bedroom.

He knew before he asked what was happening. "Is it time?"

"Don't you think it's bout time for it to be time? Yeah, it's time! Now don't just stand there! Go call Doc Rankin!" She had that sense of urgency that only one in distress, surrounded by those not totally connected to their plight could muster.

George took off like a flash and hit the landing and the front door at the same instant he began screaming for John.

John burst from the barn before George could call him twice. "She ready?"

Somehow finding himself out of breath, George urgently yelled back. "Yeah! She's ready! Go call Doc."

"I ain't got no change! I'll get him!" John shouted over his shoulder as he neared the end of the drive at a fast gallop.

"John, take Buck!" George yelled.

In the distance George could make out John yelling back at him. "Too, slow!"

He knew John was probably right. In the time it would take him to find change and get to the public phone down on Hebron Avenue, or the time it would take to saddle Buck, John would have covered the three quarters of a mile to Rankin's house. He remembered the way John used to run when they were back down in Georgia. George bolted back up the stairs. "I'm here, Baby!"

"You here? Where Doc?" She was quite agitated.

"I sent John…"

"John? You sent John? John don't know nothin' 'bout gettin' no doctor? Why didn't you go like I asked ya?" She was very agitated. No sooner had she gotten the words out of her mouth than she moaned loudly and sprawled back with her back arched as she absorbed the pains that wracked her pelvic area. John reached out to touch her arm and she slapped his hand away. That act seemed to bring her back. "Oh, Son, I'm so sorry. I'm actin' like a crazy Minnie jackameena!" She suddenly laughed the laugh of someone who does so to keep from crying. "Where's Doc?" she screamed. She was agitated again.

"I know, Baby! It must hurt something awful. Doc's probably only a couple of minutes away. Let's pray!" He reached out his hand and she grabbed and squeezed it with supernatural strength as she once again moaned in agony through clenched teeth.

She looked at him through wild glazed eyes and said, "You pray! I'm screamin'!" as her voice got progressively louder throughout her short statement. She was sweating at her forehead, and the soft black hairs that so delicately framed her face were pasted to her skin. She moaned again and rolled slightly on her side facing George.

Benny was down in the front room, not knowing what to do to help. He just sat and listened and waited. He had never been around a woman in labor before. His father yelled down to him and told him to start a big pot of boiling water. "Poppa, what are you gonna cook?" he yelled back upstairs.

"It's not for cooking. It's for Theresa. The doctors always ask for it when they're helping a lady give birth."

Benny got some urgency in his voice. "Alright, Poppa, I'm gonna do it right away."

They heard the front door burst open and then they heard John yell up at them. "I got Doc, Pank. He comin soon as Miss Lucie get done dressin'. She wants ta come too!" The clatter of the engine of the Model T could be heard through the open door. "They here already, Pank. They comin'!"

John had to step aside as Lucie Rankin ran past him and rushed right up the stairs. She was trying to calm Theresa even before she got to the room. "We're here Theresa. Everything is going to be fine. You just hang on Honey and pretty soon we're going to have ourselves a beautiful baby."

Doctor Rankin was just a few steps behind her but he was gaining on her as they climbed the stairs. He was silent. He figured Lucie would do enough talking for them both.

Theresa felt comforted as soon as she heard Lucie's voice. She had always had good feelings towards the Rankins, especially Lucie. She was always seemed so concerned about people, and she was very unpretentious. They had all gone to church a few times and spent a few Sunday afternoons sharing dinners and sharing time while George and Doctor Rankin talked shop about the farming business and very often, about horses. They had grown quite close during her pregnancy, and every time she went for her check up, one or both would tease her about naming the baby after one of them. She never told them, but she and George had agreed that since they had introduced her to the tonic, which she felt helped her conceive, they would be honored to name their firstborn after such genuinely nice people like the Rankins.

The Rankins dismissed George shortly after they got there. In those days, it was common for the father to leave the room while all the labor activity was going on. George and John and Benny sat together at the kitchen table and talked and ate apple pie and drank milk. They told Benny about the race John had won on the day that his father had first met Theresa. They made plans to buy a sleigh so the horses could pull them through the snow-covered fields, but before he would go to bed, Benny wanted his father to tell him the story about Dynamite; again!

"We had that bull a little over a month, and we could tell he wasn't gonna be pleasant to be around. He didn't even warm up to the cows, and you know that's gotta be a mean ole bull if he doesn't like cows." George waited for the giggle he knew was coming from Benny; after all, they had been through this ritual before. Then he continued. "We had to keep him penned up most of the time. Well one night during apple harvest, just about the time it was getting to dusk, Theresa was preparing some apples to can some applesauce and she decided she should go out and use the "little house" before it got too dark. Well it seems that somethin' about Theresa that night agitated that bull, because as soon as he saw her he started acting up. We don't know how long he was loose, but somehow that bull found a way to chew right through that rope and got loose. Theresa saw him try and jump the fence but he just crashed onto the top rail and flailed around until he broken enough wood to pull himself over the top. That was a big ole bull."

This was the part that Benny was waiting for, when he and his father teamed up to make the story funny. "How big was he, Poppa?"

"Why Son, he was so big Ned would hide in the shade of his shadow on a sunny summer day!" George would always make up something new, and no matter how silly it was, it would make Benny laugh. "Well anyway, when Theresa saw he was loose and had bad intentions towards her, she ran into the "little house" and locked the door. She was screaming for all she was worth. The next thing she knew she heard a huge bang and felt the floor vibrate, and the whole outhouse seemed like it was gonna' tip. About this time, I heard her screaming and I high tailed it up to where I heard her voice coming from. She kept calling me and I kept running and yelling 'here I come'. I heard the bull huffing and bellowing and heard him hit the outhouse a few more times. I realized what was going on and I ran over to the side of the pen and got the pitch fork I kept there just in case ole Dynamite ever got out of hand."

He was getting to the part of the story that Benny liked to hear the most, and he was anxious to hear his father tell it. "Watcha' do then, Poppa?"

"Well son, I ran up on that bull like Sir Lancelot and rammed him right in his butt with that pitch fork!"

Benny was laughing again when he asked, "What'd he do then, Poppa?"

"Well he screamed a bull scream. Awwrrrrrr!" George made a sound that was his best imitation of a screaming bull.

By this time, Benny was laughing nonstop. "Then what happened?"

"That bull turned real quick like he wanted to come at me but by the time he spun around at me, I caught him right in his nose with the fork and he screamed again, and turned away just as fast as he had turned my way and ran off into the pasture."

"What happened to Dynamite then, Poppa?"

"Well I called this dairy farmer from across town and I asked him if wanted him on the hoof or chopped up into steaks, and he said on the hoof. Lucky for ole Dynamite 'cause I was about to go into the meat business!" George was playing to Benny then, because he loved seeing his son laugh; especially at his sense of humor.

"How come y'all ain't never tole me bout dat befoe?" John asked, very surprised that something like that would fly so far under his radar.

"Man, we don't ever get a chance to tell you anything. Shoot, some days you're off and gone before you even brush the dust off yourself, and then you show up in the morning all bright eyed and clean. Whoever she is has your full attention." George took advantage of the moment to let John know that he didn't much care for John's behavior.

"Shoot George, a man's gotta have some company every once in a while. B'sides, I gotta' look out for my future. Y'all ain't gonna be wantin me to be stayin' round here much longer, what with y'all startin' ta have kids an all. If she anything like my Momma, once she start, she gonna be spittin one out bout every year." John tried to prepare George for the idea that he felt it was time for him to move on.

"John now you know you're no bother here. You'll always have a place in my home. In our home."

"Yeah Uncle John, if it gets to be too many kids, me and you can share my room." Benny added, as he addressed the only man he could call his uncle. As much as Benny felt a part of the lives of Ma Nellie and his grandfather, he felt more secure with each person that came into his life that he could call family. You'd never know that Theresa wasn't his mother. They genuinely loved each other. He called her Momma very early in their relationship.

"Well thanks nephew, but there come a time in every man's life when he know it time ta spread his wings," then John suddenly reached out with both hands and began tickling Benny under both arms. "and I'm startin ta feel like the eagle I am." They started tussling and they didn't hear Doc Rankin coming down the stairs.

"I'm glad to see somebody's feeling loose. She's doing well, just the stuff women have to go through but she's doing fine. Lucie is soothing her like a mother cat with her kittens." Doctor Rankin said. "George, what do you have cold to drink?"

"We have water and milk. That milk goes pretty good with that apple pie Theresa made."

"That sounds like just what the doctor ordered!" Benny was the first to laugh but they were all looking for excuses to yuck it up at that point. "You know George, she's not delirious or anything, but she keeps saying she hopes her baby isn't 'marked by no bull'. She really seems to be fretting about that."

"Doc, you just missed the long version of that story, but here it is in a nutshell." George went on to share the saga of Dynamite. "After that fool bull ran off, I went to her to see how she was doing, but before I could ask her how she was, she asked me if Dynamite was gone. As soon as I said 'Yeah' she busted out of the door, bolted past me and sprinted right into the house. You wouldn't believe a pregnant woman could move that fast. When I got into the house, she was standing in the middle of the kitchen just wringing her apron and standing stiff and straight as a statue, but all the time shaking like a leaf and moaning as if she was in pain. Tears were running down her face like she was crying on the inside. I put my arms around her and tried to sooth her, but she stayed like that for about fifteen minutes. When she finally loosened up, she was saying the same thing; 'I don't want my baby marked by no bull.' I knew what she was talking about. It's an old wives tale that a baby will take on some of the traits of whatever might scare the mother during her pregnancy. I've been working on that one ever since."

"Yeah, I've heard that bunk before, myself. She'll know it's just a bunch of phooey in a while. So you sold that old bull, huh? Did you get most of your money back out of the deal?" Rankin asked.

"Maybe you forgot who you're talking to. This is George Washington Cohen. You know I made money on that deal, and he promised me a puppy when his mutt has pups the next time."

This was the first Benny had heard about a puppy, and he was very excited. "We're gonna get a puppy? Oh boy, I can't wait. When are we gonna get it?"

George had let that one slip. He had no idea when the dog would drop another litter, so he hadn't planned on letting the cat out of the bag at this point, because he knew Benny would worry him every day about a puppy until he showed up. "Benny, now I don't know when the dog is gonna have puppies again. It could be in a couple of months, or it could be a couple of years."

Benny looked at his father with his 'gee, I'm really disappointed, Poppa' face. "I can't really wait a whole year, Poppa. Can't we go somewhere and get a puppy sooner?"

"Benny, we'll see what tomorrow brings, but every time you ask me about that puppy, I'm gonna add a week onto when I go get you a dog. Deal?" he asked his son as he stuck out his hand.

Somewhat defeated, Benny took his father's hand and shook and said, "Deal!"

Just as Doc was about to finish his pie and milk, they heard the door open to the bedroom upstairs and they could hear Theresa in her agony playing background to Lucie announcing that "She's crowning, Charles, we're going to need you up here."

Rankin jumped to his feet and walked the few steps to the base of the stairs. He turned back and looked at George and said, "We'll know soon if we name it Charles or Lucie. Either way, it's going to be a beautiful baby."

Very early on Monday morning, January 12, 1920, the first of the many children they prayed for was born to George and Theresa. As promised, they named her after Lucie Elizabeth Rankin. Well, not quite. Mrs. Rankin's given name was Lucretia, but they all agreed that they wouldn't lay that one on the baby, so she was named Lucy Elizabeth Cohen. The Rankin's were doubly honored because they were also asked to be the baby's godparents.

George was there to witness the slap on the fanny that startled the baby and caused her to take her first breath. They wrapped her in a warm blanket and laid her on her mother's chest. They were both spent, but Theresa had enough left in her to unwrap the baby and give her a full inspection. She looked at George and finally spoke through a smile that fought its way through her fatigue. "She's beautiful. She's perfect. I was so afraid..."

"Praise God she's fine, and that ain't no bull!" Even Theresa had to chuckle at George's very intended pun. He bent and gently kissed her, then softly touched the blanket wrapped around his daughter. He and Theresa just looked at each other for a few moments and smiled. He held her hand until she drifted off to her well-deserved sleep.

That next Sunday, George began his tradition of fixing Sunday morning breakfast for his family. He told Theresa to stay in bed with the baby, and he would fix her a breakfast fit for a queen. Benny was still asleep, but he and John worked together to fix a hearty breakfast. John peeled and cubed potatoes and skinned and chopped onions for a pan of country style home fried potatoes. George flowered and seasoned the chicken livers that he and Theresa loved so much. They fried some bacon for Benny, but there was enough for everyone to have some bacon along with the rest of their breakfast. George scrambled a big pan of eggs. The one item on the menu that he was most proud of though, was the hoecake he had learned to make from watching Theresa fix them on Sundays. A hoecake is an old Cherokee delicacy that can best be described as a giant biscuit, but only better tasting. A true hoecake is cooked in a skillet on the stove top. It's cut in wedges like a pie, or often, everybody just grabs a chunk. It was said that it got its name from the fact that the Native Americans used to carry a batter mix with them into the fields, and at lunch time, they would mix water or milk, if available, and make the dough. Lore has it that they would take the hoes they were working with and clean them off and heat them in a fire. They would put the dough batter on the heated hoes and hold them close over the fire without burning the dough. In short order, their lunch was done, and that's how it got the name of hoecake. Theresa had learned how to make hoecakes from her mother who had learned from her mother before her, who had learned from Sara's grandmother.

"She know yet?" John asked.

"How is she gonna know unless you told her?" George responded.

"I ain't said nothin', so then I expect she don't know!"

"I expect. Now just keep it tight!"

"You ain't said nothin'" John reassured him.

George left John to tidy up as much as possible while he went to get Theresa and Benny. He went and woke Benny first and had him get washed and presentable for breakfast, then he went down the hall to his room and gently opened the door. He knew Theresa was awake but he wasn't sure about the baby. He whispered "You sleep?"

Theresa gave him that 'dumb question' look and quipped back at him in a mock whisper. "How can a lady sleep when she knows that a beautiful man like you is just downstairs? Besides, all those aromas got your daughter hungry. She got an early breakfast and I think she may be out for the count. Breakfast sure smells good."

"You need any help with the baby?"

"No. I'll be down in a couple of minutes."

"Alright, Baby. It's waiting for you."

Everyone raved about breakfast. Lucy woke up on cue just as they finished up. George told Benny to take care of the kitchen as he announced that he and John had business in Hartford. He had to twist the truth a bit to get Theresa off his case. She was very curious as to why he needed to go to Hartford on a Sunday if he wasn't going to church. He told her it was the only day to see about getting some extra help around the place. She wasn't satisfied with his response but that was his story and he stuck to it. When she saw them hitch both Ned and Buck to the surrey, she knew he had plans to haul something back home, because George usually just let Buck pull the surrey unless there was some weight being taken over a distance; she just didn't know what kind of surprise he had in mind.

About three hours later, Theresa was lying down with the baby when she heard the rumble of the surrey's wheels at the front of the house. She gently straightened her arm to release the baby from her human cradle so she could get up and peek out the window to see what her big surprise was. Before she could get to the window she heard George calling her from the front door.

"You decent, Baby?"

Unable to resist the temptation, she yelled back, "I'm always decent!"

"Well, grab the baby and come on down, I've got a big surprise for you!"

"Okay. Give me a minute and I'll be right there. I gotta change Lucy!" Theresa paused for a couple of seconds before she continued. "Unless you want to!"

She caught him off guard and he was at a loss for words. "No. That's alright, Baby. You do that so much better than I can."

"Ain't that the truth? Can you pull them diapers off the line? She just bout gone through another batch! I'll fold 'em when I get down."

George went back to the utility room where he had strung up a clothes line for use during the cold months. He kept his ear pinned to the front of the house to hear if that tell tale third step squeaked when Theresa came down. He got back to the landing just as Theresa started to descend the stairs. He rushed up about six steps and reached for the baby. "Here Baby, let me take her." As he took Lucy out of her arms and cuddled her close, he gave Theresa a kiss, and grabbed her hand and said "Come on in the parlor. I've got a surprise for you." as he led her down the last few stairs.

With a false air of astonishment Theresa asked, "A surprise? You got me a surprise? What in heaven's name could it........." Her question was answered before she could finish her teasing as she reached the bottom of the stairs and was able to see into the parlor. The shock froze her and her emotions immediately overwhelmed her faculties as she peered through her fingers while she held her hands over her face to stifle her scream and to cover her eyes as if she were preparing her eyes for a different truth when she removed them. Her feet danced in place as almost simultaneously her arms spread out and up as she screamed, "Momma! Momma! It's you! You're here! How did..."

Her words were blocked by the force of Sara rushing into her open arms and embracing her as they both pressed tear moistened cheeks against each other. Theresa was openly sobbing tears of joy. It had been three years since Theresa had gone back home to see her parents.

"And Alice! Look at you. You came too!" By that time Alice had already come over and joined the group embrace. They all just held on to each other and jumped and squealed in unison.

Sara was the first to pull away as she turned towards George and held out her arms. "Let me see my baby." She first embraced Lucy and held her close to her as she walked across the parlor to the divan. Almost as if savoring the unwrapping of a Christmas gift, Sara laid Lucy on her lap and very delicately began to peel away the layers that wrapped her. Sara let out a noise that sounded as if her breath had been taken from her, before she spoke. "Thank you Jesus! She so beautiful. I prayed for this moment; ta be able ta hold the first born of my daughter. Thank You, Lord. Theresa, she so beautiful. She look just like when you was a baby. I hear she got our eyes."

"Yes Momma, she does. She is beautiful. Sometimes I have ta pinch myself. She's just so perfect."

Her daughters had come over and joined her on the divan, each to a side of her, as they admired Lucy, who was beginning to stir from all the noise and activity around her. Lucy brought her hand to her little pink face and rubbed the back of her hand across her nose. She turned her head toward her mother and slowly opened her eyes, squinting as if trying to stop the invasion of the soft light that kissed the parlor on that mid-January afternoon.

"Awe, looka there, she tryin ta see her Momma!" Alice cried out.

"Doc says she can't see much yet, but I swear she looks at me when I'm talkin to her." Theresa said as she moved the blanket back slightly off her face so that it wouldn't interfere with her line of sight.

"Look at dem eyes, Pank! You right. She is perfect." Sara couldn't stop smiling. Her cheek muscles were beginning to burn but she still couldn't wipe the smile off her face. Lucy turned her head to the sound of her grandmother's voice and appeared to stare at her for a second and then she smiled. "Look Pank! She smilin' at her grandmomma!"

They sat like that for a couple of hours filling each other in on their lives and making a big deal out of everything that Lucy did. They talked about Kay and she said he was doing fine, and that he was growing by leaps and bounds. He was 10, and he was a big help to her father in the fields. She couldn't get over how much he looked like John. Sam was really attached and was as much the cause of him not coming to Connecticut as anything. Sara wasn't pushing that point either. Theresa had resigned herself that her mother and father would raise him, because there was still the issue with his father.

After George and John came in from tending to the horses, George just watched and sat silent for the most part. John involved himself a little in the conversation, but he too deferred to that special mother/daughter bonding that created a camp that didn't call for outsiders. After a while, after Lucy was asleep, the three women went to the kitchen to fix Sunday dinner. It was late so they decided to keep it simple; fried chicken, cabbage, and potatoes. George had dressed the chickens the night before, as it was his plan to fix dinner when he returned from Hartford. He did offer to follow through on his plan, but the women would have none of it. They all kept saying flattering things about him to the point of causing embarrassment for him and jealousy for John.

"Hey, how bout me. I helped pay for y'all ta come up heah too, ya know. I went and gotcha wit George too, and, on top of dat, I was gonna help cook too! So how bout dat?" John was picking at his sisters and his mother. All the while he was talking, his playful slaps at them kept rhythm with his words.

"Awe come heah baby. We know you one of a kind!" his mother said as she grabbed him and hugged him and rocked him a little bit. His sisters joined in and hugged him and kept on with a steady stream of the most exaggerated compliments they could think of, until he left the kitchen and joined his brother-in-law in the parlor. John got out his guitar and George got out his little accordion and they sang hymns and ditties and whatever crossed their minds. The more George thought about it, the more he considered this reunion and first meeting as a very special occasion. His joy and enthusiasm was growing by the minute, and it was infectious.

Benny was surprised to see everyone when he came in from sledding with some of the other boys in the area. His father and uncle hadn't filled him in for fear he would let the surprise slip. Sara and Alice couldn't get over how he had grown. They hadn't seen him in three years, since he and his parents had come down to visit. A boy grows a lot between 9 and 12. He had lost most of the softness of childhood and was taking on the transforming characteristics of an adolescent; an increase in size, the beginning of muscle definition, the promise of facial hair, and a slight change in the voice. Benny also received a barrage of compliments about his size and good looks. Theresa bragged about his grades in school, about how much help he was around the farm, and about his popularity with a lot of his classmates, especially a couple of farmers' daughters.

Her mother and sister stayed almost two weeks. They had a wonderful time reminiscing and sharing their plans for the future. It saddened Theresa that her mother didn't have any life plans except living a long and obedient life; to her God, her husband,

and to her role as a mother for her children. She had grown past the point of hope for change in her circumstances, although she did say that she would love to come live with her daughter. However, Sara knew her husband would never be able to leave the land he had worked so hard to be free himself from. She called the land cursed that so inexorably bound him tighter with each passing year. He could never leave, and she would never leave him alone. They never talked about the finality of his sentence; their sentence. As Sam had grown older, and as his children had sought their own freedom, unwilling to share in his exile from hope, it became more and more apparent that whatever false sense of hope he ever had of escaping this enslavement structured by velvet chains, was as fruitless as seeking that patch of ground where the rainbow descends to kiss the earth. Even in his resignation to that life that vexed his spirit, Sam was not without joy. His sense of humor was intact, and he came to understand the value of what he was blessed with; a mighty God, a beautiful wife, children who would not have to share in his plight, and now grandchildren who would be so separated from his fate that they might only hear of this place that stole his freedom but that had to release his prayers.

It was decided that Alice, would come and stay with her sister and her family so that she could help as the children came. Theresa was confident that more were coming, and she knew that female family nearby would be a tremendous blessing, especially since her roll business was still a big help in taking care of the extras around the house. It also gave her a sense of accomplishment. Her years of working as a member of a family that worked for a common cause had left her very uncomfortable in the role of a housewife. Alice was 19 now, and had grown into a lovely young lady, and Bradley Quarters had nothing to offer her except winding up with a man with the same hope for freedom as her father. She would return home with her mother. John wanted to take some time during the slow season to go see his father and his sisters and Gabe and his old buddy, Jesse. When he came back in a few weeks, he would bring Alice back with him.

On the afternoon before they left, Theresa was in the kitchen and her mother was standing on the back porch wrapped in a blanket with her face feeling the heat of the kiss of the afternoon sun that hovered silently in the deep blue of the winter sky. Theresa watched through the window of the back door as her mother would lift her arms, palms up, every few minutes, as she praised God. The afternoon was as beautiful as one could hope for in early February in Connecticut. It was just above freezing, but the air was calm and dry, so the sun's affect on the body was magnified. When she came in, Theresa could tell that had been crying. She went to her mother and hugged her and hid her face in the nape of her neck. "I know, Momma. I'm gonna miss you too."

Sara chuckled as she returned her daughter's embrace. "My tears are of joy, not of sorrow. In da Bible, God calls everyone to a place dat He want dem ta be. He called Moses to a place; he called Elisha to a place; he called Abraham to a place; an he called Paul to a place. It was da place where He planned dem ta do whatever He made dem ta do. When I looked over dis beautiful land dat you an George own, my spirit tole me dat dis is yo place; not jes because y'all own it, but cause He gave it to ya. Last week, when my cousins come by, we talked bout da story of da chief. Dey got dat story up heah jes like my Momma tole it ta me. Dis is da land where my Momma an her sistah left from. Dey was sayin' dat word round da family up in dese parts is dat God brought you back to da very same place dat da chief last saw his chirlrens ride off inta da trees. Ain't dat somethin'?" She asked as she pushed Theresa away from her and led her to the table so they could both sit and talk.

"Yeah, that's really somethin', Momma. Do you think they're right? Do you really think that God really worked all this out so that I could come back and claim the family land?" Theresa found it all too hard to believe, but all indications were that it was at least partially true; her family had originally come from Glastonbury, and her grandmother and her great aunt were stolen away by slave traders on their way to go stay with family in the south to avoid the forced exile that led to the Trail of Tears, born in Andrew Jackson's hatred for Native Americans. It turned out that the tribal people of Connecticut were too dispersed to be rounded up en masse as they did with the Cherokee and other great native nations. The land was somehow bought by people who claimed to have deed to it, and the chief and his aging and dwindling tribe were set to wander once again.

"I was jes thankin, Pank. Yo life is so blessed. I don't thank I ever even dared ta dream you would have what ya got. I was jes thankin' God. I praise 'em fo da fack dat my foist bone daughtah will live a far bettah life dan I ever did. An it jes seem like God got His hand all ovah dis. My daughtah is da one dat return to da land we got stole from us, an my gran daughtah will be a princess in dis Grasmere. Y'all done returned stead of comin to dis land. Y'all returned ta Grasmere. I'm gone miss bein' heah wit y'all. You an George sho made my time heah like a fairy tale come true. I'll never forget it." She stood up then and turned to the door leading to the vestibule. "I best be gittin started on gittin packed." Without turning to look back at Theresa, who she knew was crying, she went upstairs.

Lucy was very fair with a head full of silky black hair, and big blue eyes that seemed to dance with joy. They danced even more so whenever her 'Daddy' came into view. Everyone made such a fuss over her. She was a very beautiful baby.

One day, when she was about six months old, they took her into Hartford to G. Fox Department Store to buy some clothes for the summer. As usual people were stopping them every few feet to compliment them on their beautiful daughter. While they were shopping, one of the sales girls was engaging Lucy. Theresa turned her head for a moment, but when she turned around, the carriage was gone. Theresa immediately let out a scream. "My baby! Somebody stole my baby. Help! Somebody stole my baby!"

George was wandering around the store, but he hadn't gone so far that he couldn't hear his wife's agonized screams. He rushed to her, but not as quickly as the frightened sales clerk who had just taken Lucy a few feet to the back of the department to show her off to her co-workers. He got there in time to hear the young lady apologizing profusely and explaining that she was only a few feet away, showing her off. George rushed right up to Theresa and asked "Are you alright, Baby?"

"No I'm not alright!" Then turning to the girl, "I know you didn't mean no harm, but you just can't walk away with somebody's baby without tellin' 'em. That just ain't right!" Theresa caught herself. She knew the girl just made a stupid mistake, and keeping at her would not fix what had already happened. While the girl, who was now in tears, was still explaining and apologizing, Theresa said

"It's alright. It's forgiven." Then looking at George, she simply said, "Let's go, Son".

Lucy was the center of their joy, but they still had a farm to run and a son to raise, and kept doing well at both. The shade tobacco experiment had worked out well, and George was making plans to convert all of his tobacco crops in '21. He had made arrangements with Stan Hale to sell his crop out of the field, so he could forego the expense of building the curing shed that added so much to the cost of entering the shade business. He conferred with Stancliffe and Doc Rankin and they both suggested he not deplete his reserves but mortgage a portion of his property to fund the expenses of the shed and additional netting and other implements he would need to operate. There would also be higher labor costs. The post war era was pulling more and more farm workers into industrial centers, and the immigrant population was not growing fast enough to fill the void. The competition for workers had driven labor costs higher. To compound the problem, that since shade tobacco required far more activity in the cultivation and harvesting processes than regular broadleaf crops, they suggested that he plan on borrowing against expected labor costs as well. The whole premise was based on his being able to pay back relatively quickly for most of it: the labor costs and other expenses would be paid back at the end of harvest. The shed could be carried over a period of two or three years.

Grasmere had done well in 1920. The crops were bountiful and it turned a good profit. The fruit and produce business was growing, as George gained more and more direct customers in the local area. His business was growing especially strong in Hartford. Benny had a regular route of local customers for milk and eggs.

Theresa still managed to make extra money by supplying rolls to The Hale House. Theresa was still taking the Lydia Pinkham Tonic, and they were both hopeful that it would work again. Things were going well, and the future looked bright.

Chapter Six

George ran into a snag when he went to mortgage Grasmere for collateral to build his shed and to finance expected labor costs for the '21 season. It seems that the paperwork that was signed between him and Evans and Rankin was not properly finalized so that the town records did not show the transfer, since the transaction was done with a written deed and a handshake between the men. In order for Manchester Lumber to fund the mortgage they had to legally reconstruct the transaction. Legally Grasmere showed as a joint ownership of Evans and Rankin. They had to "re-sell" Grasmere to George with the proper warrantees completed as well as the mortgage documents being filed with the town of Glastonbury. The portion of Grasmere that Evans' original deposit with Rankin could buy, had stayed with Evans, but he was ready to sell it, and George was willing to buy it, so George added another 10 acres of land to his farm. Once all the mess was cleared, he got his money. His plan was to pay off the lumber company and Evans within two years

That Christmas, George finally had to break down and buy Benny his puppy. He had tried to show his son the importance of keeping his word, so he reminded him that the puppy wasn't coming because he constantly broke his word and kept after his father about when he could have his puppy. It had been a while since Benny had asked, so George saw Christmas as being a good opportunity to get the puppy, before Benny asked again and he had to hold off longer!

Christmas eve, after Ben was asleep, and after all the presents were wrapped, George walked down the road to pick up the puppy. They kept the pup in the room with them to keep him from crying and giving away the surprise.

"Our family sure is growing, isn't it?" Theresa said as she gently stroked the sleeping puppy.

"Yeah, it sure is, but that's how I always wanted my house to be; full of love and full of people to love each other. We're really blessed that way."

"Well it's just gonna keep on getting better."

He leaned over and kissed her on her forehead as he said, "I know that's right. In fact, if you want to give me my birthday present a couple of hours early, we could be looking at a new family member round about peach harvest time." He tenderly rubbed her belly as he teased her.

"Well I was thinkin' more like in July!" she quipped back as she pressed the back of his soothing hand.

"Naw Baby, you must've missed school that day but it's gonna take 'til; let's see." As he began counting off the months on his fingers. "Actually, it'll be more like apple harvest time."

"No Son, it's gonna be more like the end of July. More like sweet corn time." She was smiling at him so broadly that her cheek muscles were almost in her eyes.

"No Baby. Look say we start counting January first to keep it simple. Then you go February, March....." Then he finally got it. "You're gonna have a baby in July?" She shook her head yes, but he didn't take the time to notice. "We're gonna have a baby in

July? You're pregnant!" He said the last word so loud that she had to remind him that everyone else in the house, including the puppy were asleep, and they certainly didn't want any interruptions, so he continued in a whisper. "Ooh woman, that's the best Christmas present I ever got. That's only seven months from now. You're gonna be mean as a snake in July. I'm gonna spend all my spare money on fans so you'll be nice and cool. I'm sure glad we got Alice here to be with you through all of that! So you seen Doc and I didn't know it?"

"Well I knew I had missed the last two months, and I could just kind of tell. If I was, I wanted it to be your birthday and Christmas present, and I was right, so here we are."

"This is gonna be a boy. Just you wait."

"Alright Mr. Cohen, how can you be so sure?"

"Because that's what I've been aiming for, and I know I hit the mark!" She slapped his arm and they collapsed into each other's arms and laughed.

Benny named the puppy Rover. He was a cute mixed breed. You could tell by his paws that he was going to be a big dog. George got the dog for free from his friend John Hoffman. George wasn't sure of the pedigree, but John said the dog's mother was a cross breed, mixed with American Bulldog and a Coonhound. She wasn't very pretty, but she was a good family dog and a great watch dog. As for the father, John had no idea. He let Molley roam free on the farm, and there was no telling who she had allowed to come to visit. It was a joy to watch Benny running and tussling with his puppy. Lucy was excited by the puppy as well. She would almost lunge out of her father's arms whenever the puppy came close, trying to reach for it. She would giggle anytime he let her touch Rover. He was just as excited by her. He was all wiggles and dancing paws as he spun in circles as she reached out to him. Lucy would squeal with delight whenever his cold wet nose would find a place on her exposed skin. George wouldn't let the puppy lick her face as he was constantly trying to do. He had always thought it unclean when he saw people let their dogs lick them all over their faces. People defended the practice by explaining that a dog's tongue is medicinal. He, on the other hand, couldn't get past the fact that a dog was one of only a few animals that could lick its own butt.

During the winter months, George had time on his hands to do repairs and to set up his business relationships for the coming year, but most of all, it was a time that he could spend with his family. George loved playing with Lucy; especially playing stinky toes; he would hold her delicate toes to his nose and sniff and say "Phew" and pull his face back and shake his head and squint his eyes. This would send Lucy into spasms of laughter. Benny would repeat what his father was doing and they would all get tickled watching Lucy's reactions.

One afternoon in late February, George was holding Lucy as he sat in Theresa's rocking chair and looked out of the window at the field they see when they sit on their back porch. She was sound asleep with her head securely nestled in the curve of his arm. He looked down at her and, without any warning, felt a sense of apprehension. She was so beautiful and so vulnerable. He realized that if he so much as turned his body in the wrong direction he could smother her. Life was fragile and the next breath is promised to no man, but it is the conscious will of God that we should survive to see the next moment. He had never dwelt on contemplating his own mortality, but for some reason, watching the large fluffy flakes of the freezing afternoon snow drift so nonchalantly to the Earth, he too felt that these moments were too beautiful to remain so. He realized that into each life some rain must fall; that there was a nugget of bitter for every bit of sweet. How and when would the dark day start? Was he prepared? Would his family be prepared?

His mind raced back to the decision he had made last fall. He had recently talked with Stan Hale, and he had suggested, based on some recent information, that George might want to reconsider going full bore into shade tobacco; not because it wasn't a hot commodity, but because the economy was still recovering from the fallout of the war. Farm land values were peaking at absurdly high levels that could not be sustained. The shift of labor from the farms to the factories were further affecting the profitability of farmers as the shortage of labor was driving labor costs to unprecedented highs. Because of the uncertainty and the huge amounts of capital required to fund the industrial revolution that was in full progress in the post war years, the cost of borrowing was high and funds from normal, credible sources were hard to come by. Stancliffe's concern was that, once on that treadmill, it was hard to get off. Even though the cigar industry had reached a peak in production in 1920, market indicators were that it was the last best year for the industry. That could mean that once the farm land value bubble burst in the Connecticut Valley, like it had already done in other parts of the country, it would be hard to get the financing needed to carry operations in the future because the value of the collateral would be diminishing, and possibly diminish to the point that it couldn't sustain the operations.

The tobacco industry was reconfiguring as the returning veterans were driving the focus of the industry from cigar product to the cigarettes they had become addicted to in the trenches of Europe during the war. Also, with the growth of advertising in more accessible media like radio and popular magazines, more and more women were beginning to take up the smoking habit, and their smoke of choice was cigarettes. The tobacco grown in the Connecticut River Valley was almost exclusively cigar related so the tobacco farmers in the region were beginning to feel the effects of that shift in demand, although it was having an unexpected effect on shade tobacco. One of the key competitors for Connecticut shade was Florida shade. Being the second domestic choice, and probably ranked behind Cuban, Dominican, and Sumatran in worldwide markets, many of the farmers down there were switching crops over to other types of tobacco. This left many cigar manufacturers with fewer options for leaf wraps; either buy Connecticut shade, or go offshore for a less desirable product. This helped keep shade a good cash crop, and leaving many growers with no reasonable option but to go for the shade option.

The problem with shade tobacco was that it was so vulnerable to disease and weather conditions. Even during the curing process, fungus infections could destroy a crop before it cured properly.

George decided to go ahead with his plans anyway. He had good council from Doctor Rankin and Nathan Richards, an attorney who was a business associate of Rankin's, and one of Rankin's Shriner lodge brothers. They were telling him that the Farm Credit Banks were giving better and longer term loans to farmers, and that they had both mortgaged through a local lumber company that competed with those banks for local business. He was very comfortable that signing a loan with such a long maturity window, and his ability to bring in superior crops he could handle the transition to shade tobacco.

Now, as he sat there holding his beautiful little girl, and knowing he had another child coming soon, he wasn't second guessing himself as much as he was becoming painfully aware that the stakes had been raised and that the days of being a casual farmer were over. His experience in applying for the mortgage showed him that he needed to get his papers in order and keep them so he could protect his legal interests. He was also concerned that if anything should happen to him, Theresa and the children would be protected.

That night, after the children were asleep, they sat in the parlor and read the Bible for while. Neither of them felt good about their sporadic church attendance, but they just didn't feel comfortable with the subdued worship environment at First Congregational. They maintained their spiritual strength and kept their focus through daily reading and prayer. When time and the weather permitted, they would hitch the horses and go to Shiloh Baptist in Hartford's north end. Services there were cut from the same mold as the services they remembered from back home. They would usually spend the rest of their time listening to the radio and singing along or just talking until they were ready for bed. Tonight, George needed to talk.

"Baby."

"Yes, Son."

"Today, when I was holding Lucy, it made me start thinking about things when I realized how much I've come to love her in such a short time. I looked at her just laying there all cuddled up in my arms so sweet and innocent and trusting and dependent. She has all she has simply because God is using us to provide it, but what happens if we aren't responsible enough to handle what He has provided? Then, I realized that I actually hold my entire family like that in some respects. Not just you and Benny and Lucy and the new baby, but all those other kids we're working on. What happens if I'm not here?"

Theresa looked at him curiously and asked, "What do you mean?"

"Well it's just that I'm the only one that knows what hole I got the money buried in."

That statement startled her. She squinted her eyes into slivers. "You never told me you had any money buried in no hole. What are you talking about? I thought the money was in the bank."

George chuckled. "It was just a figure of speech. All I was getting at is that you don't know all the details about our business. You don't know how much I spend. You don't know who I buy from. You don't know if I'm payin' them or if I owe them money on an account. What's my deal with the coal man?" George quickly threw at her to purposely get her off balance.

"Oh Son, I don't worry about all that stuff. You take care of all that. I don't want to get in your business. You do it way better than I can."

"You didn't answer my question. What's my deal with the coal man?" He repeated himself more assertively.

"I don't know. I just know that he comes before we run out of coal. It's something I don't even have to worry about."

"That's just my point. You don't know anything about how Grasmere does business. For your information, we barter. I supply his fruit stand with fruit and vegetables, and he pays me in coal. We keep a record that we both sign, and at the end of the winter, the first of April to be exact, he either pays me or I pay him. I can go on about a lot of little holes I got money hid in, but I think you get my point." He pulled her around to look at him, because she had turned her face to the wall while he was talking. When she turned towards him he saw she had a very hurt look on her face. "Baby, what are you looking like a wounded puppy about? I'm not upset with you or anything. It's just...."

"I know what you're doing, Son. You're trying to prepare me to be without you here to take care of me. What's wrong? Are you sick? Are you leavin' me?" She was getting more agitated as she spoke, and her words were coming in the short staccato pace and tightened controlled tones of one who was being squeezed by sorrow.

"Whoa! Whoa! Where's that pretty little head of yours going? There's nothing wrong with me, and there's nothing wrong between us! It's just that I realized that if something happened to me, you wouldn't know the first thing about our business. So, if you had to run the farm, or if you had to get someone to run the farm, or if someone tried to take advantage of you, you don't know enough to keep things going the way I would want to see you do it. I need to let you know more about what I do, and how I do it. That's all I'm saying!" He was holding her to him now, and pushed her away to arms length so he could look in her face and see her relief, but he was disappointed by what he saw.

Theresa was looking down and shaking her head from side to side. "Son, we ain't talkin' 'bout this. What are you doin', tryin' to conjure up trouble? You're always gonna be right here to take care of me and however many kids the Lord decides to give us. I'm trustin God for that, and if I take my trust from Him by makin plans for Him to fail me, then I don't really trust Him. Now, do I?" Her tone had become almost defiant as she spoke.

George chuckled, more because of his anxiousness to respond than any amusement he got from her statement. "Theresa, now you listen to this, and don't ever forget it. We may make pacts with God, and we may pray to God, but we'll never change His mind. His divine plan for our lives will be as He planned it before He first called our names. When He calls us, it may not seem like the best day to go, but it is. He doesn't make mistakes, and His mind is far too high above ours for us to even to begin to expect that we know what He plans to do, and why He does it, and how He does it, and for what purpose. He tells us that He comes at an unexpected moment. Baby, I hope I live a hundred years, healthy and full of life with all our children and grandchildren and even great grandchildren around me; all doing well and full of good health. But I know I could drop dead tomorrow. It doesn't mean that God didn't answer my prayer for long and abundant life. It just means that His plan was for me to serve a purpose in this life and then come home. It is only there that He has promised the abundance and longevity so many of us assume is our right in this life. His word even says that a man's life is short and full of trouble, but He swore by the blood of His Son that we can't even imagine how wonderful our lives in His Kingdom will be. He wants us to be ever ready; ever mindful of our responsibilities. If He didn't want it that way, He would send birds to bring us everything we need while we did nothing more than sit around and do whatever pleased, us at the moment. Remember this: 'All things work together for the good for them that love God and are the called according to His purpose.' The good things and the bad things that come our way, ultimately happen to perfect us into being the person He chose to conform to the image of Christ." He was holding her close to him again, as he spoke, and he felt her calming down. He held her at arms' length again to check on the effect his words had on her. She was calmer.

"Son, you shoulda' been a preacher." She teased as she pulled herself back into him. She was talking into his chest as she continued. "I understand what you're sayin'. God is not a genie in a bottle for us to use. It's just that it's so scary to plan like that. The thought of being without you is way more than I want to even think about right now. I know you're right. We'll do better." She looked up at him and forced a slight smile.

1921 was an eventful year at Grasmere. There was a lot of excitement in April when George and his crew and some of his neighbors got together and built the massive tobacco barn. They bought all the lumber and fasteners and hardware from Manchester Lumber. They supplied the blueprint. It was the same blueprint that everyone in the area used to build their tobacco sheds. They called them barn raisings, and they were usually a big social event. Neighbors and friends would gather around and the men would build all day and the women and children would cook and serve. The older boys served as "go fers" to keep the fasteners and hardware and tools supplied. George and John and three other men that worked on the farm had spent the last few weeks getting things prepared. They cleared the land and graded it for the footings and support piers. The plates were measured and cut, as were girts and braces and rafters. All the components were assembled and strategically placed around the perimeter of the construction, and ready for the invasion of self proclaimed carpenters to raise the shed. Shed may be a misnomer for these structures, because of their size. George had plans for a 30' X 90' building. It was their simplicity that distinguished them from barns. They were basically four walls of flat boards on a solid frame. Some of the cladding boards in the wall were hinged to allow them to open and serve as a ventilation system. Inside, they were basically a wide-open space with support bents, or columns strategically spaced to support the beams that the tobacco was hung from to dry.

That day, people began coming around 7:30 in the morning. They were mostly friends and neighbors and business associates and their families, but there were several people there that George did not know. When all was said and done, he had about 25 men, with about 20 of them being able to do more than stay out of the way. Doc Rankin and Stan Hale came, but mostly socialized and handled a few convenient tasks. Nathan Richards came and did likewise for a while, but left after being there a short while. George had Richards figured out fairly quickly. Doc Rankin had pulled George aside and told him that Richards was anxious to meet Theresa. Richards seemed a bit jittery when he introduced them. He was very respectful and courteous, but he just seemed a bit stiff.

After Richards left, Doc Rankin pulled him aside. "Sometimes I think I get too much satisfaction out of mischief. I just had to put Richards out there like that. He said something that bothered me."

"What'd he say?" George asked.

"Well he found me as soon as his lazy behind got here and we were just looking around at all of the people here and putting faces with names and women with men. You know how that goes. Well, after about five minutes of that, Theresa came out of the house carrying a big baking pan. He pointed at her asked, 'Who is that?', and I told him she was 'George's wife', and he asked me, 'George who?', and I told him I meant you. I guess it was before he thought, but he said 'But she's a..'. Guess my eyes must have told him to shut up, but anyway he seemed very surprised. He said he always thought you were Jewish. Well I filled him in on the situation and he just seemed to be a bit uncomfortable with the whole thing. That's when I called you over to introduce Theresa to him. I figured that if we were all going to be working together, he had to get over it, and the best way to do that is to humanize that which is villainized."

"I was wondering why he seemed so jittery. He was trying too hard to smile, but I couldn't figure out why."

"Well, now you know. I think he was more embarrassed than anything else. He'll get over it; or he won't. I bet he's not the only one here that's surprised to find out you're not a Jew. I hear that a lot. I correct some, but some I don't, depending on the circumstances."

"Doc, today it doesn't much matter. As long as they can swing a hammer and don't disrespect my family, their aces with me! Let me get these guys goin on that west side frame." With that, George walked away. He knew what Rankin was talking about. He was positive that some of the people that he was doing business with would have never let his foot in the door if they had known his heritage. He knew his name threw some of them off. His name explained the less than European flavor of his hair and his lips. His light skin and his blue-gray eyes sealed the deal for those predisposed to believe it. He never had that problem with black folks, they seemed to figure things out pretty quickly. When he was with Theresa or Benny, there was never a doubt. He was also very aware that there were plenty of people who were fully aware of who and what he was, and it made absolutely no difference to them. He was as certain that most of those there that day were like that, and that those who weren't, when confronted with the truth, would not change their relationship at all. He trusted that Richards was in that latter category.

There was plenty of food and the atmosphere had more of the flavor of a picnic than a work day. It reminded Theresa of her church fair down in Stewart County, except people weren't dressed in their best. Children were meeting school mates in a different environment, and found ways to enjoy each other. Many of the wives were meeting each other for the first time, and enjoyed getting to share their common interests, and comparing recipes. Theresa was being pampered by everyone. She was 6 months pregnant, and it was very obvious. It was annoying her because she didn't feel debilitated, and she had to spend far too much of her time explaining that she was okay to handle being the hostess of the event. The food was wonderful. There was plenty of fried chicken and hot dogs and many versions of baked beans and potato salad and macaroni salad. There were pans of rolls and other kinds of breads and desserts. There was punch made from Fruit Smack (the predecessor of Kool Aid) and juice, and soda. As usual, Theresa was besieged by requests for her roll recipe, and she was always prepared with her pat answer that it was a trade secret, but she was sure to remind everyone that they were for sale at the Hale House.

Lucy was walking well by then, so she was exploring her steps and mingling with the crowd, under the watchful supervision of her aunt Alice, and an occasional inspection by Rover. No matter what he was doing, and he found plenty to do, he came looking for Lucy every few minutes, almost as if he was just checking on her. She got a lot of attention, but didn't seem to pay much attention to anything or anyone in her constant exploration of life. That all changed when she met Viola. Viola was not quite as big as Lucy but seemed to have the same motor skills and curious nature. She was a cute little blond that contrasted with Lucy's dark haired exotic appearance. They grabbed on to each other and just enjoyed being around someone close to their own size. Everyone was making a big deal over how cute they thought the pair of them looked playing together. Soon Theresa saw a very pretty blond woman come and brush the dried grass from little Viola's knees after she tripped over someone's foot. Theresa saw it as an opportunity to introduce herself so she could maintain contact with Lucy's new found friend.

"Hi, I'm Theresa. I'm Lucy's momma." She offered the young woman her hand and smiled.

"Hi, I'm Florence, and I'm Viola's mother." She took Theresa's hand and returned her smile. "I'm pleased to meet you. Your daughter is gorgeous!"

"So's yours, and they seem to really like each other. How old is she?"

They filled each other in on the particulars about their children. Florence explained that she came to meet some people, and had seen Theresa with Lucy in the market and walking down the street and wanted to meet her. She figured they were about the same age and had little girls the same age in common. She was the daughter of Mike and Fannie Roberts, who lived down Oak Street at the next house. She explained that she had recently lost her husband who had died a few months ago from a job-related injury in a factory, and she and Viola had moved in with her parents. That immediately touched Theresa's heart, not that she had any experience with feeling what Florence must be feeling, but because she so deeply dreaded ever feeling the emptiness she imagined that Florence must be feeling after being so finally torn away from the man she loved.

The day was filled with a great sense of community. It was a genuine culture that had evolved in Glastonbury. People stuck together, even though they might not always choose to be together. There were many distinctly different communities in Glastonbury because of the rural labor revolution that was going on at the time. Farmers' children were moving into manufacturing jobs that were evolving in the big cities, and even in the smaller communities like Glastonbury, people were coming from all around the world to fill the gaps. There were large Italian, Eastern European, and southern black populations that were forming bonds within their own cultures, but where there was commonality, the communities had little problem blending together to get things done. Barn raisings were almost a symbol of the commitment to set aside the differences that can plague us if we allow them. It was almost redemptive that from time to time for the entire community would come together.

At the end of the day, the shed was, for all intents and purposes, up and ready for company. They had gotten a hand from a crew from Consolidated Cigar Company that had just moved into a complex at the far end of Oak Street. They were working on the factory, but were also the same crew responsible for building their sheds. They were a big hand in shortening the group learning curve, although many of the locals had helped others in the community and had also gained some valuable on the job experience recently. One of the foremen had explained to George that Consolidated was very keen on their people becoming a part of the community because their success, as a cigar manufacturer, was greatly impacted by the growers in the community. Although they had bought several tobacco producing farms in the area to grow their own crops, there was no way they could meet their own demand from their own crop production. There just wasn't enough available farm land in the area. He had told George that they considered themselves a potential customer as opposed to a potential competitor. CCC would not be selling their crops on the open market like George. He also let George know that someone from the company would probably approach him at some point to contract for his crop. George was grateful for the help and for the information but gave no indication about how he was affected by the information.

George had been selling his raw shade crops to Hale because he didn't have the proper facilities to properly cure and ferment the product. Most of his broadleaf crop was bought by some New York buyers who processed tobacco for the local cigar manufacturers. There were hundreds of them in the New York area. They were a vibrant but diminishing market, as Consolidated Cigar and

General Cigar began marketing national brands like Dutch Masters, White Owl, Roberts Burns, and the like. The appeal of the local and regional brands was losing ground to the giants. Still, in 1921, they were a strong, viable customer base for the independent farmer. Now, with facilities and the expertise, Grasmere would be able to cure the tobacco as well, which added considerable profit to the harvest. Some of the smaller manufacturers required that the grower ferment the leaves as well, but this stage was one that allowed the manipulation of several steps that could distinguish the final taste, color, and texture of the leaves. Some manufacturers preferred to buy the leaves before this step was performed so they could create their own signature flavor. The other opportunity was for the grower to create his own unique wrapper through this process and sell directly to the brokers for the smaller manufacturers who needed this service.

Outside of the normal little surprises that life delights in presenting, that spring went very well. Everything was growing well; the crops, Lucy, the baby in Theresa's womb, the puppy, and their social circle. It seems that the barn raising had opened the doors to friendship. Doc Rankin took his role as godfather very seriously and came and checked on Lucy frequently; often several times a week. He also kept his eye on Theresa and saw to it that everything was going well with her pregnancy.

Even Nathan Richards paid a few visits. He was concerned about the impact of the conglomerates coming into the area and buying up so much of the crop production. He was trying to politic for the Farm Bureau members to resist selling out to Consolidated either thru selling their land to them or by contracting their crops for prices that were set before the free market established fair crop market values for the year. When he came, he always presented himself as friendly and caring. He was personable and always brought candy for Benny and cookies for Lucy. After his first visit, when the puppy snapped at him when he tried to pet him, he always brought a piece of meat or a bone for Rover, but his reception was always the same. Rover just growled at Richards every time he came by. Theresa took note of that.

Florence Roberts and Theresa became fast friends, even though Florence was several years younger than Theresa. They had a common bond in the girls, and Theresa took it upon herself to keep Florence's spirits up as she healed from the loss of her husband. Lucy and Viola delighted in being with each other, and they gave their mothers a couple of hours a week where they didn't have to be concerned about how their babies would fill their time. Theresa had Alice to help her, but Florence welcomed the time of freedom to hang out with an adult without her focus being on Viola.

Theresa went into labor on July 20th, and her entire support team was around her; George, Alice, Doc and Lucie Rankin, John, Benny, and her new best friend, Florence. During the night, one of the women was always there with her to fan her and keep her cool. Doc would check on her every once on a while, as would George.

The men took up their positions around the kitchen table. Benny was the first to abandon ship. He went into the parlor and the softness of the sofa seduced him into dreamland. Rover followed Benny. George, John, and Doc kept each other amused with foolish stories and jokes. They tried to wager on the sex of the baby, but they all were betting on a boy.

When Florence walked into the kitchen, their banter stopped. She said, "Don't let me stop you fellahs, I just came down to get some ice." as she walked to the ice box. She pulled the small pot of ice chips George had set in the ice compartment, but the chips were stuck together. She got the pick and began chipping gingerly at the pot.

"You need some help wit dat?" John asked.

She never turned around when she declined his offer. "No John, that's alright. I've got it."

They all sat there, silent as they watched her body jiggle slightly each time she brought the ice pick down into the pot. Florence was a very shapely, full figured woman, and watching her walk was an adventure. Seeing her working away at the ice was hard to turn away from. George noticed the looks on the faces of his comrades, especially John, and he had to chuckle. When she finished, she stretched up on her toes with her arms over her head. She then put her hands on the edge of the sink and stepped back a few steps and arched her back as she raised her chin to the ceiling to stretch the fatigue out of her body. She held that pose for only a few seconds, but it was long enough for John to silently lose control of his expressions. When she stood up, she rotated her head a few times.

"Boy that felt good. I was getting a bit tight from all that fanning. It's pretty hot up in that room." The mist of sweat gave her smooth caramel tanned skin a patina that made her look like she was made from silk.

John was the only one to speak. "I bet it was hot up there!" He had planned that his double entendre would be more subtle than it turned out being.

Her demeanor never changed, nor did she say another word as she turned and left the kitchen. George did catch a slight upturn to her already smiling lips and a quick side glance at John as she had to walk close to where he was sitting to exit the kitchen.

After George heard the third stair from the top give its tell tale signal he finally let loose and laughed.

"Man, that was something else, and I bet she didn't have a clue what she was doing!" Doc added.

"Oh I thank she knowed what she was doin'. She jes tryin' ta catch my attention!" John declared.

"That's your sister's new best friend, and she'll scratch your eyes out if she thought you were trying to take advantage. You've been up north too long. You forgot that the looks you were giving that woman would have gotten you hung in Georgia, and those words would have gotten you shot on the spot!" George teased his bother-in-law.

"Man it wasn't me doin' nothin but lookin at what she was doin. Sides, you didn't catch dat look she give me when she walked by me? She jes bein frisky an friendly, an so am I!" John defended himself well.

They all had a good laugh, then moved on to other topics. The sun would be up soon. John was the next one to succumb to the softness of the divan, very soon after he excused himself from the hard kitchen chair to rest his back for a minute. He didn't wake again until George came and shook him and said, "Wake up John! It's a boy. It's a boy!"

"Everybody doin okay?" John asked as he slowly became fully awake.

"Just fine, but Theresa's mighty sore. He's a pretty big boy."

"How big is he?"

"Almost nine pounds!"

"Dern! Dat's a big ole man chile! Good, we don't want no scrawny men in dis famly. Did ya name him after me?" He was only half kidding.

"No. I owed Doc one more. His name is Charles William, after Doc, but I promise, we'll name the next boy after you."

John looked up at him through eyes that weren't totally adjusted from his deep sleep and said, "Yeah, you bettah, else I'll tell Pank bout how you was lookin at dat woman tonight!" He threw his hand up as soon as he said it in anticipation of the smack to the head he figured was coming. He didn't prepare in vain.

Chapter Seven

George's first full-fledged venture into shade went as well as could be expected. There were some losses to blossom rot, but other than that, he got the crops in and cured in good fashion. Demand for Connecticut shade was at an all time high. Richards had told him that he had heard there were about 17,000 acres of tobacco under shade in the Connecticut River Valley that summer. The extra profit in delivering cured tobacco was a tremendous boost. He had an in with some of the New York brokers. They loved Connecticut shade for their custom cigar making customers. They preferred to ferment the tobacco themselves because they had a winning formula that delivered superior wrapper leaves. His father had connected him with some of his cousins from New York, via letter. There were a few of them that had connections in the cigar industry, and George sent many customers his way. As his reputation for quality tobacco grew and product was in high demand, he never forgot the men who gave him his start.

Some of his Jewish family were very welcoming and embraced him because he was family, but many were very reluctant to foster any kind of relationship because his heritage was not truly Jewish. The elder Cohen was somewhat notorious because of his perceived rebellious attitude towards his family. He never let them direct his life because of their disapproval of his relationship with Nellie. Some were dismayed by the attitude he displayed in his youth and considered him an outsider. There were others who were delighted that he was a man that stood by his convictions.

There was a pocket of them that had become Messianic Jews, who regularly came and fellowshipped with George. These were not converted Jewish Christians, but they held on to all their Jewish customs, ceremonies, and beliefs except that they believed that Christ was the awaited Messiah. It was not uncommon for George to don a yarmulke, (the little "beanie" type hats you often see on Jewish men at their religious ceremonies) during his sessions with his cousins in the parlor. He didn't practice Judaism, but he was intrigued by his heritage and the traditions of that part of his family tree. Their discussions usually centered around their common beliefs in New Testament teachings, although they had a few doctrinal differences. All things considered, that was to be expected. Their bond was in their heritage and their love of Jesus.

After that year's harvest, George bought a 1919 Model "T" Ford from a widow who had inherited the vehicle but had no interest in driving. Doc Rankin took him out a few times and showed him the mechanics of handling his new auto, and in short order he was driving; not well but adequately. It would take several weeks of trial and error driving before he became skilled enough to be considered a good driver. By Christmas that year, he felt comfortable taking the family to church in it. Up to that point, he had only used it for late season deliveries of apples and greens from his fall crop. It certainly made his trade in Hartford easier to get to, but he still had to use Buck and Ned when he was taking large loads to the regional market.

March of the following year, in just over 17 months, he paid off the 3 year loan to Manchester Lumber. He didn't need to get any financing for the labor or other expenses for the 1922 crop, because he had done well enough in '21 that he had it all in the bank. He kept his money in Stan Hale's bank. It just seemed like the right thing to do. He was prepared to pay Evans off early as well, but decided it would be best to keep an extra cushion, just in case. That year went well, and the night of Little Charlie's first birthday party, Theresa told him she was pregnant again. She was expecting another January birthday! So now, all of their children, Benny, Lucy, and the new baby, would be January babies, except Charlie, who would be the only summertime birthday they could celebrate! Theresa and George were both born in December; she on the 10th and he on the 25th.

There was a small piece of Grasmere that was just wooded land. George did not have the time nor interest in developing it because it flooded quite often, and the soil was full of rock and clay. Doc Rankin happened to know a young immigrant Galician (now part of Poland) who wanted desperately to own some land. Joseph Garay said he could work any land and, in time, grow crops on it. It was perfect timing for George. He paid Delbert Evans off the Monday before his birthday, and sold the small plot to Garay for almost the same amount of money the Wednesday after. George was quite proud of the financial prowess his wheeling and dealing demonstrated. Almost no money left his hands to claim full ownership of a bigger and better parcel of land.

When January came, so did the baby, just as expected. The baby was a beautiful baby girl, who looked very much like Lucy at birth; very fair, with blue eyes, and silky curly black hair. They named her Nellie, after George's mother. When they called to tell Ma Nellie that she had a namesake, she screamed with joy on the phone and vowed to get to Connecticut as soon as she could to see her grandchildren. She wouldn't plan on coming until the threat of winter had passed.

Lucy had just turned three years old, 3 days before the baby came, and her mother told her that her new little sister was her birthday present. She was thrilled to have a newborn baby in the house. Lucy had been only eighteen months old at the time, so she had been too young to appreciate Charlie showing up! She was excited by the fact that the new baby was a baby girl, just like her, and that she had to help Momma and Aunt Alice take care of her. She delighted in getting her little sister things when she was asked to. Her face would always take on a somber demeanor at first, to denote just how seriously she took her assignment. So pleased was she whenever she completed her assigned duty that she couldn't help but to smile when she handed the diaper, bottle, or whatever it might be to her Momma or her aunt. She especially liked it when she had to lie down in the afternoons to help put baby Nellie to sleep. They told her that if she took a nap that it would help her little sister sleep better, so she never resisted nap time anymore.

They went into 1923 with great expectations that the market for tobacco was continuing to grow. In April, George bought more land that bordered on Grasmere from Nathan Richards. Stan Hale warned George against the purchase because he felt that the farmland value bubble that had begun to deflate around the country would soon have its affects in Glastonbury as well. George felt he could get a tremendous gain in crop values, even if the land values began to shrink. Even more importantly, the property had an existing shed that Richards wasn't using, and as an incentive for George to grab the property, he "threw it into the deal". He planned to escape the property as soon as the valuation problem became a local issue. It was good land, accessible to his systems, and he expected high yields.

Richards' motivation in selling the land was not altruistic. He had the same impressions of the market as Hale. His hope was that he had sold the land at its peak, and that he would be able to buy it back at the bottom of the cycle and reap the profits while essentially holding on to the land.

Meanwhile, Consolidated kept driving the price of land higher as they sought to buy more prime tobacco land. They still had heavy demand for better quality cigars, and needed the quality wrap that would distinguish them from their lesser competitors, and keep them on even ground with General Cigar that was buying up the land in nearby Windsor and Enfield. The crop values were also being shored up. Both Consolidated and General were busy contracting independent farmers to sell their crops in advance of the season for a predetermined price. So far, this had worked to their advantage. The crops were usually worth more than what they had contracted them for, but it also reduced the risk of failure for the farmers. The differences were marginal, but that's where the money was made in large corporations that were successful; on the margins. George, like most independents, was able to negotiate higher prices as the market price continued to rise, but they also bore the risk of crop failures due to disease or weather related calamities. In a good year, shade had about a 15% crop value shrinkage due to breakage, blossom rot, storm, insect, and disease damage. It was not unheard of, however, that there was as much as 35% of the crop damaged in a bad year.

Richards was still a proponent of the independent resisting Consolidated to protect the integrity and self control of the farming community. There were those who felt that Consolidated was actually a definite benefit to the farming community by keeping the price of land high in a national economy that was headed in the opposite direction. George could understand both arguments, but held on to his independence. His position was supported by his confidence in his ready-made market for his crop through his New York connection.

The year didn't turn out quite as well as other years for the tobacco crops at Grasmere. With more acres under cover, and with a shortage of available labor in the Connecticut valley, it was more difficult keeping the pests from the plants, and avoiding the plants' flowering which led to a higher than normal amount of blossom rot. George lost about 20% of his crop, but it was far better than some. He heard some numbers from farmers in the area as high as 30%. Still, it was a profitable year for Grasmere. The tobacco crop still made a profit, and the other crops were profitable as well.

When Labor Day came, George and Theresa once again hosted their annual cookout to celebrate the end of tobacco harvest. Their first was a couple of years ago, and it was a big hit with their friends. The size of the crowd increased each year since, as their circle of friends grew, and as more friends asked if they could bring someone, 'just this once'. It didn't take long before people started calling it a tradition, so the crowd just grew year after year, and everyone knew what to expect. There would be plenty of food. John would come over about two in the morning and he and George would slow roast a hog in the same kind of pit he and his father and brothers had made for Theresa's wedding. Theresa made a huge batch of her rolls, of course, and would make a couple of big pots of greens. Alice would make potato salad, and they would team up and fry chicken on an almost continual basis from about noon of the day of the picnic until well into the afternoon. The other families all volunteered to supply different things, and the wives all bought one or more of their specialties.

There were basketball and baseball games, and races for the boys and young men to show off their prowess. The men laughed at the efforts of their comrades that dared try to compete with the teenage boys in foot races. They held their own in the ball games. Some of the less energetic men played horseshoes. The young girls had races too, and many of them participated in rope jumping contests. There was always the annual kickball contest that pitted mixed teams of both sexes of all ages. It wasn't pretty, but everyone had a lot of fun.

Theresa was tired from all the preparations, but it was a good tired. She sat on the back porch and looked out over the field behind the house; the one that made her fall in love with Grasmere. She felt such a sense of peace and belonging as she surveyed the normally tranquil scene filled with people she knew and genuinely cared about. She could see Lucy and little Viola running around like antelopes. As she watched her firstborn, she mused over the fact that she would soon be four years old. How different her life was from the time she feared she would never have a child. Charlie was out there somewhere with his father, and she had another baby in her arms. She felt very blessed.

She had just nursed Nellie who was almost 9 months old and already testing her legs. She loved to "stand" in her mother's lap and get bounced up and down as Theresa sang a little ditty. "Shout! Shout! Shout the devil down! Shout! Shout! Shout him in the ground!" She would half sing and half speak as she helped

Nellie 'jump' to the beat. After each round, Nellie would let out a belly laugh and begin bouncing herself up and down to let her mother know it was time to go at it again. She could keep this up for an hour if you let her. Thank God for Alice!

She wasn't aware that George, who must have gone in the front door, came up behind her and kissed the top of her head. "Hey baby! Taking a break?" he asked facetiously. He knew she had been going non-stop for the past two days preparing, and that she would be on-call constantly for the rest of the day as everyone looked to her to co-ordinate everything from food to bandages!

"Hi Momma. I wanna huh, Momma. I wanna huh!" Little Charlie said as he leaned out of his father's arms and reached for his mother. They knew what I 'wanna huh' meant. That was Charlie's two year old language for letting his mother know he wanted to be nursed. Lucy was weaned relatively young at about two and a half. She already had two and had one on the way, so Theresa decided she needed to get one of them 'out of the kitchen' so to speak!

George spun a bit to keep Charlie from getting his hands on his mother. "No 'huh' now man, we're gonna get rolls and juice and chicken! What do think about that?"

"Shickem? Yea, shickem. Duice!" Charlie quickly forgot about liquid lunch. He loved chicken. Especially the livers.

"Yeah man. Shickem!" His father teased as he winked at Theresa.

She smiled at him and mouthed the words, "I owe you one!"

George gave her 'that' smile and mouthed back, "I'll see you about that tonight!" as he raised his eyebrows rapidly in succession, suggestively.

"Why George Washington Cohen, get your mind out the gutter!"

He quickly retorted, "That ain't no gutter, and I wasn't thinkin' 'bout using my mind!"

They both laughed and he kissed her and held Charlie out to her so he could kiss her too before they each went about tasks at hand.

If it weren't for Florence Roberts yelling out a general announcement that it was "time to give these nice folks a break", about 10:30, people might have stayed there a few hours longer. At about dusk, John had started playing his guitar and singing upbeat songs. George got his accordion and a couple of the men kept harmonicas in their pockets for moments such as these. A couple of fellows from Hartford were there with another guitar and a saxophone. Alice got out a collection of pots and served as the drummer. People started dancing and singing and very few of them left. Most of those that did leave had young children that had gotten sleepy and cranky and made it unbearable for their parents to stay. Florence's proclamation got everyone in a more considerate mode and people began to wind things down shortly thereafter. As it was, the last of the stragglers, John and his 'friend Miss Davis', and Florence and a sleeping Viola, didn't leave until almost 12:00. To their credit, they stayed around to help Alice and George get things back close to normal. Theresa watched her babies and Viola while her mother helped in the kitchen.

George thought he caught a meaningful glance between John and Florence as they accidently touched each other while clearing the counters. George's mind raced back to the night Charlie was born, and the heat he thought he felt between these two. George quickly dismissed his thoughts. After all, Geneva Davis, John's live-in 'friend' was in the same room, but he did notice that she always seemed somewhat quiet when she and Florence were in the same space. John offered to walk Florence home, and he would carry Viola for her. Florence coyly refused to impose, but didn't resist much when John insisted, so the four of them were headed out together: Viola asleep, Florence and John all smiles, and Geneva not so much! He was tired but George figured a better course of action, from many perspectives, would be for him to give them all a ride in his Model "T". They all seemed happy to accept, except that John cut him a funny look when the two women were ahead of them walking out of the house. That look supported the wisdom of his decision.

He wasn't gone long, but when he got back, Theresa had just finished her bath and was sitting on the side of the bed combing out her hair. He looked over at Nellie in her crib, and she was fast asleep, looking like a little angel wrapped in her soft pink blanket. He knew Lucy and Charlie were sleep with their Aunt Alice.

"Wow, what a day! It was beautiful, but I swear it seemed I was doing something the whole day! But it sure was a nice time!" George said as he began taking off his clothes.

"It sure was. And it sure was!" she laughed. "I brought you up some warm water so you could wash up before you got in the bed."

"Why, thank you, but what are you trying to say?"

"Oh, Son, you know I'm just trying to help you get some of the tired off you. You been going all day, and it was hot and dusty out there! And..."

His laughter interrupted her defense. "Hey Baby, I was just kidding. I know you were just being sweet. Lord knows it's gonna feel good! Thanks, baby!"

She kept talking while he was in the dressing area, washing himself. "I'm sure glad Florence spoke up and got those folks to thinking about leaving. Everybody was having such a good time that I bet they would still be here if somebody hadn't said something. I can't imagine what it's gonna be like next year. Every year there seem to be more and more people. I mean a lot more people!"

"I know, but every year it gets better, and we know more and more people. I am getting to notice that people start getting extra friendly and helpful in August! What's up with that?"

"Awe Son, stop acting the fool." Abruptly shifting topics, she said "It was nice of you to give John and them a ride home!"

"Yeah, you said it right: John and them. You know, I'm feeling like there's a little something going on between John and Florence; and I think that Geneva has her suspicions too! That's why I gave them a ride. I don't think Geneva liked the idea of John carrying Viola home for Florence."

"Now Son, don't start no rumors about stuff you don't know nothin' about."

"What are you talking about? I'm not starting rumors. I'm talking to my wife in the privacy of our bedroom. If I can't express my feelings to you, who can I talk to?" He was only half teasing. Her statement had perturbed him a bit.

"Whoa there Mr. Cohen. I didn't mean nothin'. I was just teasing with you. I've seen it too. I even asked Florence about it. She admits that there is some attraction between them, but there is too much stuff in the way for them to do anything more than flirt every once in a while."

"I knew it!" he proclaimed, as if he had just hit the winning run in the ball game his team lost that afternoon. "Why didn't they get together?"

"Well let's see: She's white and he's black and that's a problem in the north as much as it is in the south. Her father would have a fit. Her daughter would have a tough row to hoe coming up. He is her best friend's brother. John ain't the most settled man you could find. Do I need to say more?"

"Alright. I see. Well at least now I know I'm not seeing things. I wonder how much Miss Davis is seeing?" he asked.

"I'm sure she will never have anything more than suspicion to concern her. Florence might like to have fun, but she would never disrespect that relationship to the point that Geneva would ever have anything real to worry about. That's the same way I used to feel about you and Ida Hale. I could tell she had an eye for you. I think she had a case of jungle fever when we first met!" Theresa teased.

"Well if that was the case, she never showed it to me."

"What "it" are you talking about her showing you?" she continued her teasing.

"Oh stop it Baby. You know I can't see any woman but you. In fact, today reminded me of the day I first saw you. I never stop thinking about that day, and every time I'm at a picnic or a fair, I think about that first glance I had of you through that crowd. Now that was some flirting. Neither one of us was trying to hide that we wanted to get to know each other better, and I am so happy we did. Thank you for being such a flirt," He paused momentarily for effect, "and for being such a wonderful wife to me and mother to our children." With that he re-entered the bedroom, dressed only in his shorts, a recent fashion item that grew out of attire introduced to the military during WWI.

"Why Mr. Cohen, you're making me blush!" she paused for dramatic effect, "Or maybe I'm not blushing. Maybe it's something else!"

"Why Mrs. Cohen, is all that talk about loose women having an effect on you?"

"Why certainly not sir. I told you before, to get your mind out of the gutter."

He blew out the light on the night stand before he reached for her. "Although it does think for me from time to time, that is not my mind, and it certainly is not the gutter it's thinking about!" With that he reached for his wife and they both welcomed the embrace.

That Christmas, his birthday present was a scroll wrapped in a red ribbon with a bow on it. When he opened it, the note read: 'Before the corn is high, you will hold me in your arms and our fourth child will be safely in mine. Happy Birthday Son. Love, Theresa." He jumped for joy.

On June 5th of 1924, John Jacob Cohen was born. George kept his promise to his brother-in-law, John, and named his second son after him. Theresa had a rough time through her labor with this one. He was a very big baby. He was over 11 pounds when he was born. Doctor Rankin thought that he might be forced to give Theresa a Cesarean, but she managed to deliver him naturally. George was right by her side the entire time; soothing her with loving words, scripture of encouragement, and prayer. Florence and Alice and Mrs. Rankin took turns with taking care of her physical needs and caring for the children. Lucy was four and a half, and Charlie was a month shy of his third birthday, so they weren't as much of a problem, in that they were both weaned and toilet trained. Nellie was still only one and a half and lacking in both graces. She was also too young to understand the circumstances. She just wanted her Momma, and it was difficult keeping her away during those hours of labor.

Two nights later, she and George were laying in bed, and she was nursing the baby, and he had her in the crook of one arm and a sleeping Nelly in the other. He chuckled and said. "The corn's not high yet."

Not missing the significance, she turned her head to him and smiled and forced her head deeper into the side of his chest as a sign.

"You better lay off the Lydia Pinkham's for a while." He joked with a straight face. They laughed until she complained about the pain in her still tender belly.

1924 promised to be a banner year for Grasmere. George had mortgaged back the parcel he had bought from Nathan Richards to him via Manchester Savings and Loan back in December of the previous year to get some additional operating capital for the '24 season. He needed to secure his labor force earlier and he also needed to mechanize a bit more to avoid the inefficiencies that had cost him 20% of his crop the previous year. He computed that the value of the additional harvest potential would offset the cost of the loan in the first year, and the equipment he would buy would last for a few years. Buck was 19, and he wasn't a good match for Ned in work tandems any longer. Not that Buck wasn't still an awesome animal, it's just that his competitive nature in tandem would have him challenging workloads better handled by younger animals. His life expectancy was at most 30 years, and if he was handled without being exposed to extreme conditions, he would be serviceable for light hauling for many years to come. He couldn't compete with Ned who was only 9 years old and in the prime of his strength. Besides, there were some real advantages to mechanizing. He used some of the proceeds of the loan to buy a tractor to help with the plowing and cultivating, as well as hauling large bins of crops out of the field.

The Grasmere crop yield for the year was exceptionally high and he had an opportunity to make some additional money on the real estate he had mortgaged back to Richards in December. There were still those speculators that were anxious to buy land in Glastonbury at a premium. George had met Frank Ronskavitz through his association with the Hales, and he was aware of the transaction George had made with Richards to buy the 3 parcels he had mortgaged in December. Because Ronskavitz valued the property for speculation, and because he had no capabilities when it came to farming, he was excited that he could get some yield value without lifting a finger. He and George made an agreement that Ronskavitz would buy the land from George. George would pay off his loan to Richards and reap a nice profit. In addition, George retained full rights to the 1924 crop, and would be allowed full use of the land and its shed until such time that the land was sold. In return, Ronskavitz would receive a portion of the yield of every future crop. This was a win/win situation for both men. Ronskavitz was betting on the escalating value of the property and what he considered a reasonable rent of the land in the way of a percentage of the crop value of one of the best crop producers in the valley. George got the use of the land to grow extra crops that would yield a good profit without the land investment. As a bonus, he got to retain the use of the shed, which wasn't even a consideration in the transaction.

It was a brilliant move on his part, and he was highly praised in the business community for arranging the transaction. Ronskavitz didn't go without his kudos as well. Richards, who was relying on the market plunging as it had been predicted by the experts, as evidenced in the reality of declining farm land values over most of the rest of the country, didn't fare quite as well. Any hope that he would be able to reclaim the land on the strength of calling his debt on the modest crop loan George had taken, didn't come to pass.

Doc Rankin' stopped by the house the day before the Labor Day cookout to drop off some soda, a cooked ham, and some of his wife's cookies. They had some people visiting who were leaving the day of the picnic, so they wouldn't get there until late. He wanted to make sure they didn't hold things up. Besides, he had an extra batch of cookies just for Lucy and Charlie. As he was leaving, he asked George to step outside with him for a moment. Doc Rankin had a warning for George. "I'd watch out for Richards if I were you. You know he's not as liberal when it comes to race and religion as he might want to make it seem. The fact that he couldn't screw you was bad enough. The fact that you were more successful than he was in transacting business with that piece of land has proven quite an embarrassment to him. I hear that he's told a few of his like-minded friends that he's got your number and you won't even see it coming."

"What in the devil is wrong with these people? Small minded fools. Thanks for tipping me off. I'll keep my eye on him, and certainly at arm's length. Rover still growls every time he comes around. So much so now that he tried to get after him once. Come to think of it, he hasn't come to the house since then." Doc and George laughed.

"Well anyway, watch yourself. The next time you need to make a transaction, check with me or Stan first. All these bastards will smile in your face, but we know who the dumb guys are. We'll help you steer clear of those idiots. Well I gotta get going. Lucey just wanted to make sure we got our stuff here early and our little Lucy and Charlie got the cookies she baked."

"Thanks for the warning and for the cookies. Now you know I'm gonna have to test those cookies before I give 'em to my guests or the kids!" George said with that mischievous twinkle in his eye.

"Yeah. We figured that you and Theresa and Alice would have to test a couple apiece before you were satisfied, but just a couple. You hear me George? I got spies around here and they'll tell me!" They laughed together and gave each other a knowing nod as Doc turned and walked to his car. The look said a lot without a word being spoken. It was a 'thumbs up' without a movement of hands.

Richards didn't attend the cookout that year, and he certainly wasn't missed. This was the best gathering they had up to that point. The weather was perfect, there was plenty of food, and it just seemed that whatever people decided to do, it brought smiles to faces.

Later that night, after everyone had gone and things were put away, George and Theresa were sitting on the back porch with little Nellie, who was desperately fighting sleep so she wouldn't miss anything, and baby Johnnie, who was in his favorite position; at his mother's breast. He was a big baby with a very determined spirit. He had a different look from his siblings. He had more color and darker eyes; a bit less broad in the forehead. George said that he looked just like Benny, who looked like his father, as a baby. George's mother, Nellie had made the same comment when she came to visit in early August. Circumstances had kept her away until then, but she finally got to meet her namesake, as promised.

"I was just thinking about Ma. That succotash recipe she gave you sure was a hit!" George said as he shifted Nellie to his other knee. She just looked at her father with those dazzling grey-blue eyes and smiled, exposing a perfect set of baby teeth.

"Yep, it sure was. I thought ole' Florence was gonna eat herself sick; Doc Rankin too, for that matter. Yeah we sure had some good food this year. Looks like all the women went out and found a way to make some dish that was just right for them to make, and they brought it here to show-off. It just seems like everything was better this year." Theresa was very excited by the success of the day, but she continued, remembering George's focus. "I sure wish Ma Nellie could have been here. She would have been so proud to see how people just fussed over her succotash!"

Suddenly, George broke out into a chuckle. Theresa asked him what was so funny, but every time he tried to tell her, he just laughed even harder. After several attempts, he finally composed himself enough to answer her.

"Remember what you told me about Lucy falling off the railing, and Ma spanking her for not being ladylike? Well I just had this vision of Lucy sitting up on the rail and all of a sudden disappearing into the bushes with nothing visible but her little feet kicking in the air!" He got that out and was off on another binge of laughter.

Theresa chuckled but she wasn't quite as amused as George was. She remembered the incident vividly. Ma Nellie was on the porch holding court with her grandchildren. Nellie was in her lap, Johnnie was sleeping in a cradle next to her rocker, Charlie, who had just turned three a couple of weeks earlier, was showing off his tumbling skills in the grass, and Lucy was nervously fidgeting between sitting on the railing and jumping off. Her grandmother warned her several times about trying to straddle the railing, and she would get down immediately, only to absent mindedly jump back up again. Well, on one of these occasions, she straddled the railing and her momentum carried her all the way over the railing and into the Lilac bush. She immediately began screaming for help.

In the same instant, Ma Nellie jumped up as she put little Nellie on the floor and screamed, "Lucy! Are you alright?", as she was running down the stairs toward her granddaughter embedded deeply in the bushes.

Charlie was just standing there and staring like a deer in headlights. Little Nellie was on the porch beginning to cry. "Ducy fall down! Ducy fall down!"

Ma Nellie pulled Lucy, who was also crying by this time, out of the bush. Except for a scratch on her arm and a smaller one on her neck behind her ear, she was none the worse for wear. "Are you alright, child?" Ma Nellie asked.

Still shaking from her fright, Lucy gave a very shaky "Yes ma'am!" back to her grandmother.

"Well that's good. You could have hurt yourself very badly doing that. Now you're sure you're okay?"

"Yes ma'am." Now more composed, Lucy answered her grandmother.

"Well that's good!" she said as she returned to her seat in the rocker. "Now come here child. Grandma Nellie has something for you." As Lucy got to within her reach, she grabbed Lucy's little wrist and pulled her suddenly to her and forced her, face down, to lie across her lap. Almost at the same second she began spanking her backside. "I – told – you – not – to – sit – on – that – rail – like – some – little – Tomboy." Each word brought another smack. They were brisk but certainly not hard. The sound was more frightening than the pain. After her brief but impactful punishment, Ma Nellie pulled the struggling Lucy back up on her feet and held her firmly at arms length as she continued her chastisement. "You shouldn't be sitting on the railing. You're a little girl, not a little boy! You must learn to act like a little lady! Don't ever straddle that railing ever again! Do you understand?"

By this time Lucy was so outdone, all she could manage was a nod and sporadic attempts at a "Yes" between her involuntary convulsions. As soon as she was free, she ran into the house as fast as her little four-year-old legs could carry her. She ran directly to her mother to report on her Grandma Nellie.

Theresa, having heard the tail end of the commotion outside, knew enough about what happened to be fully aware of what Lucy was trying to say between her convulsions. All she got from her mother was to be pried off of her leg and told, "Your Grandma was right. You shouldn't have been up on that railing like that. Now stop crying or I'll really give you something to cry about!"

At that moment Ma Nellie walked into the kitchen and looked lovingly on her frightened little grandchild and said, "She could have gotten hurt. I want to make sure she remembers that sitting on the railing is out of bounds. I hope I didn't frighten her too badly!" They both exchanged a knowing look as Ma Nellie knelt and gave Lucy a hug.

George broke his reverie. "Yeah, Ma can sure show you what she means!" They both chuckled. "I sure wish she was closer so she could get to know her grandchildren better. By the next time we see her, Johnnie will be walking and most of them will be in school."

"Yeah, I miss her too, but she wants her life the way it is, and we have to be glad for her that she has peace in her life. I know she is happy for us and what we have here. God puts us all where He wants us to be. We're blessed, Son."

George reached out and caressed her cheek with the back of his hand. "Yes, Baby, we have been very blessed! Thank God for Jesus! I know our family will continue to be blessed. I want the best for my wife and children. I want them to be able to go to school and become whatever they desire to be. Look at Lucy. She's so bright. Why can't she be a teacher or a doctor or a lawyer? And Charlie, he can be the same, or maybe turn this farm into a great empire like the Hales or the Cullmans up in Windsor."

Over the next few years, their family continued to grow and prosper. Grasmere was doing extremely well. The value of the crops continued to rise, and the economic woes of most of the rest of the country had not hit Glastonbury yet.

Their fifth child, a beautiful baby girl that they named Lillian was another January baby. She was born on the second day of the new year in 1926. She was healthy and full of life. Like Johnnie, she had a slightly different look from her sisters. Though not as fair as her sisters, she had a very pretty light brown complexion. Her eyes were dark like Johnnie's. She had a head full of curly black silky hair. She had a slightly more delicate look than her sisters. They said the angels danced for her because she was always looking up and smiling for no apparent reason at nothing in particular. George was boastful about his beautiful children and his large family. "The Lord commanded us to be fruitful and multiply so that's exactly what I am trying to do. And we're not done yet! Even the plants are fruitful and multiplying!" He would boast. On the day of Lillian's first birthday, Theresa told George she was 3 months pregnant. Her quiet little birthday party turned into quite a celebration for the Cohen family as the joy of yet another child blessing their lives emphasized the milestone in the life of their youngest.

By the beginning of February, Theresa was complaining of being lightheaded and the severe morning sickness and breast tenderness that had plagued her during the early part of her pregnancy just seemed to stop very abruptly. Doc Rankin said that this was due to some abnormal hormonal shifts and suggested she stay off her feet as much as possible. As a strong young mother with five little stair steps running behind each other, she found that to be almost impossible to accomplish. After a few days, however, she noticed some spotting, and this time Doc Rankin was more adamant about staying off of her feet. George assured her that he and Alice could handle the children, and that he just wanted her to focus on keeping the baby growing in her womb safe. After a few days of bedrest she felt stronger and began doing very minimal things to help Alice (George wasn't as much help as he proclaimed himself to be.)

On the morning of the fourth day back on her feet, she screamed for George as she went to bath herself. She held up a bloody cloth to George and didn't have to say a word. Besides reading her expression, he knew the significance of the bloody cloth. He comforted her for a moment and then called Alice to stay with her while he called for Doc Rankin. Doctor Rankin and his nurse were there in a flash, but it was too late to affect any difference in Theresa's condition, and she had a miscarriage. She had been carrying twins; a boy and a girl.

To Theresa, hearing that she had lost twins that had depended on her body to sustain them for four and a half months was like losing a child she had come to know and love. She was devastated and felt a tremendous amount of guilt for not being a better patient and adhering to absolute bed rest until the doctor had cleared her. In an attempt to console her, Doc Rankin very possibly made the situation worse.

"Theresa, I know you are hurting right now, but you'll feel better day by day. Just thank The Lord for those five beautiful little ones you've got running around now. They need you at your best."

Very lethargic, either from the physical trauma or the emotional devastation, Theresa's response was barely audible. "I know I'm gonna be alright. I know my little babies are with Jesus already. It's just that..." She couldn't finish her sentence as she began to sob.

George, who had yielded the space at her side on the side of the bed to the doctor as he examined and consoled her, rushed to her side and effortlessly pulled the doctor away and took his place. He put his cheek against hers and felt the coolness of her tears as they wet him as he spoke into the hollow of her neck. "Baby, I know it's hard right now, but we have to trust God that he does what's best. Maybe there was something wrong with them or maybe God saw something awful happening to them in the future and loved them too much to let them come into this life to suffer. We don't know, but His word says that all things work together for the good for them that love God and are the called according to His purpose. It's just that sometimes we have to wait a while to see the good in a situation, but we know it will come, because it's His promise. We'll be fine. Maybe those were the angels that Lil is always smiling at, and maybe they escaped heaven to come play with her but their Father found out where they were and called 'em back home before they got in real trouble!" He chucked after saying that, hoping she would appreciate his humor. She understood and smiled weakly to pacify him.

Doc Rankin was preparing to leave and said "Theresa, I'm going to leave now. Physically you have nothing to worry about. Just rest for the next couple of days. You should expect some light spotting for as long as a week. If you get to be tender in the tummy, or start running a fever, or if you smell an odor down there, or if you start bleeding heavy, then call me, because it may be a sign of an infection. You're not going to feel much like doing anything for the next couple of days, and that's fine. It's normal and it's your body's way of saying 'take a break and recover'. Your system will be fully recovered by the time your next monthly comes on you. Are you still taking that Lydia Pinkham's?"

"I stopped after you told me I was pregnant." She mumbled; barely audibly.

"Well, let me suggest you stop taking it from now on. You don't seem to have a problem getting pregnant anymore. That's for sure.

And besides, I heard a couple of reports that if it over stimulates a woman, that there are some ingredients in it that can cause a miscarriage. We don't..." he did not get the chance to finish his sentence.

From somewhere she found the energy to let out a primal scream and then a heartbreaking plea, "Oh Doc, please don't tell me I killed my babies. Please Doc. I didn't know. I didn't mean to. Oh, Son. Oh, Son. What have I done?" Her tearful plea turned into body wrenching sobs.

Both George and Doc tried their best to console her and assure her that she had no culpability in the miscarriage at all, but she would not be consoled. Soon, George asked that everyone leave him and her alone. He held her and rocked her and sang "His Eye Is On The Sparrow", a favorite of hers. He remembered when he first heard it. They had just gotten serious about each other and her mother and sister Mary and she sang it one Sunday afternoon in the parlor after they had discussed the sermon of the day. He sang a couple of stanzas and then just hummed until she fell asleep. Sporadically her body would yield to an involuntary shudder that always comes when we are calming down from a major cry, but God gave her the peace of sleep.

There was an air of sadness about Theresa for weeks. There was a late season snowfall and George piled the whole gang up in the sleigh he had bought when Benny was an only child. He knew she loved the sleigh rides with the kids and it always made her happy to watch the sheer joy on her children's faces at the exhilaration of Ned and Buck hurtling them effortlessly over the meadows of Grasmere. She smiled but her cheeks didn't kiss her eyes like they used to. She laughed but not the deep laugh that used to pierce the cold winter air like a melody to the rhythm of the percussion of the hoof beats that shook the very earth beneath them. Her eyes looked but they did not see much more than the apparitions she hoped would be a visitation of the angels that fled so abruptly out of her life. She did what she could to spare her family from the pain that still scratched too close to the surface of her emotions.

As the months progressed, she seemed more vital, but George couldn't find his Theresa. Not the real Theresa; the one who was so open and full of spontaneity. He spoke with her often about the sovereignty of God and how He wants us to accept what life brings as part of our life set of circumstances, designed to help us mature in our relationship with Him, as we grow through them. Nevertheless, He is, and always will be, behind the scenes moving us to higher levels in His kingdom. He constantly reassured her that she did nothing wrong and that his mind could not even conceive of trying to invent any animosity towards her, and she loved him for that. In many ways they grew even closer, but it was different during that season of their lives.

Life progressed as normal, otherwise. The farm continued to do well. Their circle of friends kept increasing, and so did their family. On the night of the Labor Day cookout, while everyone was still dancing, Theresa made him dance with her and then spun them out of the group and off to the side. They were both huffing and puffing a bit. Her eyes danced long after her feet had stopped, as she wildly stared at him and laughed. Then she boldly kissed him after she had wiped the dewdrops of perspiration that had come while they were dancing. He noticed that she had a real smile; the kind that forced her high cheekbones almost into her eyes. The kind he had missed seeing on her face for so long. Seeing her this vibrantly alive was infectious and he broke out into laughter as well. His amusement was simply in witnessing her joy. "What's gotten into you?"

"Doc just left, and he finally told me!" She spun again and laughed again.

"He told you what?"

"He told me he wouldn't tell me until I went to see him tomorrow at my appointment, but he told me just before he left!" She was still smiling at him strangely.

"Okay, Theresa! Calm down now, Baby. What did he tell you?" His last question was delivered loudly and deliberately almost as if speaking to someone impaired.

"We're gonna have another baby, Son." She answered him as if he was impaired. "What do you think he could have told me that would have made me this happy?" She jumped up and wrapped her arms and legs around him as soon as she said it. She caught him off guard and off balance and he stumbled back as her weight hit him and they fell onto one of the tables. They and all of its content spilled over onto the ground. They sat there and hugged and laughed even after the crowd had gathered around to make sure they were alright.

George kept saying to everyone that came over to help them up and who asked if they were alright, "We're gonna have a baby!" Those who knew the story of Theresa's miscarriage and her subsequent depression, were moved to tears to see their friends so genuinely overjoyed. Those who didn't know, walked away suspicious that George and Theresa were given to too much strong drink.

Later as they lay in bed, they were thrilled that the day had gone so well and that everyone had so much fun. They laughed at falling over the table and at the suggestion they heard that some people had thought they were drinking.

"Do you remember the night of the Fourth of July, after the kids tried to burn down the house?" She was referring to the episode where George had given Benny and Lucy and Charlie some sparklers to play with. He had left Benny in charge of his younger sister and brother, who were seven and a half and almost six. They did well except that Lucy threw one in the air and it landed on the roof of the front porch. It sat and smoldered for a while but no one paid any attention to it. Suddenly it burst into flames. George ran and got his ladder and John, who was there for a family picnic, and Benny passed him buckets of water until the small fire was under control. There was very little damage done, but they praised God that it burst into flames while they were nearby to react. What if it had smoldered until after everyone was asleep?

"Yeah, I remember that night. It was a bit scary after we really thought about what could have happened." Then another memory stormed back to him. "Oh yeah, and I remember something else about that night. That fire seemed to have got you all hot and bothered. Yeah, I remember that night!"

Smiling sheepishly, she simply said, "I think it was that night!" They held each other in their joy. She, because she felt that God was giving her a sign that whatever caused the miscarriage had been purged from her life; he, because it did him so much good to see his old Theresa back.

Yvonne was born on April 7th of 1928. She was another blue-eyed fair skinned little girl. Well, not really so little. She was 10 lbs at birth. Not so much fat but long limbed. Unlike her sisters, her hair was thinner and blonde as opposed to their thick curly black tresses, but she was beautiful. She had facial features more like her father, as did Benny, Johnnie, and Lil.

One morning, after she and Alice had all the children settled, they sat there at the kitchen table drinking their morning cup of coffee. Alice looked at her sister holding Von, who was fast asleep, in her arms. She noticed tears in her eyes. "What's da mattah, Pank? Why you cryin'"

Theresa looked at her sister and tried her best to give her a smile. "I was just thinkin' about my two little angels. I was just wondering if they would have felt like this in my arms. I was wondering what I would have named them; maybe after Momma and Poppa; Sara an Sam. That would have been nice. Or maybe we could have named the boy George. After all, he got three boys and ain't none of em named after him!"

Alice, being very meek, interrupted her sister as delicately as she could. "Hey Pank, don't do dat. Don't go getting yourself all depressed pullin up the past when God done give you such a beautiful chile to fill da hole dem two left. Why she bigger den both them woulda been combined!" Alice's humor did not go unnoticed, and her sister smiled at her politely.

I know what you're thinking Baby Sis, and I appreciate where your heart is. It's just that I want those two little angels so bad, and its like Von is a really beautiful blessing, but in my mind she is in addition to, not in place of. It's going to take me some time. I keep wondering if I had trusted God instead of that damn Lydia Pinkham stuff if I would have my two babies now."

"Pank, you don't know da mine of God, but you do know da word of God, an His word is all about reconcilin' and restorin'. He wants you whole. Let go an let God do His work in you. Remember, God controlled whether those babies came into this life or not. It was His decision; not yours. Do you remembah what Momma used ta say? 'Don't doubt da Lord.' He too wise ta make a mistake an too lovin' ta do evil. Trust dat He did what was best." Alice's voice was filled with compassion for her sister.

"You know Sis, I really believe what you say! It's my unbelief about what I did that's causing me the problem!"

"I'll pray for yo freedom from yo own chains that hole you prisoner. Walk in peace. Yo time ta walk wit dem chirlren ain't fo dis life. It like God gave you a glimpse of heavin. Dey gonna be dere waitin fo ya!" Those words got a genuine smile out of Theresa.

"Out of the mouth of babes. Thank you, Sis. You just said some things that truly touched my spirit and I receive them, in the name of Jesus. I am declaring a healing in my life. I rebuke any foul spirit that comes against my mind. God has not given me a spirit of fear, but of power, and of love, and of a sound mind. I declare myself healed and hidden under the blood of Jesus. Amen!" Theresa reached out and grabbed her sister's hand. "Really. Thank you! I'm gonna be okay!"

"An da church said, Amen!" They laughed at her impersonation of Deacon Bryant.

Chapter Eight

The stories of farm bankruptcies were rampant in 1928. Nevertheless, with few exceptions, the Connecticut Valley was feeling the benefit of being the best resource for a product with a small but consistent demand. There was a small downturn in the overall demand for cigar wrap, but it hadn't been manifested at the high end of the product category yet. Consolidated was still seeking leasing agreements with farmers in the area, but its all-out assault to buy farm land had subsided. That was due mainly to the fact that the speculators had driven the price of land to the point that it was far more beneficial for the major producers like Consolidated Cigar to pull back on the growing business and concentrate on the cigar making business. They had driven most of their smaller competitors out of the market, so their competition for the crops was minimized. It was now a buyer's market.

George's consortium of private cigar makers was feeling it, and the number of them in the business continued to decline. As a result, George had contracted a portion of his crop for purchase by Consolidated at a pre-determined rate. This was less profitable than what George had been doing over the last few years, but it was far less risky. Beyond the risk of crop shrink due to natural disaster and disease, there was the very real risk of customers not being in business at the end of the harvest to buy the crops they had agreed to buy. For George, because of the reputation he had for growing fine quality, his risks in that area were far less than for most, but he felt that this year, given the general economic conditions, a hedge was in order.

Nathan Richards and a few of his supporters were still strong proponents for control of the market by the independent grower and used their influence wherever possible to minimize the successes that Consolidated might have made in the market. It was their opinion that if they could keep land and crops out of the hands of Consolidated that Consolidated would somehow creep back out of the market which would do several things for the Glastonbury economy. First it would raise the tax base by creating what they felt would be higher profits from selling to independents. They felt that a growers association would be a far better support system than banking on the nobility of what they still considered a foreign corporation. This despite the fact they had established their headquarters just down the street from Grasmere on Oak Street. The other key issue was land values. A huge fear was that Consolidated could at any time find a preferred source for their wrap product in a market that could provide similar quality at a much lower price than what was available in Connecticut due in part to the high cost of lands that their market activity had artificially escalated. The more town land that they owned, the greater the risk would be if they decided to abandon the market at some time and sell their land off at prices that would crash the local real estate values. Because of that, they constantly put pressure on the locals to minimize their dealings with Consolidated.

On the other hand, Stancliffe Hale and some of his supporters were as adamantly convinced that nurturing the relationship with Consolidated was the best course of action for the growth and stability of the wealth of the town. So far, they had been a real benefit as far as stability was concerned since the reality was that neither the Businessman's Association nor the local banks could offer little more than loans when a farmer got behind the eight ball because of a poor crop. Consolidated eliminated the risk.

There was constant jockeying for support of one philosophy or the other in local elections for town, county, and state officials, as well as in the selection of officers of locally influential business associations like the Farmers' Bureau.

As things turned out for George, he probably could have waited another year to get into bed with Consolidated. He was still able to attract enough independents to replace those that had failed. They came at some of his local friends' and competitors' expense, however, because the customers were not new to the market; only changing suppliers. The quality of George's crops, due to his superior growing and cultivating techniques, made his product extremely attractive. The portion of his product sold to Consolidated was about 8% under priced compared to the price from the independents. On the other hand, any major shifts in demand or increased shrinkage due to natural factors would have easily eaten up that difference very quickly. Most of the local farmers understood the nature of competition that came about due to normal business activities, but some took it personally when you got the upper hand in a business transaction.

George had such an encounter in the fall of 1928. It was about two weeks after the annual cookout and George ran into Paul Bender, another farmer, while he was picking up some staples for Theresa and some candy treats for the kids.

George spoke first. "Hi Paul. Missed you and the family at the cookout this year. How's everything going?" Paul barely grunted in response, so George pursued the conversation. "Hey man, are you alright?"

"Yeah, I'm fine, I'm just not in the talking mood."

George laughed, trying to use humor as a door opener to get his friend to talk. "Well that's a first for that mood for you, isn't it? You know, not talking! That's a first!"

If looks could kill, George would have bled to death right there on the general store floor. "How can you expect me to have a normal conversation with you again after what you did to me and my family? Or maybe you thought I wouldn't find out!"

A bit taken aback, but sincerely concerned, George asked "What are you talking about, man? I haven't had anything to do with you or your family or anything concerning you since I last saw you stuffing your face at my cookout this time last year! Now tell me how I harmed you!" George found he was getting angry at the accusation.

"You sold quite a bit of tobacco to one of my best customers, and because of that I had to sell what I usually sold to him on the hustle at the last minute. He didn't even tell me he had already bought from you until I chased him down when he didn't show up this year!"

"Man I don't know who you're talking about. My customers have changed some over the past few years because so many of the makers are dropping out of business or selling out to General or Consolidated, but I never chase after anybody else's customers. They come to me asking if I have enough yield to take them on. If I do, I sell them. I don't ask where they were buying from. I just give them my price and commit my harvest to them. If one of your customers came to me and bought tobacco this year it was just business. I'm sorry if he screwed you, but that was him, not me!" George became conscious of the other people around him about halfway through his statement and toned the latter part down in volume, but not in intensity.

"Well why do you have to go after my customers all of a sudden? You certainly seem to do well enough that you don't need to take from me!" Paul hadn't lowered his volume nor his emotions.

"Look man, I'm in the tobacco business. If someone comes to me, I am assuming they want what I got more than what the next guy's got. I don't offer to beat anybody's price and I don't make promises I can't keep about quantity. My price is my price. It's based on what I know I can get for my product. People like my product, but then again, I work extra hard to make it that way. Now I am assuming there was something that sent your customer into the open market. You need to talk with your customer and find out what you did to lose him. I'll guarantee you one thing, it wasn't about price. Your name always comes up as a place that potential customers can buy shade broadleaf cheaper than they can from me, or most anybody else, for that matter. I never try to beat your price because I don't have to. I get what I ask and I usually have a waiting list. I didn't break what's broke in your business, and beyond the advice I just gave you, I'm not in the business to fix it. I'm sorry you're pointing your grief at me, but I suggest you look in a different direction."

"Don't you even want to know who it is?" Paul asked, as if that would be a factor in the direction of the conversation.

"No. No I don't" George surprised him with his directness. "No Paul. That won't make any difference to me next year. If he comes to my door, and we agree to do business, I'm gonna sell him. I assume that since you know who he is, you'll take that advantage and make your best effort to win him back. I hope that whoever he is doesn't show up at my door. I wish you the best of success, but if he does, and we agree to do business again, then I will do business with him again. Just know this; I expect no quarter in fair business dealings, and I give none. That's just the way things are. If you get over your mad, you and the family are always welcomed to the cookout. In fact, you're welcomed any time you show up at my door, unless you're coming with some more dumb crap like this!" George smiled and smacked him on his shoulder to emphasize the forgiving nature of his ending statement, but that went over like bad breath on a dentist!

Paul violently pulled his shoulder away from the friendly smack as his red face got redder, if that's possible. "Why you uppity Jew Ni.." He stopped abruptly, catching what he was about to say, suddenly embarrassed at his attitude.

George's reaction was emphatic and instantaneous. He extended his index and middle fingers in tandem and shook them under Paul's nose. "Fool! When you pray tonight, thank God He didn't give you the nerve to finish what you were trying to say. Now you best turn your sorry ass around and take your hatred somewhere else. I'm done with this!" George took his hand out of Paul's face and turned to walk away. He got about two steps when he heard a desperate Paul call his name.

"George! George I'm sorry. You know that's not me. You're right about everything you said. My head got screwed up. I've been listening to the wrong people. I'm sorry. I didn't mean to say..."

George cut him off in mid sentence. "Paul, out of the fullness of the heart, the mouth speaketh! You've got some things in you that you need to fix. Let's give this some time and we can talk when we're both a bit more level headed."

Sheepishly, Paul looked George in his eye and promised he would see him soon so they could talk.

After they had put the children to bed Theresa looked at him and said "Son, do you mind telling me what's bothering you?"

"I didn't do a good job of hiding it, did I?"

"When you get mad, your jaws shut tighter than a bulldog and that little muscle in your jawbone twitches like it has a mind all its own! And those fingers, they make it sound like Indian war drums. We been together now eighteen years. There ain't much about your ways I don't know. Now what's wrong?" Theresa demanded.

"It has nothing to do with you! I had a fight with Paul Bender today."

"Paul Bender? I hope you didn't hurt that scrawny little...."

"No Theresa, it didn't quite get to that." He went on to describe the incident to her. She was surprised to hear how Paul would gain so much animosity without at least giving George an opportunity to explain himself, if he needed to.

"Gee Son, that's too bad. The way him and his wife act with us you would think he was your best friend. You never know. So who do you think he meant when he was talking about listening to the wrong people?" She already knew the answer but she wanted to hear George deal with the issue.

"Nathan Richards and that bunch of course, unless there's another pocket of bigots around here. It must really be eating away at them to see us doing so well. We have to watch our backs with these fools. I guess there's no magic land where people can just be people together."

"You know what they say, Son. Birds of a feather flock together. When times get rough, they start to peel the onion, one layer at a time."

George smiled and looked quizzically at her. "And just what does all that philosophizing mean, Miss Theresa?"

"I got your Miss Theresa! What I was saying before I was so rudely interrupted is just that people always shed the most uncomfortable things first, so when it comes time to protect their little worlds, they tend to start peeling people like they peel an onion. First to go is the layer with the brown skin. It's so different it's really easy to peel away. I think we all do it. It's not just them."

"You're probably right, Baby, but I desperately hope that time proves you wrong. We have seven children and I would hate to think that they'll miss out on the things we've worked so hard to give them because some fool decided that they were the first to be peeled when it was time to compete for opportunity. That's why I want my children well equipped with education. I'll make sure they have an inheritance to get them off to a good start, but I want them to have the moral fiber and education to make it work for them. Promise me Theresa, if I go before you, that you'll see to it that our children are prepared. I'll make sure that you are in a position where you can care for them. Grasmere will sustain you all."

"Now Son, don't go startin that talk again. You know I don't want no parts of it. I truly believe that if anything ever happened to you, I would just curl up and die. I hope you bury me, and not me you!" She was sincere.

He reached out to her and pulled her to him. "Stop being such a little sissy! The Lord will keep us, no matter what the circumstances, but you can be assured of this one thing; that through Him, we will always be together." As they walked upstairs to bed, he had one more thought to share with her. "You know Baby, there are always going to be evil spirited people, but we can't let them hinder us from seeking the company of those with beautiful spirits. Too often, people select an onion by its skin rather than its meat. One thing I want our children to always remember as wisdom: you never judge a book by its cover. That's important for us all to remember."

She smiled a smile he couldn't see. She thought, 'You are a wonderful man, and I love you.' But, she simply said, "Amen Reverend Cohen!"

Her behind was almost at his eye level as they climbed the stairs so temptation got the better of him so he smacked her right cheek as he said, "I got your Reverend!"

She shrieked and began giggling. "And I say Amen again!"

The year was flying by. Yvonne, the new baby, was growing by leaps and bounds, and she was such a happy baby. By the time she was six months old, she was almost jumping out of the arms of anyone that held her when she saw her father come into sight. All of his children reacted to him like that, but he was creating a very special bond with Von. He would always go right to her when she reacted and lift her and twirl her around and kiss her plump cheeks. She was a beautiful little girl. The rest of the crew would also storm him when he came home, and he would lift and twirl and kiss them all in the special way he knew each of them preferred. Lucy and Charlie, because at 8 and 9 they had outgrown their turn on the daddy ride, got hugs and kisses and more meaningful inquiries about their days. Nellie had started school, so she now had more to share as well.

Even though there were no new births, Doc Rankin was a steady fixture. Beyond his frequent trips to drop Lucy, Charlie, and Nellie off after they had stopped by his house on the way home from school for some of Lucie Rankin's cookies, there were several incidents that required his attention.

The first was back in the summer when Lucy and her Aunt Alice were returning home from making their milk and egg delivery run. Lucy stepped in a bumble bee hive and was stung many times. Alice had fought them off her and raced her home. She had over a dozen stings. It was good that they were bumble bees instead of yellow jackets, who also nest in the ground. They are far more aggressive and would not have been driven off as easily. As it stood, Lucy swelled and developed a fever and felt ill for four days, but by Friday of that week she was back in school.

The other involved Johnnie. He was quite a handful; always running and jumping and climbing. He was fearless. One day in the early spring, just after Yvonne was born, George was pulling out of the driveway in the car, on his way to the market in Hartford. He had already told Johnnie he couldn't come. Just as George was gaining momentum as he drove down the driveway, Johnnie ran and jumped on the running board of the car. George didn't know this had happened, but Theresa was helplessly watching from the kitchen window. By the time George had picked up enough speed to enter the highway, Johnnie lost his grip and fell off the car and into the street. George, totally unaware, kept going. Theresa yelled for Alice who made it out to Johnnie before Theresa could. He had several bumps and bruises on his arms and legs and head. The worse was a big lump on his head. Thankfully there were no broken bones. The bump caused quite a bit of swelling on his head but it went away after a few days.

It wasn't six weeks later that he fell off the seat of the tractor and had one of the tiller blades impale is head. That was a close call, but again he was blessed with a narrow escape from serious damage. His father felt guilty about both situations because he had exposed his son to the danger that caused him the injuries, but everyone did their best to assure him that it was Johnnie's nature to get himself into scrapes!

Despite all of that, it was a good year in the Cohen household. They had a beautiful Christmas together, and all the children except for Yvonne, were old enough to appreciate it. They got everything they asked for and then some. It was George's 46th birthday and he had everything he had ever hoped for, and he wanted his children to bask in the same joy and security. He took the kids out on the sleigh and they had a wonderful time as Buck and Ned lumbered across the rolling meadows of Grasmere. Even Rover went along for the ride, at least part of the way, until he got too excited and jumped out of the sleigh and was chasing after the family on the home stretch. At 8 years old, he was still surprisingly spry.

They had four birthday celebrations that next month. They celebrated Lillian's 3rd birthday on January 2nd. Lucy's 9th birthday was on the 12th, and Nellie's 6th was on the 15th. Then on the 29th Benny turned 21.

They began the planting in April. George already had his buyers lined up, and there was not much of a change from the previous year, although he shifted a couple of independents. A couple came and a couple went. He had been doing well enough that he didn't need a crop loan for seed and equipment and wages. He had his money in hand; some in banks; some hidden away.

The general talk around town was that some farmers were forced to specialize in other crops because the demand for shade from their customers was shrinking. The discussions concerning Consolidated were becoming more heated. In late May they called for an important town meeting to elect officers for the town planning committee. Nominations were to be entered and voted on at the May 29th meeting. Officers would be elected at the June 1st town meeting.

George got the notice about the meeting on the 11th of May. They wanted to give a three week notice of the vote. He decided then that he didn't want to go. He had grown weary of all the political talk, and preferred not to get involved. People were getting very emotional about their position on the issues. He knew that Stan Hale was up for the chairmanship and figured him to be a lock for that office. It wouldn't matter if he showed up or not. Besides, it was the wrong time of year to be spending energy on anything other than getting his plants off to a good start.

It was going to get very busy, so he decided to take Theresa out to Hartford on Friday night to make up in advance for the time they wouldn't have together. It would be a special night out just for the two of them to visit some good friends, without the crew tagging along. Alice was more than happy to watch the children. Lucy was a mature 9-year-old and could help care for Lil and Von.

They got dressed in their best night-on-the-town clothes. She wore a simple form fitting wool suit with a long skirt and a short jacket. The suit was a navy-blue cloth with very fine polka dots lined up in straight rows that gave the impression of being pin stripes. She wore a white blouse that had lace ruffles at the bodice and on the cuffs. The collar was high. She completed the outfit with a cameo broach. Her hair was parted in the middle and pulled back loosely and finished off in the back with a French roll.

George was in a very stylish dark grey three-piece pin stripe wool suit. He wore a light blue shirt with a white collar and cuffs and a bold geometric wine and tan tie. His polished black shoes were decorated with white spats. He topped it all off with a black stingy brimmed derby.

George smiled brightly when he first saw her dressed with just a hint of makeup. Her heart skipped when she saw the look of adoration on his face and she did a slow pirouette followed by a curtsey to acknowledge his obvious show of appreciation of her looks. For him she raised an eyebrow and nodded. They stood for a second and admired each other.

"Why Mrs. Cohen, after all these years, you still take my breath away. You look so beautiful, Baby."

"And so do you Mr. Cohen, but if looking at me takes your breath away, then stop lookin'. As fine as you are tonight, I think you're gonna need all the breath you can catch when I get you back home!" She said giving him an exaggerated once over.

"Uh huh! I hear you talking stuff now, but that same fineness that takes my breath gives me extra inspiration, and I don't need much breath when I'm inspired!"

"You just ain't gonna let nobody out talk you Mr. Cohen; now are you?"

"Not as long as I'm breathin'!" they laughed themselves all the way out to the car. They knew they were a sharp looking couple.

At the Morelands, they had a great time catching up on life and world events. They shared their stories about their children, friends, and their neighbors.

They all had a huge laugh at George's expense when she told them about the meal Florence Roberts' father had prepared for them. Unfortunately, or fortunately as it turned out, Theresa wasn't feeling well and had to send George alone. He made apologies for her absence. They were disappointed but understanding. Mr. Roberts fixed the meat and Florence prepared all the rest of the meal. During dinner, George continually commented on how good everything tasted. He kept inquiring about the kind of meat it was, but they kept evading the question. After dinner, Mr. Roberts finally addressed George's question.

"Now George, you kept on asking what kind of meat that was that you were enjoying so much at dinner. I didn't say anything because I wanted to see if you could figure it out. Do you know what it was that you just ate?"

"No, sir. I can't say that I can identify that taste, but it sure was good."

"You just had you some skunk meat!" Florence and her father laughed when they saw the look on George's face.

George jumped up instantly and ran out the front door and tried his best to heave it back up but it wouldn't come up. Later on, Florence would tell Theresa that George literally turned green the instant he heard what he had just eaten.

Mr. Roberts came out on the porch and asked, "What's the matter George? My family loves skunk. You gotta admit that it's mighty tasty!"

George wanted to hit him or, at the very least, curse him out, but out of respect for his age, and the fact that he was a good neighbor and his wife's best friend's father, he simply said, "I better get going. I don't want to get sick in your house."

Theresa was very sympathetic for George when he got home and told her about dinner. What kind of people eat skunk? They should have told you before you ate it! Are you okay? Do you want some tea to help you digest it? She hit all the right buttons, but after George had gone to work the next day, and she saw that he was alright, she told Alice. After the proper expressions of concern, they looked at each other and burst out laughing hysterically. Their laughing episodes continued to break out spontaneously throughout the day. They even made a sign by pinching their nose and making a stinky face, which would instantly bring the other to side splitting laughter. After dinner, Alice did it when George turned his head and they started laughing uncontrollably. Only after George insisted that they tell him what was so funny several times, to the point of becoming aggravated, did they finally let him in on the source of their delight. His first reaction was hurt that his family would find such an awful thing happening to him to be funny, but Alice brought him back to reality.

"Bro George, ya gotta admit dat it pretty funny dat you could eat a whole meal of skunk meat an enjoy it an not git sick 'til ya found out it was skunk." She was talking to him calmly and looking at him sincerely, before she added, "Shoot, it a good thang dey tole ya what it was. Otherwise ya woulda been askin fo some ta take home fo yo lunch taday!" She said it in such a way that she barely made it through the statement while keeping a straight face. When she finished speaking, she instantly bent over and squeezed her stomach as if that could stop the cramping spasms that danced to the melody of her laughter. Theresa, then George followed suit.

Theresa told the Morelands that George still feigns anger at Florence every time she comes to the house, but Florence, being Florence, turns the tables and teases George unmercifully about the incident.

They had a great time that night and on the way home Theresa looked over at him driving with the bright moonlight hitting his face and said, "I get the feeling sometimes that I loved you even before I met you. I can't explain it, but you are such a part of me now that I can't remember how I felt before I was loving you!"

"And I hope that never changes. I hope we still love each other this way when we're too old to speak! 'Til the cows come home!" He smiled at her.

She reached out and touched his thigh. "Yeah, 'til the cows come home!"

When they got home she showed him just how breathtaking she could be, and he showed her just how inspired he was. They fell asleep smiling and holding each other close.

That following morning, George was up and out before Theresa even woke up. She made a cup of coffee and a grilled cheese sandwich and had Lucy and Charlie run it out to the field for their father. He was busy supervising the setting of the poles in the shade fields, but he sure appreciated the breakfast. Lucy and Charlie raced back and he just barely beat his sister.

It was a nice day, and the entire family was out doing chores or playing when George came home for lunch. Nellie was the first to spot him coming up the trail. "Look! Look! Here come Poppa!" as she took off running towards him as fast as her little legs would take her. Johnnie flew past her and Lucie and Charlie soon overtook him. Lillian tried to catch the crowd but she was left way behind. Yvonne had only recently taken her first steps. They mobbed their father like ravenous wolves on a ham bone, and he loved every minute of it. The boys were running circles around the crew who had all seized various parts of their father. Lucy was the most considerate. She was holding his hand. Nellie was draped around his neck, getting her horsey ride, and once little Lil caught up to them, he scooped her up into his arms and she played with his moustache while he walked. As they approached Von, he shifted Lil to the arm that Lucy was holding on to and used the free arm to scoop up the baby.

"Hey, ya got any room for me?" Theresa joked as she came up to him and kissed him. "You snuck out on me."

"I was gonna wake you, but I didn't want to get inspired again!" They exchanged a knowing look. "Besides, I got out real early. We got a lot to do, and the guys only work 'til 3:00 today. Tonight's their night to howl!"

"Uh huh. Just like last night was yours?"

"So-to-speak!" He began peeling himself free of the crew as he approached the stairs. He only had about twenty minutes to eat so he could be there when his work crew finished their lunch break.

It was getting dark before Theresa saw him leading the cows back up into the barn as he finished his day. When he came in the door he looked dog tired.

"Long day, huh?" She commented as much as she was asking.

"Sure was. Not bad for an old man with just a wee bit of sleep!" he said as he reached her and gave her a little peck on the lips. "I'm hungry. As long as that ain't no skunk I'm smelling, I'll be down in about ten minutes. I gotta wash up. I smell like a skunk myself!"

"No Son. You smell like a man; a real bona fide man." She said smiling at her husband. "By the way, that's a spaghetti recipe I got from Jo-Anna Saglio. Hurry up, it smells good and I'm hungry too. I'm waiting to eat with you."

"Okay. I'll be right back. Promise!"

She waited about a half an hour before she got concerned. She called him once and got no answer. All the young ones were asleep so she didn't want to yell again and take the risk of waking them. As she was climbing the stairs she could hear snoring from her room. She smiled. She decided he probably needed rest more than food. She would let him sleep until his hunger woke him. Whatever time that might be, she would get up and fix his plate. Just as she was turning around to go back down the stairs, she heard an unearthly screaming sound coming from outside or upstairs. She couldn't tell which.

Lucy, who had been in her room reading, came charging down the hall and overtook her on the stairs. "Who's that Momma? Who's screaming?"

They were rushing down the remainder of the stairs together while Theresa was answering her question. "Oh no Lucy; It's not a who, it's a what." In whatever time passed between confusion and recognition, she was whisked back in time to the night Ole Man Mose died; the day she first saw George. It was the piercing shriek of a screech owl and grew louder and more insistent with each passing second. She screamed for George, but by this time the turmoil caused by the unwelcomed visitor had roused him and he was already headed down the stairs. He ran past her and out the front door and immediately turned to look up at the roof as soon as his feet hit the ground. The owl saw him before he saw it and it had already stopped screeching and was taking flight when George looked up. He watched as it disappeared in the coal black sky, lit only by the first quarter moon and the flickering light of the thousands of shimmering stars that served only as silent witnesses to his escape. It briefly reappeared as it flew across the stingy backdrop of the moonlight.

Theresa was in a frenzy. Alice looked like she had just seen a ghost, for she too remembered that night almost eighteen years ago to the day. Charlie and Johnnie were asking Lucy what happened, but turned to their father when he walked in the door.

"Did you get it Poppa? Was it big? Was it scary?"

"Now calm down everybody. It was only an owl; a small owl at that. It really doesn't sound any worse than a nervous horse! Now stop worrying, it doesn't mean anything." He said it as convincingly as he could.

Theresa and Alice just looked at him. Then Theresa said, "Son, we gotta pray. We gotta pray for deliverance from that death spirit that these birds bring with 'em. You remember Ole Man Mose. I'm gonna call my Momma an tell her and my family to pray for us!"

"Well, I don't have a problem praying, but my God is bigger than any owl or any force behind any owl. God is our protector and our provider, and unless it's his appointed time, no owl can speed it up, and no prayers can slow it down."

"Are you saying that prayer doesn't help? Are you saying that if we pray for deliverance or healing and God answers the prayer that the prayer didn't matter?" Theresa was confused by his statement.

"When we pray, God already knows the answer before we ask for help. If we have enough faith in Him to humble ourselves and pray and turn to His ways, He will attend to our prayers. Of most importance is that we trust and rely on Him. Sometimes He allows things to frighten or concern us. If we turn to Him, it will work out to our good and His Glory, even though the immediate response isn't what we want to hear or when we want to hear it. It all works together. He wanted us to be here having this discussion so that whatever happens next in our lives, we will understand that, if we pary, it will be as He planned it. In His plan, it is important that the owl screeched. God doesn't always answer yes you know, but He always answers right!" Theresa and Alice were looking at him strangely now. Lucy was trying to grasp what he was saying. Charlie and Johnnie abandoned ship as soon as they heard them having a 'God talk'.

"I still don't understand. Are you saying it's useless to pray?"

"No. You have to really understand the nature of God to really understand how He operates. He is a being with no restrictions except those He chooses to put upon Himself, and because of His righteousness, He will never deviate being what He says He is. He is omnipotent. That means that He has all power in His hands. Nothing can happen that He can't stop, and nothing can be imagined that He can't create. He is omnipresent. That means that He is everywhere at the same time. He is omniscient. That means that He knows everything there is to know about everything that has ever happened or will happen. God is immense, so He is bigger than anything we can imagine. In fact, he is infinite. He has no bounds by time or space. He is eternal because He has always been and will always be. He is not restricted by the confines of the universe. He is precognitive. He sees into the future because he planned the future. Whatever the circumstance, He knows best how to handle it. He is immortal. That means nothing can destroy Him. He is immutable. That means that He never makes a mistake in deciding what is right, so He never has a need to change His mind. God is Holy so He has no pleasure in evil. God is sovereign. That means that He doesn't have to answer to anyone for what He plans or does, and we should find comfort in that because He never makes a mistake. Finally, God is love. His plan is based on His immense love for us. He so loved the world that He gave His only begotten Son that we might have the right to life, and that more abundantly. He has assured us that all things are worked to our good (either in this world or the next) and His glory." After all that, he paused to look at them. "God's word is filled with instances where He requires that we pray, and we should because He commands us. He also tells us that where two or more are gathered in His name that He will be in our midst, so we should pray with and for each other, but never does He say that He will change His perfect plan to accommodate our puny interpretation of what we hope to be the right outcome. He answers prayer as a sign, and He even influences our prayer in the person of the Holy Spirit whose job it is to give us what we need to pray for, even hen we don't realize it. Look! It's deep! Just keep on praying. He will answer either yes, no, or later. Either way, be prepared to accept that His will is the perfect solution to the situation, even if it seems like an awful idea to us at the time! Jesus is the perfect example! He asked for relief but got the cross. Not what He wanted, but it is what God needed Him to do. Ultimately it is what allowed Him to fulfill His purpose of being the only sacrifice fit to redeem man and save him from his sin. Jesus is esteemed above all in heaven, so that's a good thing for Him. He showed us the reality, power, presence, and love of God, and that glorifies Him! All things work together for our good and to His glory."

Chapter Nine

George was just walking back to the house from the mail box when he heard a car pull up beside him. It was John Hale, Stan's son, who was now a constable. He looked like what George imagined Stan would have looked like at 26. He got out of his car and approached George with his hand extended.

"Hi Mr. George."

"Hi John. Haven't seen you in a while. How's Alice? I hear you all had a baby girl a while back! Congratulations!" George gave his hand a final squeeze and a hearty pump as he finished his greeting.

"Thanks Mr. George. Her name is Judy. She's almost eight months old now. Boy, time flies. You and I haven't talked with each other since the cookout. That was the best one yet! I loved that little band you brought in from Hartford! I don't think I ever danced so much in my life!"

"Yeah. They like coming to the cookouts and we love having them, so it works out good for everybody. So how are things with you?"

"Pretty good. I'll tell you, I never knew constables had their hands in so much stuff. I said I didn't want to be a farmer because you guys put in too many hours, but I swear I think I'm coming out on the short end of that stick!" John laughed and then changed his expression. "Mr. George, my dad asked me to come by and make sure you plan on being at the nominating meeting tonight. It's real important because Richards and his group are really out there rallying as many people as they can to be there to support their side." John was very active in politics like his father.

"Well John, as a matter of fact, I just told Theresa this morning that I had made up my mind not to be there. I've just got so much going on right now, getting the crops in and off to a good start, I just can't take the time." John looked disappointed. George continued. "Besides John, your father is a lock. He's been in charge of so much in this town, who else can compare as a choice for town planning committee chairman? He won't miss my vote."

"Unfortunately, too many people seem to feel that way, and there is a real possibility that Evans or one of his cronies will be the only choices on the election ballot for Friday. Most everybody is planning on coming out on Saturday evening for the vote, but they'll only have the choices of those nominated. My father needs his support with him tonight."

"It's that serious, huh? I really wanted to stay out of the political stuff, because I can honestly see merits in both sides' arguments. I expected that your father would be the one to lead us to a peaceful co-existence. I don't have that same confidence in Richards. Well, you know I'd cut off my arm for your father if I thought it would make a difference. I'll adjust my plans. I'll be there. What time is it again?"

"Six thirty sharp!"

"Tell your father he can count on me."

"We never doubted that." John tipped his head to George and left.

The trip to the mailbox had taken more time than he planned for. When he got back to the house, he just dropped the mail on the table, grabbed his sandwich, guzzled down his tea, and gave Theresa a peck on her forehead as she sat there holding Yvonne. "Just spoke with John, Jr. He said that Stan will really need some support tonight to get nominated for the chairmanship, so I'm gonna go to the meeting after all. Can you have my black suit and a white shirt ready for me? I'm gonna take off early so I can be there by six thirty, but I don't want to lose too much time, so I'm gonna be rolling fast when I get back to the house."

"Alright Son. Sounds like they got some mess going on down there. You sure you want to be getting involved in all that?" She was concerned.

"No, I don't think there's much to it. It's just that those voices that want to be heard need to let them be heard. If anybody's gonna be representing Grasmere's interests in the decisions this town makes, I want it to be Stan. I'll see you in a few." With that, he left and closed the door behind him.

Theresa stood up from the table and watched him from the kitchen window as he disappeared around the far side of the barn. She felt very clingy to her family ever since the incident with the screech owl, and she found herself praying several times a day for the safety of her family; especially for Lucy, Charlie, and Nellie as they went to school, and, of course for George. She had sent a letter to her mother and told her about the owl. She got a letter back within two weeks, which was pretty fast turnaround. Her mother said that she and her father and the rest of sisters and brothers were holding them up in prayer, but she also mirrored what George had said. 'Don't forgit where your strength come from. He makes all the decisions and he don't make no mistakes.'

About five fifteen, George came barreling into the house and yelled out that he was home. He took the stairs two at a time as he headed up to the bedroom to wash and change clothes. It took him a little over a half hour and he was back down in the kitchen.

"Why Mr. Cohen, you sure you going to a town meeting? You look like you're dressed up to meet some floozy. You best not be messing around on a Georgia gal; she'll hurt ya!" Theresa teased. "You look very nice, Son. Now you be careful and don't be down there getting yourself elected to nothing. I barely see you enough now as it is!" She said with that mischievous gleam in her eye.

He reached down and let Yvonne grab the finger she was reaching for, and kiddingly said, "Tell your Momma to stop picking at me!" Then, turning to Theresa he asked, "Where are the rest of the kids?" Yvonne was the only one he saw.

"Oh, Alice is reading the little ones a story. Charlie and Lucy are doing their homework. I'm getting ready to call them down to dinner. You got time to eat with us?" she asked.

"No, I'm gonna get going. No sense in going through all this," as he gestured towards his attire, "and not being there in time to vote. I'll eat when I get back. Love you!" he said as he bent and gave her a kiss. Then he turned and gave Yvonne a kiss on the cheek.

Theresa kissed the air as she tried to reach his cheek while he was kissing hers. "I love you too!"

"I'll be back as soon as it's over."

"I'll keep dinner warm for you."

"Smells good! What is it?"

"Skunk stew!" She laughed at his reaction. He went from his bright smile to a mock serious face. "No, Son, I fixed you a beef stew."

"Sounds good. Can't wait! See you later, Baby!" He closed the door and she listened as his hard heels announced his steps off the porch and into the hard gravel. She got up in time to watch him get into the car. He turned and waved as he ducked into the car as if he knew she would be watching.

As soon as he was out of sight, she called everyone down to dinner. Dinner always seemed so much more civilized when George wasn't there. That's because they knew that their father was the boss, and he would let them get away with things that their mother wouldn't put up with. He would be tickled by some of their antics and thought they were cute. She on the other hand, was most interested in getting through dinner without any of them making any unnecessary mess or messing with one of their siblings and causing them not to eat. All that meant extra work for her, and she knew how to nip that in the bud.

It got to be about nine thirty and Alice said she was about ready to retire for the night. Theresa, who had gotten very quiet, said, "Something's wrong!"

"Whatcha' mean?" Alice asked before the implications struck her. "Oh, wit George? He fine. Dey probably jes celebratin' or somethin'"

"My spirit has been really uneasy for the past hour or so. It's not like him to stay after for any of those meetings; especially during the week; especially when he's hungry." Theresa was becoming more and more agitated as she spoke.

"You still spooked bout dat owl, ain't ya? Trust God, Pank! He'll be comin' in any minute. You bess make sho his food warm! I'm goin ta bed. Them crumb snatchers of yourn bout wore me out taday! Night!" She gave her sister a finger wave and headed up the stairs.

As soon as Alice hit the creaking stair step, Theresa began praying. She was praying out loud for about a minute when she thought she heard something on the porch. Her first thought was that it might be a prowler or someone who knew George was at the meeting and trying to get in the house. Her mind was racing as she moved toward the kitchen to get the meat cleaver. As she walked past the door she heard a different sound. This was like something was scratching at the door. At about the same time, she heard Rover's bark; the one he used for when he wanted to be let in. Relieved that it was only the dog, she just opened the door. Her heart felt as if it leaped into her throat. As she threw the door full open, she screamed, "Oh, my God! Oh, my God! What happened to you?" George was leaning against the door post. His legs seemed too wobbly to support his weight. As she went to help steady him, he fell into her arms, but she couldn't handle his weight and its momentum, and he fell onto the kitchen floor. She was kneeling at her husband's head instantly.

He tried to support his torso on his elbows, as his legs kicked frantically beneath him as he valiantly tried to stand up. "They poisoned me, Baby!" His voice was raspy and soft and it appeared to take all his strength just to say that.

His hands were cut and the forearms of his suit were frayed and dirty as if he was using his arms to propel himself. He was covered with dried grass and the knees of his trousers were completely worn through, and she could see that his knees were scraped raw and were bleeding. He reeked of vomit. There was a hint of alcohol. He was wheezing as he tried to breathe.

"Had to crawl home. Left car. Can't drive. Not drunk. Get help." Theresa was rubbing his head and crying when she snapped out of the place she was and mobilized to help her husband.

"Alice! Alice! Come here quick! It's George, Alice. Come help me, It's George!" she screamed at the top of her lungs.

Alice sounded like a heard of horses as he raced down the stairs to her brother-in-law. "Oh my God, Pank! What happen ta him?"

"They poisoned him, Alice. He said they poisoned him. Help me get him on the couch." They both draped an arm over their shoulder and grabbed one his legs under the thigh, just below the knee and lifted. The adrenaline almost made him feel weightless. They moved briskly to the sofa they had in the kitchen area and laid him on his back. As soon as she had him steady on the sofa she told Alice to stay with him.

Theresa frantically dialed the operator for Doc Rankin. "This is Theresa Cohen. It's an emergency. Connect me to Doctor Rankin. Please hurry!"

Doctor Rankin told her to keep him as still as possible and only give him small amounts of water if he asked for it. Until they could pin down the type of poison it is, they want to prevent vomiting as much as possible. Some chemicals such as petroleum based compounds and alcohols have fumes that, when vomited, can enter the lungs and cause pneumonia. He told her he had an ambulance on the way, and that he would be right there.

Lucy was the first one up. They hadn't heard her come down stairs until she started crying. "Poppa, Poppa, What did they do to you Poppa?" She was kneeling by his side. He raised his hand slightly to acknowledge her and turned his eyes to her and gave her the best smile he could muster, but it wasn't much more than a grimace.

"I'm gonna be alright!" was all he could say as he wheezed between words.

Theresa was standing there and she knew that he would not want the children to see him like this. By this time, they were all standing around crying and calling out to their 'Poppa'. "Alright now. Y'all go on back up to your rooms and let your Poppa rest. He's gonna be okay." It took the last bit of composure she had to get that out.

Alice took over at that point. "Alright y'all. Ya heard yo Momma! Gwine on back ta bed. He gonna be fine." Most of them were still crying, but they were obedient.

Soon after, Doc Rankin came. His eyes were red when he came through the door. He came right in without knocking and went directly to his friend on the couch. He knelt by his side. "Hey man, looks like you got a hold of something bad. How does your stomach feel."

George saw the redness in Docs eyes. He wondered if he was sick too, or if he had been crying. Were the tears for him? Was it as bad as he feared? "It burns like crazy, Doc. Are you okay?"

"Me? It's not me stretched out. Me and Stan both got a bit of a stomach ache but it's nothing like this. You been drinking?" Rankin asked as he bent nearer to George to smell his breath.

"You know I don't drink like that. I had a sip of that stuff they called peach brandy for the toast afterwards. That's it!" George was beginning to pant.

"Alright George. Relax and no more talking for a while." Rankin stopped long enough to lift the blanket Theresa had put over George and saw the condition of his knees and winced. He knew that wound was very painful, though not nearly as painful as the healing process would be as the scabs on the flexible joint would take a while to heal. "One last thing George. Did your stomach start to ache before or after the brandy? Just say before or after."

"After. Right after. I..." As he was talking, Doc put his finger to his lips.

"Stop talking my friend, I heard you. Now rest. The ambulance was already in Hartford, so it's going to be a while before they get here." He got up and nodded to Theresa that she should take his place next to her husband.

George's eyes were closed and his breathing still had that wheezing sound. His hands were too cut up and tender to hold, so she just put her hand on his forhead and gently rubbed and soothed him in the way he loved her to sooth him. He smiled and he moved his hand and placed it on hers. Then his smile faded and he appeared to go to sleep.

Theresa rode in the ambulance with George and the nurse. Doc followed. He seemed to drift in and out, but he did softly call her name once. She whispered that she was right there with him. He gave a weak smile and drifted back off to sleep.

Theresa waited outside of George's room while the doctors examined him to try and determine exactly what was wrong. She heard him moan once when they were undressing him. The nurse had missed a piece of cloth that was stuck to his knee wound, and it tore the newly forming scab from his leg when they pulled his pants off.

After about an hour, Doc Rankin came out. "Well there's nothing more we can do here tonight. They pumped his stomach so no more of whatever it is that he took will get into his system. He's pretty knocked out. He won't even know you're here. Why don't you come on back home and get a good night's sleep? We'll come back in the morning!"

"I know he can't hear me, but I just want to kiss him goodnight." She didn't wait for a response. They had cleaned him up. He looked like he was sleeping peacefully. She stood there for a moment just looking at him and her heart was breaking. She thought she had cried her tear ducts dry, but more found their way down her cheeks. She wiped at them just before she bent to kiss him so she wouldn't drop tears onto his face. She tenderly kissed his lips and lingered close for a second and whispered. "Goodnight Son, my shining knight. Keep the faith. I'll pray your strength. I will be here in the morning." She saw a tear in the corner of his right eye and wondered if he was as frightened as she was.

That next morning, Doc was there by 6:30 to pick Theresa up to return to Hartford Hospital. They hadn't gotten more than three hours sleep. They were both in their own reverie on the ride in. As she looked at the sun peeking over the hills in nearby Manchester, she was reminded of that day almost eighteen years ago when she and George first arrived in Glastonbury. A lot had changed but much was the same. The roads were better and there was more traffic, but the river still flowed south, and the majestic cottonwoods still waved to the heavens along its shores, and the light of the morning sun still danced on the face of the water like the silver sides of fish jumping for joy. How their future had seemed so full and challenging. Now, those once future years seem to have blended into a lightening streak headed back down the road to yesterday. As she remembered that day so long ago, she also wondered if her fairy tale ended last night on this dark road when she last heard him whisper her name.

When they got there, Doc told her to "Go to your husband. I'll check on his chart to see how he's doing."

When she went into the room, her spirits were dashed when she saw him exactly like she had left him. The tear was gone. She was wondering if it might have been hers. Other than that, he looked like he hadn't moved a muscle. She bent and kissed him, again wiping away the tears. Last night was the first night they had slept in separate places. In fact, except for nights she was going through labor, it was the only time they had slept in separate beds. She bent and kissed him tenderly on his lips. He smiled almost imperceptibly, but she was sure she saw him smile. "Good morning, Son. I'm right here with you. Me and Jesus. We're right here, and the children send their love. It's okay to rest."

Doc Rankin came in and looked him over, only touching him to feel his pulse. Keeping his eyes on George, he began speaking to Theresa. "They gave him some Morphine for his pain. That's why he's knocked out. Besides he's very weak from his ordeal. He's got a low-grade fever and chest pains. Theresa, there's a chance he's got Pneumonia. It's possible that while he was vomiting last night that some particles might have gone into his lung and caused an infection. They're going to take X-Rays later. I don't need to tell you that Pneumonia is serious." He still wouldn't look at her.

"Oh my Lord! Jesus please help us. Have mercy Lord. Raise him up Lord and heal him." She didn't take her eyes from her husband.

She laid her hand on his chest and continued to intercede for her husband.

After about two hours, Doc said that he would have to go. He knew that Theresa wasn't ready and offered to send someone to pick her up. She was expecting that Benny would be out soon so she banked on getting a ride back with him.

Doc hugged Theresa and was about to leave the room when George suddenly coughed. He coughed several times and after each cough he moaned. Then, he was quiet. Doc came back to his bedside and felt his forehead. He was hot. There weren't many remedies for bacterial infections in those days. Penicillin was just discovered in 1928 and not ready for use yet. Sulfa drugs were still a decade away. The best treatment for pneumonia in those days was to put the body in position to help itself fight the infection naturally. Cold compresses and baths were used to keep the effects of the accompanying fever down, as well as to shock the system into a combative mode.

Benny and his fiancé, Ruby, arrived just before noon. He had just gotten the news. When he got there his father was coughing and moaning. A nurse was holding a cold compress to his neck. Theresa was seated next to George with her eyes fixed on him. He was shocked to see his father in such a state. He walked to Theresa and kissed her. "What happened, Momma?"

Theresa stood and hugged him and suddenly just broke down and sobbed as she held on to this symbol of her husband's flesh. In that moment he reminded her so much of his father. Memories kept flooding back as she remembered when George first told her about his children; about when he first brought Benny to meet her family; about watching him and his father tussling in the hay piles back at Grasmere; the argument they had when he decided to leave Grasmere at the age of 20. It took her a while to compose herself enough to relate the events of the previous night to him. Benny was furious to think that someone would poison his father like some animal. The fact that he could not direct his anger just made it even more frustrating.

They gave him more morphine to help him escape the pain of pleurisy that had settled in his chest. They stayed until just before dusk, when Benny said that he would have to go, but he would be happy to give her a ride home. It was almost as if he could sense they were leaving. He lifted his hand and said, "Hey Baby. Hey Son. I'm gonna be alright!"

"I know you are Poppa!" Benny said as he leaned over and kissed his father's forehead.

"I love you, Son. We're all praying for you." She bent over him and tenderly kissed his lips.

As she was bent over him, he reached out and pulled her head closer to him. His voice was very soft and filled with the sound of escaping air. "Baby, if I could just have some of your greens and some corn bread, I think that would give me the strength I need to get better. Would you bring me some tomorrow?"

She planted her cheek against his and whispered, "You know I will. I would do anything for you, Son; anything in this world."

True to her promise, she brought collard greens and cornbread to him on Friday, but he couldn't eat them. He didn't have the strength to lift his head from the pillow. He was coughing a lot that day, and every time he did his body was racked by the pain it caused in his chest. He was taking very shallow breaths to keep the pain down as much as possible. They had to give him another shot to give him some relief. She looked at him and wished there was some way to take some of his pain away; something she could do to help him breathe. But all she could do was to sit and watch as one frustrating day rolled into the next. Each time she left, she left with high hopes that the next time she saw him he would be feeling better and able to give her that smile that told her how much he loved her. Each day she returned, he was a bit less of the man she had hoped to find awaiting her. Deep in her heart, she was beginning to doubt if he could pull through.

That night, she wanted to leave early, because she had to catch a trolley tonight. She wanted to get home in time to call Mrs. Bradley and have her relay a message to her mother. His parents didn't know about this either. She had been so busy running back and forth she hadn't taken the time. When she left, she bent over and kissed him tenderly on his lips, and said "Good night, Son. Good night my shining knight. I love you more than I could ever put into words, but I know that you know that. I'll be here with you tomorrow, and for as long as it takes for us to get better. I love you, Son!" The tears were streaming onto his face, but she didn't wipe them off. She knew that if it were her, she would want to feel them there. She assumed he felt the same.

Her mother was shocked to hear that George was in the hospital. "Oh, Pank, I'm so sorry ta hear dat. What happened? Did he get hurt or is he sick?"

"Both actually, Momma." She gave her an abbreviated version of the events that led up to the call.

"Dem damn devils. Dey jes mad cause a colored man doin good right up in dey face!" Sara forgot that Mrs. Bradley was right there. Mrs. Bradley wasn't trying to eavesdrop, but she was genuinely concerned about Theresa. Sara didn't care at the moment and Mrs. Bradley didn't mind a dose of the truth. "Keep on prayin, baby. Me an yo Poppa gonna be prayin wit ya." Mrs. Bradley was animatedly nodding her head and folding her hands as if to pray and then pointing from her bosom to the phone. "Mrs. Bradley say she be prayin fo y'all too! Remember Pank, keep yo faith in Jesus. Say hi ta Alice fo me and ta all dem granchirlrens. Bye, Bye." Just hearing her mother's voice gave her a sense of peace.

She dreaded making the next call. Ma Nellie is so close to her son. She takes pride in everything he does. She knew this would knock her mother-in-law for a loop.

Ma Nellie asked the same questions as her mother. Was he injured or was he sick? Her answer and her explanation was the same. Ma Nellie was maintaining her composure extremely well. "Well Theresa, the hospital is the best place for him right now. Don't worry! Keep the faith! He's from good strong stock. He'll get better in no time. I'll call his father. I'm sure he'll want to call you. I'll tell Inez when she gets in. Now stop fretting my child. You've got to be strong for all my little babies."

"Alright Ma Nellie. I'll call you in a couple of days and give you an update. Bye now!" When she hung up the phone she felt relief that it had gone as well as it had. After she thought about it awhile, she had a change in how she felt the conversation had gone. Either she didn't convey the gravity of the situation well, or Ma Nellie was in denial. She hoped it was the latter.

Benny came and got her on Saturday, and they went out to the hospital together. When they got there, George already had a visitor and seemed to be faring better. He was still coughing and obviously it still caused him pain, but he seemed to be risking deeper breaths, and that seemed to be energizing him. One of his cousins from Hartford was there. As soon as George's father had called him, Bill jumped in his car and drove out to the hospital. Bill Cohens had a furniture business in Hartford and he and George were very close. They would find a way to spend some time together almost every week. Bill had bonded with George from the beginning and was the most consistent friend he had in that part of his family.

Bill hugged and kissed both Theresa and Benny, and whispered "Trust God, he's going to be alright. We're in prayer for him." He then turned back to George and reached out and laid his hand on his forearm. "I'm leaving now my cousin. I leave you in good hands; both here and up above. Your family loves you, but Jesus loves you more. Sometimes we go through things, but the key word is that we go through. Believe that, and never lose faith in God." He bent down and kissed George's forehead.

George seemed to be mustering strength, and before Bill could stand back up straight, he was speaking. "Bill, I thought you knew me better, but you speak as a fool. I may lose this flag, but I will die with the staff in my hand." He reached out and changed the positions of their hands and put his hand on his cousin's forearm. Almost as if to say 'You sought to comfort me, now let me comfort you'. He then went into a fit of coughing that took a while to subside. That seemed to drain whatever small boost of energy he had. He lay quiet for a while. Then he turned his head toward Theresa. She noticed how dull and weak and sunken his eyes looked. He gave her his best attempt at a smile.

She smiled back at him as she felt her throat tighten and the tears began their too familiar trek down her face. "And I love you too! You don't have to speak, Son. I feel the message from your heart. You have already told me all you need to say. I have already told you all you need to hear." She stood and bent over to kiss him. Her tears flooded his face as she lingered at his lips.

She went to wipe the tears from him, but he said, "No. Those are mine."

She just smiled at him. She had been right. They had the same spirit. He soon drifted off to sleep and the nurse came and gave him his shot. She told Theresa that he would be out for a while and that she should go get some rest. "This could go on for days and he needs you to be strong. I promise to take good care of him. Me and his Father." Theresa looked at her and smiled.

"Thank you. I know you will." She turned and kissed him tenderly on his lips. "Good night my shining knight. Good night Son. Benny, kiss your father good night." When she turned to leave, she didn't look back.

Theresa was up early, preparing herself to go visit George. She hadn't been able to sleep after she woke up in the middle of the night. It was about three in the morning when she woke. She felt a cool refreshing breeze cross her face and in an instant it was gone. That troubled her, yet she felt a peace about herself. She was combing her hair when she heard a knock at the door. Benny sure got here early, she thought. She put on her robe and went down to the front door. She pulled back the curtain to make sure of who it was, and it wasn't Benny. It was Doc.

She opened the door, and as soon as she saw the redness of his eyes, she knew. As soon as he saw the expression on her face, he knew she had determined the purpose of his visit. To eliminate the chance of breaking down during any attempts to verbalize what his face so obviously bespoke, he simply shook his head 'No'

"Oh no! Oh no! Oh, my God, no!" She was screaming, he held her, but even though her face was buried in his chest, her screams pierced the early morning air as they stood in the open doorway. It sounded like a heard of stampeding horses as little feet hit the floor and came running to their mother's side.

Little Nellie was the first one there and she was holding on to her mother's thigh and trying to calm her mother through her own tears. "Don't cry Momma. Momma, don't cry. Please Momma."

Alice was by her side in a flash and helped Doc mover her out of the doorway and on to the sofa in the parlor. Theresa just couldn't be consoled. The children were all over her, begging her not to be so sad, all the while suffering their own brand of sorrow, expressed in sobs and moans and streams of tears. Alice, though not immune from the pain of the moment, took the position of consoler. She hugged each of the children and assured them that their father was with Jesus now and that he was happy in heaven. It kept them from completely losing it. Lucy was devastated, and Doc was spending time with her. She was nine years old, so she understood the concept of the finality of death far more than her younger siblings. Charlie and Nellie, being eight and six, were aware and were suffering that pain as well as the helplessness of watching their mother so distraught. Johnnie, Lillian, and Yvonne were reacting to the situation of seeing their mother in pain as much as anything.

Alice made a pot of coffee for Theresa, Doc, and herself, and put a pot of hot chocolate on for the children. It was about an hour before they could calm Theresa down enough to talk to her reasonably.

"Pank, I can't say dat I know how ya feels, but I do know how I feel, an it can't be nowhere near as bad as you feels, an it hurt real bad. But ya know George, an right now he would want ya ta put it in da Lord's hands. He won't kicked out of dis life, but da Lord call him home. It was His choice dat dis was de time fo George ta come back home. It was His choice. Ya know how George always talkin bout how all thangs works ta da good? Well dat mean dis too. We might not like it, but God know what He doin. One thang fo sho, Bro George ain't sufferin no mo, an dats good, ain't it?" She hugged her sister and rocked with her for a while. "Now let's drank us some coffee an start handlin dis thang!"

Theresa's heart smiled, but her lips could only quiver in their feeble attempt to chisel free of the grief so deeply etched in her face. She did nod at her sister to let her know that her words were appreciated. Eventually, she gathered herself and said, "I gotta call Ma Nellie and Momma, an let them know. Oh my God, this is going to be so hard. Lord, remove this bitter cup. Nevertheless..." And with that she walked to the phone.

She heard Mrs. Bradley's voice answering, "Hello?" It was still only eight in the morning.

As soon as she heard the familiar link to her memories and her mother, she began to weep again. She could get out "Hello, Mrs. Brad....", and she broke down again.

"Pinky, is that you? Pinky, is it your husband?"

She was relieved that Mrs. Bradley could decipher the purpose of the call and, at least, save her the pain of speaking those words.

With a quivering voice she answered. "Yes, he....." Her sobs came on her again.

"Oh my God, Pinky, I am so sorry. Here chile, let me go get yo momma. You hold on now. I'll be right back."

Sara evidently had come to within earshot when she heard the phone ring, because Mrs. Bradley turned and there was Sara taking the phone out of her hand. Her sorrow welled up quickly and her voice was already wavering when she spoke to her daughter. "Oh my baby. My po lil Panky. I am so sorry. He was such a good man. I am so sorry."

Hearing her mother's voice was a comfort. She felt strong enough to speak. "Momma, I know he's not suffering anymore. My baby sister reminded me of that." as she nodded at Alice and managed the hint of a smile. "That's a good thing, right? It's just so hard. We've been bosom buddies for eighteen years, on top of being husband and wife. We have so much together, it's just hard trying to imagine going on without him."

"I know Pank, but it ain't nothin' new undah da sun. God made us so we can handle times like dees. It gonna be hard, but I can assure ya dat you will make it. Thangs will git bettah, bye an bye. Jes keep trustin God. Da Fathah know bess what ta do, and when ta do it, whethah we likes it or not. One thang fo sho; dis too shall pass."

"I know Momma. Thank you for soothin' my spirit. I trust God, and I know it will get better day by day, but I can't imagine ever feeling whole again. Just pray for me and the kids. Tell Poppa I love him, and let him know that the strength he made sure I had in the Lord is all that's letting me stand. I gotta go. I gotta call his mother. That's going to be so hard."

"I know chile. We gonna be prayin yo strength in da lord. Bye Pank."

"Bye, Momma." As soon as the connection ended she broke down again. Alice and Lucy and Nellie and even little Lillian were right there hugging her. Lillian was only three and a half, and too young to grasp the full situation, but she knew her Momma needed a hug. Yvonne just sat in her high chair, but it even seemed that she was quiet because she knew that her Momma needed more attention than she did.

She gathered herself as she heard the phone ringing on the other end. As soon as she heard the click indicating that someone had picked up the phone, she started crying again, and it was difficult to get the words out. "Ma Nellie?"

"Oh my God! Oh my God, Theresa. Tell me my son is alright. Please Theresa, tell me."

Through her sobs, she confirmed the worst. "He's gone, Ma. He's gone. Our George is gone on home." They cried together.

Theresa heard Inez' voice in the background. "Ma, what's wrong?" Then, without any words passing between them, her spirit confirmed to her what was going on at that moment."That's Theresa, isn't it? Oh my God. Sweet Jesus. My brother. Oh, my God. Ma I'm so sorry. I am so sorry for Theresa." She hugged her mother. They all cried together, right there on the phone.

After awhile, Ma Nellie said that she would call Theresa tomorrow when she was more composed, and they hung up. It was the beginning of a sad, sad day.

The undertaker came to the house late on Sunday afternoon to discuss arrangements. He was on his way to go pick up the body. He asked Theresa when she would like the services and she told him the quicker the better. She did not want that anticipation weighing over her head nor the children's. She wanted an open casket, and she wanted his funeral and wake to be held at Grasmere. She really felt strongly about his final return to Grasmere. The undertaker said that he could get it all done by Tuesday. Theresa was surprised at how quickly the turnaround would be, but she said that would be fine, unless her mother-in-law would need more time to get there. If she had a problem making accommodations that quickly, then she may have to move the date back. She asked him to give her a minute and she would try to confirm that while he was there.

Ma Nellie said she was too upset to make that long trip, and besides would rather remember him as she last saw him. She said that Inez was already on her way as they spoke and would be there by mid-day on Monday. She gave the times and asked that Benny be there to get her.

Theresa gave the undertaker the suit that George had worn the night they visited the Morelands. She loved that night. It was the best of their last days together.

He said that he had always admired George, and that he would make a special effort to make sure that he had everything ready so he could bring the body to the house on Monday evening, and make arrangements for the funeral on Tuesday.

When he left, he tacked a big black wreath to the front door; a sign that there was mourning within that house. The wreath had black shiny leaves that looked to be made of leather.

People had begun coming, even before the wreath was hung. Doc and Lucie Rankin were the first to arrive, and they, along with

Florence Roberts and John and Geneva, almost took up residency until after the funeral.

Over the course of the next three days, the house was filled with friends and wellwishers. They brought food and memories and both kept the house as full of good spirit as possible. Theresa had her moments, but the constant flow of people, and the showering of good wishes and heart-felt caring among friends kept her from collapsing. She could almost feel the prayers of those that weren't there as well.

She had unexpected reactions to some of the people who came by. When Stan Hale's youngest, Katie, came by, Theresa broke down for the first time in several hours. There was something in seeing her as a beautiful twenty-one-year-old woman that flooded memories back to when she and George had first come to Glastonbury. Katie, then only two years old, had been part of their welcoming committee when they drove up to the Hale house that day, and she and Katie had a special bond until time, teenage hormones, and distance changed the relationship, but not the affection.

When the Morelands arrived, their presence reminded her of that last wonderful night that they had spent 'out on the town'.

Paul Bender and his wife came in. Paul walked to her very sheepishly and she could see that he had been crying. He couldn't speak at first but he came up to her and pulled her to him and just hugged her longer than she expected he would. When he pulled away, his eyes were wet, and he looked at her and nodded his head and gave her a smile contorted with an effort not to weep. He pounded his chest twice as if that could speak for his heart and turned and left.

Janice Bender came up to her as soon as Paul turned away. "Theresa I am so sorry about George. If there is anything you need." At that she pulled closer to Theresa and whispered. "Did George tell you about that ugly scene between him and Paul?"

Theresa knew exactly what she was referring to. "Yes."

"Well, Paul had planned to apologize to George after the meeting, but he was waiting for a moment when he could be alone with him and he never got the chance. It's just eating him up inside that things were said that should have never been uttered and he never took his chance to apologize. He's just torn up with guilt and grief. He really did like and admire your husband, you know." She was looking pleadingly into Theresa's eyes as if she could issue some sort of absolution.

"Janice, George and I talked that night. He had assigned it to Paul's head and not his heart. Tell Paul that if he had been able to get to George that night, he would have gladly taken his hand in friendship." She gave Janice a quick hug and turned to greet their neighbors, the O'Connells.

Janice grabbed her arm and pulled her back toward herself. "Theresa, thank you. I know your plate is full right now, but I got some more I want to talk with you about." She gave her a knowing look as if she wanted to share a secret and turned and slinked away.

Theresa just smiled and turned back to the O'Connells. They had spent a lot of time with the O'Connells. Their son, Raymond was Charlie's buddy, and he practically lived there.

By 7:00 Sunday night, Theresa was exhausted, and Doc Rankin told her she should go upstairs and get some sleep and he and her family would gracefully wrap things up for the evening. She gladly accepted the offer and went to bed. As she undressed she began to cry again. It was so strange to be in that room that they had shared and not expect him to 'be along shortly'. It was so hard to grasp that she would never hear him say those words again. As she got in the bed, she said, "Oh my God! Never is such a long, long time." She stuffed part of the pillow in her mouth and held the rest close to her face and just screamed a scream only she could hear until she fell off to sleep.

The undertaker brought George's body to the house about 4:30 Monday afternoon. The wake was scheduled for 7:00. The children were in the kitchen with their mother. Alice directed traffic. Inez had come in earlier and she was upstairs napping.

As they rolled the big chestnut casket in, all was silent. Alice turned to Charlie and said, "Go git yo Aunt Inez up. Tell huh yo Poppa home!"

He looked at her as if it just struck him at that moment that his father was in that big wooden box that those men just rolled into the parlor, and his eyes welled up in tears. Alice, seeing the plight of her nephew, came to his rescue and said that it was okay, and that he should stay and take care of his momma.

They all stayed in the kitchen while the men fussed with the casket and the floral arrangements. This gave Alice a chance to get back down with Inez. They went into the kitchen and waited with Theresa and the children until the undertaker came back into the kitchen.

"Now I want you all to go in together, but I want you to go in order. Theresa, I want you and your son here, to go in first." He gently took her elbow and Benny's and stood them side by side. "Now I want you to take the two eldest children by the hand and follow close behind Theresa." He said as he led Inez and Lucy and Charlie into place. "And you," he said, speaking to Alice, "I want you to stand back with the little ones and let them come up as they get comfortable." Once he had everyone in place he asked, "Okay, is everyone ready?"

No one responded by word or gesture. He slowly brought them into the room. As soon as Theresa was at an angle that she could see George, she quickly let go of Benny's hand and rushed to the casket, crying out loudly, "Son! Son! Oh, Son! What have they done to you? My God! My God, why did you let that happen? That man loved you so much! Why did you let that happen?" Inez and Alice quickly broke protocol and rushed to her side. Benny was also trying to console her but he quit to find his own release.

Inez began wailing. "Oh my sweet brother. I am so sorry. I am so sorry. We're going to miss you so much."

Lucy was begging her father to get up and Charlie was yelling that his Poppa was dead. Johnnie was mimicking him, and Nellie was desperately clinging to her mother and proclaiming that everything was 'going to be alright, Momma'. Lillian screamed and put her hands over her eyes. She was only 2 ½, but her natural brightness and the maturity that comes from being a middle sister, allowed her young mind to understand the situation when she saw her father lying in that big wooden box. She kept repeating "Poppa, Poppa, Poppa!" Alice could see that she was traumatized, and quickly scooped her up. Yvonne was just 14 months old, and she took the same posture as Lillian, who she idolized.

Ever the tower of strength, even Alice broke down and moaned. It was in part her sadness for George but probably more for the pain she saw that those she loved so deeply were going through right now.

 Florence was the first to come to the house, and Theresa asked her to be the hostess while she and the family went upstairs and got dressed for the wake that evening. Close friends began coming about 6:30. About 6:45, Theresa and Inez and Alice and the children were led back into the parlor. They were more reserved now as they were led to a row of chairs right in front of the casket.

Every few minutes, Theresa would stand and walk to the coffin and look down on the man she loved so deeply. "Oh Son! Why? Why? Why? I love you so much. Why did you have to go?" There were always those nearby to comfort her.

Lucy was the most grief stricken of the children. She seemed to be in shock and kept asking her father why he wouldn't get up so she could talk to him. She would be the last one standing many nights, and against her mother's wishes, her father would intercede and would let her stay up late while he read and she cleaned her nails and rubbed her hands through his wavy hair. There was a particularly close bond between them because of that. But then again, he had a way of making all his children feel particularly special by the special parts of his life that he shared with each of them

For the next hour and a half, they sat there, in and out of moments of control, and received all the wellwishers who seemed to come in waves.

Tuesday, the funeral was scheduled for 2:00 in the afternoon, at the house, like Theresa requested. They crowded as many people as would fit into the parlor and kitchen areas. Some had to stand on the front porch. The pastor from the First Congregational

Church had a commitment to eulogize a friend in another part of the state, so Theresa had to solicit the pastor from Shiloh Baptist in Hartford. Truthe be told, it was her preference. They attended First Congregational because it was the community church and it was expedient, and the word of God was taught there with great clarity. But, when they wanted some down-home Baptist, get you jumping, and clapping, and praising type worship, they would attend Shiloh Baptist in Hartford; Pastor W.A. Hubbard's church. The Morelands went there as well, and they had made the arrangements for Theresa. They even brought three members of their choir to sing.

Pastor Hubbard read the scripture. " 'For we know that if our earthly house of this tabernacle were dissolved, we have a building of God, an house not made with hands, eternal in the heavens...... Therefore we are always confident, knowing that, whilst we are at home in the body, we are absent from the Lord: (For we walk by faith, not by sight:) We are confident, I say, and willing rather to be absent from the body, and to be present with the Lord.' I have read in your hearing Second Corinthians chapter 5, verses 1 through 8. May the lord add a blessing to the reading and hearing of His word." Without any additional fanfare, he sat and the two women and the man he had brought with him got up and sang "How Great Thou Art." They sang acapella, and they harmonized beautifully. The man was heavy set and very dark. His teeth looked like pearls set against the blackness of his skin. His voice was full and rich and deep, and contrasted beautifully against the soprano and alto of the two women. This was one of the songs Theresa had requested, because it expressed his sense of reverence for all that is of God. When they got to the final verse;

When Christ shall come, with shouts of acclamation

And take me home, what joy shall fill my heart!

Then I shall bow, in humble adoration,

And there proclaim, my God, how great Thou art!

Theresa lost her composure while sitting there looking at the joy of her heart stretched out cold and lifeless. She envisioned him rising to meet Jesus on Sunday morning still holding onto that staff that served as a symbol of his faith. Her crying had a cascading effect throughout the gathering and things got emotional for a while

Inez represented the family in acknowledging the kindnesses of those who had come and expressed themselves so lovingly over the past few days. She also read the obituary from the Hartford Courant. She corrected the error they had made which stated that he had passed in the afternoon, as opposed to the morning. She held up well.

After the ensemble sang "Amazing Grace", Pastor Hubbard stepped forward once again. "Giving honor to God, on behalf of the officers and members of the Shiloh Baptist Church, we bring our greetings to all here assembled, and I give my condolences to the bereaved family of Brother George Washington Cohen; Theresa Cohen his loving wife, his adoring children; Benny, Lucy, Charles, Nellie, John, Lillian, and Yvonne; and to Inez Griffen his admiring sister, Alice Fantroy his devoted sister-in-law, John Fantroy his faithful brother-in-law, his parents and in-laws in absentia, and to all those who are gathered here because he in some way touched your life.

At this moment, I know your sorrow has no measure and there is no hiding from your pain. The one thing I can tell you is this:

your husband, your father, your brother, your friend, is now with the one who loves him the most. And be assured of this one thing; God was not taken by surprise when he showed up. He had a celebration planned at an appointed time, because precious in the sight of the Lord is the death of His saints, and Brother Cohen showed up right on time. But on this side of glory, we are left wondering. I hear it at the beds of the sick and the afflicted; at the coffins and gravesides of the deceased. Why? Why Lord? Why now? Why him? Why her? They were so young! Why didn't they get their three score and ten?"

Theresa, I used to watch you and brother George come into my church and you were such a lovely couple; apparently perfectly matched and filled with love for one another. I could see it written all over your faces. He blessed you with seven beautiful children together. You have a successful farm here at Grasmere. Your Labor Day cookouts are anticipated by folks far and near. You are well liked and respected by folks of every race, hue, and religion. Both of you are devoted to lifting the name of Jesus. So why? Why amid all that goodness? Why amid all that success? Why in the midst of all that love? Why with all these dependent children? Why amid your praise, prayer, and devotion would God allow your husband to be struck down in what appears to be the prime of his vigor and productivity? Have you asked that question Theresa?"

At that, Theresa moaned "Yes! Oh yes! Why, Lord, oh why?"

"He won't answer you directly, but He has assured you in so many ways that He is in control. There are rumors going around that George may have been poisoned. We may never know for sure, but one thing we do know is that it did not catch God by surprise, nor was He impotent to stop it if it were His will to do so.

Our natural tendency is to question God when we don't understand His motivation behind certain things, but the truth is He don't owe nobody any explanations. Just know that He is God, and His ways are far beyond our ways. His knowledge is far beyond our knowledge. He does what He wants, when He wants, where He wants, why He wants, and how He wants.........."

As he proceeded Theresa was amazed at how much of what he said reflected what George had said to her and Alice the day they talked about praying away the power of the curse of the screech owl. It was as if George was still teaching her from his grave. God is too wise to make a mistake, too powerful to be overcome, and too loving not to care. True trust in Him is not only to believe in all the wonderful things He can bring our lives, but to trust that whatever comes in our lives, He has allowed for our ultimate good and to His Glory. Her conscious thoughts went back to the Pastor.

"So my brothers and sisters, once we accept that father knows best then we can rejoice, like Paul, no matter what comes our way. In the book of Philippians, fourth chapter, that wonderful fourth chapter of Philippians, in the eleventh through the thirteenth verses, Paul says when talking about concerns over his earthly condition, Not that I speak in respect of want: for I have learned, in whatsoever state I am, therewith to be content. I know both how to be abased, and I know how to abound: everywhere and in all things I am instructed both to be full and to be hungry, both to abound and to suffer need. I can do all things through Christ which strengthens me."

"God has a plan and we all have a purpose. George Washington Cohen has fulfilled his purpose as a part of God's plan. There are some in His plan who are the objects of His affection and others who are used to help in the plan to fulfill the objects of His affection. God has given it to all of us to decide which we want to be. The decision is whether or not we decide to accept the blood of His Son Jesus Christ as our savior and redeemer. When George Washington Cohen was on that bed on Saturday afternoon and telling his cousin who warned him to keep his faith, I heard that brother George told him "Man, you speak as a fool. I may lose this flag. This flag of my mortal life, but I will die with the staff, the staff of everlasting life through my faith in the finished work of Jesus Christ, in my hand. Now that's good news, folks. Faced with death, and I believe we know when the Lord is calling us home, he declared that his faith is in the promises of God. Everything will work out for our good and to His glory. Even when I face death, I know that yea though I walk through the valley of the shadow of death, Thou art with me. He says 'Let not your heart be troubled: ye believe in God, believe also in me. In my Father's house are many mansions: if it were not so, I would have told you. I go to prepare a place for you. And if I go and prepare a place for you, I will come again, and receive you unto myself; that where I am, there ye may be also. And whither I go ye know, and the way ye know'. That's John fourteen one, verses one through four. And in those final hours, as he was laying on what some might call his death bed, but I call his springboard to everlasting life, his spirit reached into second Timothy in the fourth chapter in the sixth through the eighth verses and cried, Father, anytime you're ready, For I am now ready to be offered, and the time of my departure is at hand. I have fought a good fight, I have finished my course, I have kept the faith: Henceforth there is laid up for me a crown of righteousness, which the Lord, the righteous judge, shall give me at that day: and not to me only, but unto all them also that love his appearing."

"I'm here to tell you that Brother George is doing fine right now. He wouldn't come back this way if he could, for eye has not seen, nor ear heard, neither have entered into the heart of man, the things which God hath prepared for them that love him. And he's saying right now, I love you Baby, but I'm not coming back. I love you Benny, but I'm not coming back. I love you Lucy, but I'm not coming back, I love you Charlie, but I'm not coming back, I love you Nellie, but I'm not coming back, I love you Johnnie, but I'm not coming back, I love you Lillian, but I'm not coming back, I love you little Yvonne, but I'm not coming back, I love you Mother, I love you Father, I love you sisters, I love you brothers, I love you cousins, I love you friends, but-I'm-not-coming-back! In a moment, in a twinkling of an eye, you'll all be here with me. You too have an appointed hour. No man can change that. God sets the clock and there is no need to change his mind. His plan is perfect and his results are sublime. Don't think death is only for the old, or only for the wicked, or only for the sickly. God uses death as our doorway, at His appointed time, to eternal life. Jesus was only 33 years old. He had done good all His life. He was doing wonderful things here on earth, but at his appointed hour, in God's prescribed manner, He called Him home when His purpose was fulfilled. When He calls you home, will you be ready to receive your reward of everlasting life, or will you serve eternity as an unwilling participant in the biggest cookout of all time?'

"Tomorrow is promised to no man. This time last week, Brother George was handling business as usual. If you don't know Jesus Christ as your Lord and Savior, I ask that you bow your head right now and repeat after me: Lord I am a sinner. I have no hope but in you. I know that you are the Son of the Living God and you have offered yourself as a ransom for my sin. I have but to believe that You are, and that You can save my sin sick soul. The Word of God says that "If thou shalt confess with thy mouth the Lord Jesus, and shalt believe in thine heart that God hath raised him from the dead, thou shalt be saved. Not by works or by deeds, but through your faith, you are saved. Amen."

The room was filled with those who were softly repeating the words, 'just in case'. His words gave Theresa some comfort, but they didn't, as he had said, take away the pain.

At that point the ensemble started singing "It is Well", very softly. The undertaker bent down to Theresa and said "It is time to close the coffin, do you want to say a last good-bye?"

Those words made her heart pound as if it would burst through her chest. She had been sitting there looking at George, and had grown to find a sense of comfort sitting there looking at him. She had not braced herself for the moment when even looking at his empty shell would be taken away from her. Alice and Inez stood and pulled her to her feet. She didn't resist.

The man with the deep voice was singing lead again, but many in the room were singing along with him. "When peace, like a river, attendeth my way, and sorrows like sea billows roll; whatever my lot Thou hast taught me to say, it is well, it is well, with my soul."

To that backdrop, Theresa looked down in the coffin at the face she loved so deeply. "My Son, My Son. I don't know how I'm gonna make it without you."

The pastor was still standing nearby and he softly answered her question. "Through Christ my dear. Through Christ. It's not just words. We can do all things through Christ who strengthens us." There was a smattering of Amens throughout the house.

Theresa continued. "I love you so much. You loved us so well. We'll miss you so much. Goodnight my sweet prince. I'll never say good-bye." Theresa bent down and kissed him tenderly on his lips. She wailed as she watched the lid slowly hide him from her. Lucy was screaming for her Poppa to get up, and was inconsolable. The other children were crying which caused their aunts to let go themselves for a moment.

The short ride to Green Cemetery was very quiet. Everyone was emotionally drained, and Theresa prayed for all their strength in handling this one last hurdle. Leaving him at the cemetery was so final; such a cut-off from her attachment to the physical reality of the man she loved these last eighteen years.

She walked slowly behind the pall bearers carrying her husband's body the few feet from the hearse to the family plot George had bought. He had done so with considerable foresight, shortly after her miscarriage of the twins. She could remember thinking how frivolous the eight-plot sight seemed to her, at the time. In her mind, their love of each other and their love of God would protect them from all harm, and they would have decades before this walk would be necessary. She now realized how frightened she was of the reality of the possible separation of her and her husband that caused her to negate its possibility at every turn. Now here she was, moments from leaving any real nearness of his flesh. Henceforth, George Washington Cohen would be a memory; a loving memory; an impactful memory; an ever-present memory, but only a memory nevertheless. Yvonne and Lillian would only have her stories and the few pictures she had to recall their father, for their memories of today will vanish with their baby teeth, and whatever fleeting recall might linger, will flee like ether when they consciously try to control the remembrance of their father. Johnny and Nellie will recall some, but most will shine like the sun in a cloudy sky, whose light will only peak through as the winds temporarily remove the clouds of forgetfulness. Lucy and Charlie are old enough that they will have these days burned deeply into their remembrance, but theirs too will dance between reality and fantasy as each passing year will add another layer of opacity to visions they hold most dear. Benny will remember most clearly, and perhaps only he of all of George's children will be able to focus on more willful aspects of his relationship and question his final interactions with this loving man. The thought that George would never see any of his other children graduate from school, or take a mate in marriage, or hold one of his grandchildren, just opened the floodgates of her sorrow that she so desperately hid behind a mask of composure. In reality, she wanted to stop willing her legs to move on to her foreboding destination, or even to stand, or her lungs to pump air and just crumple into the greening grass and lay beside her husband and float away to the tranquility that only death could provide. What joy filled the prospect of one more dance with her Son in the meadow behind the back porch at Grasmere and then rising together to the Everlasting.

She was only barely conscious of the Pastor's soft but pervasive voice as he stood beside the open grave and recited the twenty third Psalm. "The Lord is my shepherd. I shall not want." She was led to a chair at the side of the grave, once the pall bearers had situated the coffin on three two by ten boards that bridged the two sides of the deep earthen canyon that would be his final earthly resting place. She felt too drained to sob at the fright of leaving the man she loved in so desolate a valley to wait, who knew how long, for their reunion.

"Let us pray. Dear heavenly Father, in as much as you have called the spirit of our beloved husband, and father, and son, and brother and friend, George Washington Cohen to his eternal rest, we return his earthly remains from whence they were composed; ashes to ashes and dust to dust. We thank you for the time we had to share with him, but now humbly yield to your greater love that calls him to your side. We ask your compassionate grace on the pain in the hearts of his wife and children and family and friends. Heal them quickly Lord. And may the wisdom from your word, opened before them this day, land on fertile ground and reinforce their confidence in the power of the finished work of your darling Son, Jesus Christ. May this serve to strengthen this family. Keep them out of the way of hurt, harm, and danger. Send your angels round about to protect them, and let the seed of your word that he planted in their hearts grow into the assurance of a certain reunion with him when they too are gathered into Your kingdom. These and all things we ask in the precious name of Jesus. Amen."

He walked deliberately to the head section of the casket and selected two white roses, and spoke as he began to separate their petals and sprinkle them on the casket. "Man goeth to his long home, and the mourners go about the streets; then shall the dust return to the earth as it was: and the spirit shall return unto God who gave it. Jesus said I am the resurrection and the life; he that

257

believeth in me, though he were dead, yet shall he live. Ashes to ashes and dust to dust. Into thine hands oh Lord we commit his spirit. Amen and Amen. Thus concludes our service. Those wishing to take a flower ..."

Theresa smiled and stepped the few steps to the side of the coffin. She placed her hand on where she imagined his heart would be and leaned over and tenderly kissed the cold wood that now separated her from his lips. "Goodnight Son. Goodnight my Sweet Prince. I love you more than you could imagine, Son. I leaned so much on your strength. Thank you for teaching me to lean on the Lord. I'm going to miss us, but I'll be back. I promise you Son. I'll be back." Her tears had wet the coffin. She didn't wipe them away. With all her strength, she turned and walked away.

Chapter Ten

All of their best friends were there at the house after the service. Their presence and upbeat attitudes lifted the gloom from the house, if not from Theresa's heart. It did give her a place to hide for a while. She was sitting with Inez and Florence when Janice Bender came up to her.

"How are you holding up Theresa?" Janice asked.

Theresa almost chuckled. Shouldn't it be obvious to everyone that Theresa was standing up totally on her ability to trust in God to get her through moment by moment? "All things considered, Janice, I'm okay." She knew her challenge would be later tonight when she was on her own.

Janice bent down and whispered to Theresa. "Can I speak with you for one moment? It's real important!"

Theresa looked at her. What could she possibly have to say that was so important that she would have to talk about it today? She sighed and immediately hoped that her distaste for this intrusion was not read into her sigh. "Okay Janice. Let's go out to the utility room." Theresa excused herself from the other two women and lead Janice out of the kitchen into the utility room. "Okay Janice, what's going on?" Theresa asked, assuming there was some blockbuster disclosure about to take place.

"Well you know how I told you Sunday night that I wanted to tell you something? I know this isn't the best time, but I don't know when I'll get to talk to you again, so I need to tell you now." She had a questioning look on her face, as if she was searching for Theresa's approval of their conversation.

Theresa wasn't feeling like dealing with whatever Janice had to say but she just wanted to get it over with. "Yes. Now what is it, Janice?"

"Well the other night, after the vote, Paul was sitting with some of Nathan Richards' buddies, and he excused himself and told them that he needed to talk with George. He said that the guys looked at each other and advised him that it would be in his best interest that he not be seen around George. He said it would be bad for his reputation. Well, Paul isn't the bravest man in the world so he just sat there."

Theresa was getting impatient for her to get to the point. "And?"

"Well, he said it wasn't ten minutes later that he saw one of the men he was sitting with over talking to Stan Hale, George, and Doc Rankin."

Theresa was getting exasperated at this point. "So what?"

"Well, two things. Don't you think it strange that one of the men who warned my husband that it wouldn't be good for his reputation to be seen with your husband was there looking like he was trying to buddy up with him no more than ten minutes later?"

"Well maybe he was just talking to Doc and Stan and George just happened to be there!" Theresa was growing weary of this conversation.

"Here's the other thing. He offered the three of them a drink out of a flask he had. Paul said he poured four glasses, and that he gave George the biggest amount, by far. They toasted and drank, and the man's glass was still filled to the same level when he pulled it down from his lips. Paul said that he cupped it in his hands so the others wouldn't see, but he didn't drink any."

Theresa just sat there looking at her incredulously. "Did Paul say anything to anybody? Those men poisoned my husband. Did he tell anybody?"

"No, and probably won't unless somebody makes him. He's afraid of those men. He's called them a bunch of ruthless money hungry scoundrels before this. I know he's shaking in his boots now that he's seen what they are capable of. I just thought you ought to know. What they did wasn't fair."

"Are you sure of this?"

"Only as sure as my husband's word, and he's a lot of things, but he's not a liar!"

"Janice, I don't know what I am going to do right now, but thank you for letting me know that. I want to see them hang by their balls if I can help it."

That night, she was surprised at how her anger at whoever or whatever did this to her family almost overshadowed her sorrow, as she lay awake for what seemed like hours. Theresa rarely drank, but that night she went downstairs and found the bottle of blackberry brandy one of George's friends had given him. She poured a cup of the sweet cordial and drank it down in one gulp. It burned going down and seemed to settle into a smoldering fire in her stomach. Her past experiments with liquor told her she had just a little time to get settled back in her bed before she was asleep. It worked.

That next morning, Doc Rankin stopped by to check on the family. The children were quiet, but most of them seemed to be okay. Lucy kept to herself and stayed in her room most of the day.

Theresa was most concerned about her. Nellie seemed very concerned about her mother, so Theresa did her best to convince her that she was doing alright. The boys went out and ran around and tussled in the hay in the barn, like they used to do with their father. Lillian and Yvonne, like Nellie, seemed fine as long as she wasn't crying.

"We're doing as well as can be expected Doctor Rankin. It's gonna be a while, I'm sure, before we're anywhere near normal. But, with God's strength, we'll make it; I'm sure."

"I know you will. I just wanted to let you know that our friendship is real, and Lucie and I will be here for you whenever you need us. When things settle down in a while and you want to start planning your future, I hope you feel comfortable coming to me to talk things through, if you need it."

"George trusted you more than anybody. You've been a good friend and a great godfather to our children. You will definitely be the one I'll go to when I'm able to think past yesterday." She smiled and gave him a squeeze around his waist as he was headed out the door. "Doctor Rankin, do you have a minute? There is something I want to talk to you about right now." As she was talking, she was walking him out onto the porch. It was a beautiful day. The sky was clear, and temperature felt to be in the mid seventies already, and it wasn't noon yet. The breeze was soft and balmy and seemed almost to caress her. She was surprised at how soothing it felt. 'Almost like a hug from God' she thought.

On the porch, he turned and asked what it was. She began searching for the best way to start. "The night George came home sick, did I hear you tell him that your eyes were red because you were a bit sick?"

She could almost see him tighten up. "Yes, Theresa. I did." He didn't volunteer any further explanation, so she continued.

"And you said that Stan Hale was sick too, right?"

"Yes. I did. I mean he was."

"Weren't the three of you together?" She tried to get eye contact but he wouldn't look her in the eye.

"Only at the end of the meeting. George and I both got to Stan about the same time to congratulate him for the nomination. We talked for a while, but that's it." He seemed very uneasy.

"Didn't some man come up to y'all and offer you a toast?"

His eyes turned sharply in her direction. She couldn't tell if she saw fear or anger. "Where did you get that from?" His voice had the same tone as his eyes.

"Is it true?" she asked, challenging what she thought was a posture to intimidate her into backing off the subject.

"Well yes. It's true, but how did you know about that? Did George say something about that?" His tone was still edgy.

"No. It wasn't George who told me. They messed my husband up so bad, he could barely talk. What little breath he had he spent trying to keep me at peace. I'm quite sure he expected that he would be able to handle it himself when he got better. No, it wasn't George." She then went on to tell him about her conversation with Janice Bender. He didn't seem surprised by any of it.

"You've got enough on your plate right now, and I didn't want to burden you with that until we had something to go on. Stan and I have talked about the fact that all three of us got sick after that drink. It could have been a benign situation, or it could have been someone conspiring to do one or all of us some harm. There's a faction of people who are money hungry and think that this is the last best opportunity to grab wealth. There are some storm clouds looming in the economy, Theresa, and the rats are scurrying to get their cheese. We didn't get anywhere near as sick as George, but neither of us has shaken it completely yet. We kind of think it was some kind of virus or something."

"If you all got it at the same time, and that drink was the only thing you did in common besides talk, doesn't that make you think?" She was getting upset with his aloof analytical approach to the situation. She was expecting a more emotional response that supported her anger and need to uncover the culprit and bring a measure of justice on his head. His eyes averted hers again.

"Theresa, there's nothing we can prove. There are even a couple of other people that were with that man that claim they got sick too." He paused and slowly shook his head as he wiped his brow and the back of his neck as beads of nervous perspiration were beginning to form. "Look Theresa, I wish we could take back that night. I wish George had followed his first instinct and never even came. I certainly wish we had never accepted that toast. Truth is, we can't take it back, and if we stay stuck back there too long, it might cause more damage than it's already caused. We can't see that there's anything we can prove. I even asked the doctors over in Hartford if they found anything, but they didn't find anything unusual except the alcohol content. It was very high for one drink, and it could be that someone slipped him some grain alcohol. If it caused him to get fumes in his lungs or if it caused him to vomit and he got fluid in his lungs, it could quickly turn to Lobar Pneumonia, which is what his death certificate is going to read. But that's all we have to go on, and believe me, there are some people involved in this turmoil that have some of the town's people pretty intimidated. I'll have John Jr. go out and ask Bender if he'll give a statement. I'm sure that little weasel won't."

They stood looking at each other for a while. Her look challenging. His imploring and apologetic.

She was expecting a reaction similar to the one Alice had when she told her. Alice was ready to go hunt somebody down and castrate them on the spot. She expected that Doc might offer anesthesia first, but that he would want to perform the surgery. For the first time, she felt disappointed in Doc Rankin.

True to his word, however, Doc came back that next day with a report. "John, Jr. spoke with Bender. He denies ever telling his wife anything about that night. His wife denies ever telling you anything about what her husband was supposed to have said. He could tell they were lying, but he could also tell that they were so fearful that they would never tell the truth. We talked and all we have to go on is that this fellow, Grayson, gave us all a drink out of a flask and that we all drank; including him. We know he probably didn't drink anything, but without Bender, there is nothing we can prove. Theresa, I'm angry that someone did that to my friend. I'm angry that they could have meant the same result for me and Stan, but unless we step outside of the law, there's nothing we can do, as far as bringing justice is concerned. For your sake and the children's, leave it alone. Vengeance is mine saith the Lord. Leave it in His hands. That's all we can do." He searched her eyes for agreement. He found none.

The household money was getting low, and she needed to get money to get the crew back to work, so she began the task of trying to uncover the financial structure of Grasmere. She found a box in the barn that he told her he kept for a rainy day. It had almost a thousand dollars in it. That was a lot of money, but nowhere near enough to pay a crew to work the farm. She searched for bank records and found some history, but nothing current. She knew there had to be a large bank account because he told her that he had more than enough money to last him through harvest. That's why he hadn't sought any financing over the past few years. He was doing well. Where did his money go? Neither Doc nor Stan could help her find out where the money was. He had closed his account at Stan's bank a couple of years earlier. Oh, how she wished she had listened to him and learned about how the farm ran and where the money was. She always ran from that conversation because it seemed to her like she was preparing for her husband's death, and she didn't want any parts of it. Now, unless they could find their money, they were in real trouble.

She went to Benny first and asked if he could move back home and help her keep the farm going. He wouldn't even give it any consideration. He seemed almost frightened by the prospect. His explanation was that he and Ruby were planning a life together, and neither of them wanted the life of a farmer. She always suspected that someone intimidated him into staying away from Grasmere. His response seemed selfish, and that was not his nature. He took his reasoning to his grave.

Next she turned to John. His reaction was different. He didn't think he was the right man for the job and didn't want to be the one responsible for keeping that business going; or not. He just wanted to stay where he was. He needed the money and Theresa couldn't promise him an income until the crops came in, unless the money turned up before then. He wasn't in a position to do that. He was helping Geneva, whose son had palsy and needed extra care. He kept his place and his job with the Carrigans as their all-around handyman and laborer. He did volunteer to give his sister his weekends and whatever other free time he could find.

She made arrangements with Consolidated for them to lease the land that was growing tobacco. The crop was already in the ground. She had no means to hire people to bring the crop through its complicated growing, harvesting, and curing cycles. Since they were supplying the labor and taking their mark-up on that as well, the return was far less than what George would have brought in.

She and Alice, with the children's help, did the best they could with the smaller vegetable crops. John and a few neighbors helped out as much as they could. They had very little to bring to market compared to past years.

Bills like property taxes, and insurance, and fuel, and electricity, and phone were piling up. She made what she could, and paid what she could. George's father had sent a few hundred dollars in June so she was pulling from that, and the little she had left from the money she had found after the funeral.

In late July, Nathan Richards stopped by the house. Rover had a fit, and Alice had to help Charlie and Johnnie put him in the barn to tie him up. He said he had "a grave matter to discuss" with Theresa. Just the sight of him made her extremely angry, suspecting that he probably had something to do, if even indirectly, with her husband's murder.

She subdued her emotions and sat with him on the porch. She didn't want him in her house. He had a syrupy sympathetic look on his face that she wondered if he had practiced. "Theresa, I never got the chance to speak with you personally at the funeral, so I want to first of all give you my personal condolences. George was a fine man, and I enjoyed my dealings with him. I've stayed away a while because I knew you had so much to overcome emotionally as well as with trying to keep things going here at Grasmere. There is something I must discuss with you, however. Before it gets too far out of hand, I thought now would be as good of a time as any to bring this matter to your attention."

Her heart was pounding so hard; she could feel it in her throat and hear it in her eardrums. She was extremely anxious, but she did her best to maintain a calm demeanor. "What is it?"

"I, along with The Savings Bank of Manchester, still hold a mortgage on this property, and we haven't received a payment in over six months. We had agreed with George that he would finalize his commitment in October when the crop came in, but it appears there will not be any crop of enough significance for that to happen." He was looking at her with that stupid, practiced, sympathetic look.

"Liar! You damned liar! My husband didn't owe you or nobody else no money. He hasn't had dealings with you for almost five years. It might be hard for me to see what's going on, but I ain't blind!"

She had stood up over him as she spoke. Her rage was uncaged and she lost any semblance of decorum. He put his hand over his head in the event she would strike him and quickly stood and backed down the steps. "Now, now Theresa. I can understand that you would be upset, but believe me; I have the documentation to prove my point." He reached in the breast pocket of his suit and pulled out a rather beefy looking document and folded it back and showed her George's signature, and handed it to her for closer inspection.

She took it and looked at what appeared to be her husband's signature, through tears of anger. Waving the document at him, she said "This is from 1924. That matter was settled in 1924. What are trying to pull?" He ducked as she hurled the document at him.

He bent and picked up the paper and shook the dust from it and returned it to his pocket. "I know this is a shock. We all agreed to keep the transaction a secret for a lot of reasons, but it is real. I have had compassion on your circumstances, and I will continue to be concerned, but at some point we need to at least discuss how we are going to get this matter resolved. Check George's papers. There should be a copy for you to inspect. I will be back soon and maybe then we can finish our conversation. Good day Mrs. Cohen."

Theresa was not feeling civil. "You popeyed snake! You lyin' Minnie jackameena! Don't you ever come back. Now get off my land before I let that dog out on your sorry ass! Get out!"

He gave her that sorry look again and turned and walked away. Just as he reached his car door, he heard a bark. He turned and saw Rover coming at him as fast as his old legs could carry him. Richards promptly jumped in the car and quickly slammed the door behind him. Rover stood outside his car door and put up the most ferocious display he could muster.

Alice and Johnnie and Charlie were running close behind him. They stopped when they got to the porch. Huffing from her short but brisk run, she looked up at Theresa and sheepishly said, "He got away!" The boys were laughing. Even through her anger, she couldn't help but join them. Seeing that old dog chase that man into his car was just too funny not to laugh at. Rover was still barking when Richards was long gone.

Theresa later learned that Johnnie had intentionally let the dog loose because that man was "bothering my Momma!" Alice was just as angry as Theresa when she heard what Richards was trying to do. They searched through everything they could find in the house, but could not find any paperwork from that 1924 transaction. She was beginning to suspect that someone had come and tampered with George's documents, because too many important papers that they needed to help their cause just couldn't be found. Not the least of which were his banking statements.

She called Doc Rankin, who she knew conducted more real estate transactions than almost anyone in Glastonbury, to find out if he understood what was going on. He said he would look into it. He had to get an attorney to force release of the documents for his inspection. His heart dropped when he saw what he was presented. It appears that George had signed a preliminary release from his mortgage with Richards and the Bank of Manchester, when he sold the land to Frank Ronkavitz. What the documentation said was that the return of ownership of the land to George was just temporary to allow the sale, and that George still had to make payments to finalize the release. Doc was sure that wasn't what happened, but they had all the paperwork they needed to make it stick.

He was very apologetic that the system allowed this kind of loophole if a man is not around to defend himself. Her lack of certain knowledge of the whereabouts of documents and the general flow of transactions that had sustained the business over the years left her totally vulnerable to this kind of fraud.

That afternoon, the sky grew extremely dark in the southwest. It was an ominous greenish grey darkness. She could tell it was a long way off, but it looked very threatening. She had Alice and the boys help her gather the animals into the barn. They hadn't finished long before the storm was upon them. The winds blew the rain almost horizontal to the ground at the beginning. Lightening was flashing viciously. This lasted for about fifteen minutes before the hail started. At first the hard beat of the hail sounded like harsh rain on the house, but soon it sounded as if a hundred rocks were being cast against every exposed surface. In those days, when it stormed, people disconnected their lights and appliances, shut all the windows, and everyone sat in silence in the dark as "God did His work." Johnnie's curiosity got the best of him and he darted across the parlor where they all had gathered and looked out the window. "Momma snowballs are coming down. Big ole snowballs."

"Boy, shut your mouth and get back over here and be quiet before God send a lightning bolt and strike you blind!" Johnnie bolted back across the room so fast a lightning bolt wouldn't have caught him if it had been sent. The hail was very short lived over the house, but the storm seemed to stall just to the northwest.

That night, the rain and the intermittent thunder and lightning continued long after the hail subsided. Just before she got in the bed, she looked out over that stretch of Grasmere that she and George had so often cherished as the symbol of their peace. As the lightning flashed in the distance, it illuminated the white nets in the fields Consolidated had contracted, and they were flying like curtains blowing through the window on a windy day. She knew they had taken a hit. She stood there for quite some time trying to remove the joy in her heart caused by her witnessing a degree of the Lord's vengeance on those taking advantage of a widow and her children. She asked the Lord's forgiveness, and for the first time in months, she went to sleep with a smile on her face.

The next day, Theresa got a call from Florence. She was telling her that the Hartford Courant had reported that the storm the night before had produced hail the size of chicken eggs. The damaging hail had done millions of dollars of damage to property and crops. It had especially hurt the shade tobacco industry. Not only were the nets torn and crops beaten to useless mulch, but the sheds in many areas were severely damaged. She asked how she and the children had fared. As best she could tell from the conversations she had with her neighbors, most had suffered very heavy losses in crops. She said that the Courant said that the crops in Windsor and Enfield were the worst hit. The storm had stalled over that area and they received worse hail damage there.

After inspection, Theresa found that there was some damage to the vegetables and fruit trees. The daylight confirmed that the equipment and crops of the Consolidated operation had suffered severe damage. She, once again felt a measure of vindication. She smiled again and continued in prayer. She was ashamed of her joy at their misfortune.

They spent one last Christmas at Grasmere. Theresa did all she could to make it a memorable Christmas. All their friends and Benny and John were extremely generous. The children had a very full Christmas. John hitched Buck and Ned to the sleigh and they pranced all over Grasmere as if they sensed this might be a final romp. Buck seemed to have wasted quite a bit since his master was no longer around, and he had been showing signs of his age, but not today. His big grey head was held high as he kept pace with Ned and seemed to be joyfully prancing under the weight of his master's precious cargo.

At dinner, Theresa set a place for George at the head of the table. She made him a cake and put one candle in the middle of it. After dinner, they lit the candle and sang Happy Birthday through their tears. They all circled the cake and blew out the solitary candle together.

Unbeknown to them, Richards had filed foreclosure papers the day before, on December 24, 1929. Four months later, on April 29, 1930, Richards was granted a Certificate of Foreclosure on Grasmere.

Stan Hale and Doc Rankin continued to be true friends. Theresa was given her old job as a cook at The Hale Tea House. Stan graciously gave her the free use of the duplex she and George had shared with Frank Saglio and his family when they first came to work for Hale's father, in 1911. Hale even went so far as to knock some walls out to make it one big house instead of two, so the children could all stay together.

In May they packed all their belongings. They had to leave Buck and Ned and the rest of the livestock behind, except Rover. Richards didn't want any parts of Rover. Benny drove the truck for several trips that day as they moved from Oak Street back to the Hale workers' quarters.

One day, shortly after they had moved in, Theresa was getting off work late, and as she stepped into the darkness that awaited her outside of the back door, there stood the biggest German Shepherd dog she had ever seen. She quickly stepped back in the door, and closed it tight. "Lord have mercy! That's the biggest dog I ever seen." She whispered to herself. After a few seconds, she got up the nerve to peek out to see if he was still there. She re-opened the door slightly and he was still standing there with his tail wagging and looking like he wanted to play. She stuck her head out the door and said, "Gwine dog! Go on now dog. Git!" He dropped to his front forearms with his hind quarters high and his tail wagging as if waiting to fetch a ball. He stood up and danced in a circle a couple of times, then tipped his head with his big ears standing at attention and just looked at her with his tongue lolling out of his mouth. He seemed friendly enough so she gingerly stepped outside. He ducked his head in a very submissive posture and slowly walked to her, all the while wagging his tail. She reached out and rubbed his head and he leaned his considerable weight against her and lifted his head to look at her. She petted him for a few seconds and then told him to go on home. He started walking slowly ahead of her. He seemed to be going her way. To her amazement, the big dog led her right to her front door. The fear she usually had going down that long dark road that led from the street to her house in back was not there this night. When she got to her front door, Rover must have smelled him coming because as soon as she opened the door, he came barreling out. She thought there was going to be a fight, seeing as how another male was invading Rover's territory. They sniffed each other and both began wagging their tails!

Every night, this dog would lead her home. The children named him Pete. Pete also walked the children home from school, but every night, he was outside that door waiting to walk Theresa home. Alice thought George's spirit had returned in the dog to protect them because he loved them so much.

They had been there a little over a year when Stancliffe Hale died on August 27, 1931. He had been getting progressively worse since about mid-year 1929. He had been elected Chairman of The Town Planning Committee at the meeting on June 1, 1929, three days after the nominating meeting George had attended. When he died, Addie made plans to move to West Hartford with her sister, and Ida wanted to move to a smaller house. They decided that something different would be done with the property the Cohen family was living in. Theresa's cousin, Aunt Amy's daughter, Arie, told her that there was an opening working for a head cook's job, and it would put her in close proximity to a lot of her cousins who had moved to Hartford over the years, many of whom had used Grasmere as a staging place for their transition from the rural south to the industrialized Hartford region. She got the job and gave her two weeks notice to Ida. Her friends in Glastonbury were happy that she was moving into a situation where there would be a lot of family support.

Two days later, Pete was killed by a car on his way to meet her at her job. The children mourned until the excitement of moving to the big city let them divert their focus, but Pete lives on in the family folklore, even to this day.

When they were leaving the Hale homestead for the last time, Theresa asked Benny to take her over to The Greens Cemetery. Alice looked at her sister. "Pank, do ya really thank ya should be gittin' all sad taday?" She just nodded.

He parked as close to his father's grave as he could. Theresa stepped out of the car and leaned back in. "I just want to talk to my husband before we go so far away. I won't be able to come as often as I do now. Benny, pull up a ways. I want to be alone with your father for a while."

Benny understood.

She walked slowly to his grave and knelt down in the coolness of the still damp grass. She patted the ground where she thought his heart might be and smiled a sad smile. "Son, I know Jesus has told you what's going on. I know our spirits can still hug each other, even though this cruel ground separates me from your arms. I am about to leave the life we knew together to find a way for me and our children. I'm not here to say good-bye, but I am here to say that I love you, and that I'll miss the time I am able to spend here with you. I will get here as much as I can, but it will be harder to get here. I know the best part of us, the part that lives in my heart, will be with me wherever I am, no matter where I go. I want you to know that my love for you will never change, and it doesn't depend on how often I can get here.

"Son, I am so sorry that I wasn't able to hold on to our dream. I should've listened to you, but it just scared me so much when you started talking about us going on without you. It's so hard. I miss you so much. I need you so much."

Lucy misses you a lot. So do all the kids, but especially her. Your boys are little warriors and they watch out for us. Nellie always watches me to make sure I'm okay. Lil and Von are two beautiful little girls. They will all know Jesus. I'll make sure of that. I'll teach them to honor their name and to love their family."

"I tried the best I could to find justice for you Son, but they just threw up blocks and covered their tracks every way I turned, but I won't never let it rest. Even if our grandchildren are still searching long after I'm layin' here next to you; right here below the spot I'm kneeling on. We'll get justice. In the name of Jesus, we won't let this slip into the shadows of our memories."

She was sobbing by this time. She smiled and patted the ground above his heart again. "We had a wonderful life together. We were so blessed to have someone in our life who loved us much as we loved them back. I still feel your arms around me, and that's how I always want to feel. If there's a way you can come visit me sometimes; come on. If there is a way, I know you'll find it. I remember that cold breeze that kissed my cheek the night your spirit went home. I remember the weay Buck showed out on that sleigh ride on your birthday. And I know you were hiding in Pete. I will look for you in every child born to this family, in every breeze that kisses my cheek; in every sunset that blesses my eyes.

"I won't let your children forget you. Not just that you lived, but how well you lived, and how much you loved them, and how much you wanted for them.

Well, my Son, I just spoke some of my heart, but there ain't enough time to speak it all. The most important thing I want to say to you is something you always knew; I love you more than I can say with words."

Before she stood, she once again patted the place where she thought his heart might be. It was wet from her tears. She rubbed them well into the grass. He would like that. She stood up and looked down and sighed deeply and said "I'll tell your children and your grandchildren and your great grandchildren about our Grasmere. I'll tell them about you. I'll tell them about the prayers you prayed for them. I promise, Son, I'll be back, and they will come with me to pay honor to you. And Son, until I come back that one last time to lay down beside you, my memories of you; my love for you; the love we shared; you will always be my sunshine on this long, dark, cloudy day!" She turned and bowed her head, and did not look back as she slowly walked away, into her new life.

Epilogue

Theresa "Pinky" Cohen lived another 57½ years after George went home; just long enough to endure just one last birthday without him. She reunited with her beloved "Son" on December 26, 1986.

Benny Cohen lived 84 years and died in Hartford, CT on August 20, 1992.

John Kayrockus Fantroy Cohen (no firm records exist of his birth and death dates) He was around 60 when he died in Hartford, CT in 1967.

Lucy Green is alive and well and is living in Middletown, CT.

Charles Cohen lived 72 years and died in Bloomfield, CT on April 6, 1994.

Nellie Cohen Wright is alive and well in Bloomfield, CT.

Johnnie Cohen lived 72 years and died in Hartford, CT on December 3, 1996.

Lillian Polite is alive and well and living in Bloomfield, CT.

Yvonne Goode Satterfield lived 80 years and died in Bloomfield, CT on December 20, 2008.

Both Stancliffe Hale and Doctor Charles Rankin became ill after that May 29, 1929 meeting and never fully recovered.

Stancliffe Hale died on August 27, 1931. He became ill shortly after that May 29, 1929 meeting and never fully recovered.

Charles Rankin died on August 12, 1934. He became ill shortly after that May 29, 1929 meeting and never fully recovered.

Nathan Richards frequently 'checked-in' on the Cohen family after they moved to Hartford; all the while insisting to the probate courts that the family could not be found.

After 'no knowledge' of the whereabouts of the Cohen family, on July 10, 1969, 3 parcels of land were awarded in a statute of limitations judgment for abandoned properties previously owned by George Washington and Theresa Cohen. At the time, Theresa Cohen and all seven of the Cohen children were living in the greater Hartford area, as they had been since leaving Glastonbury in 1931.

About the Author

Chuck Goode was born in Hartford, CT, in 1949, into a working class family that put great value on the importance of bringing honor to God and family. Influenced by a strong father, a loving

mother, and an encouraging family, Chuck was able to navigate through the pitfalls and traps that ensnare so many in the inner-city. He showed creative gifts at an early age.

An excellent student and athlete, he received many scholarship offers from universities throughout the country, but he cherished UConn. It was also the best opportunity to stay connected to his family.

Family has always been a key element in his life, and a primary consideration in many of his life decisions. He and his wife, Cleta, are blessed with 4 children and 10 grandchildren. Though now residing in Virginia Beach, they love to gather at the old homestead, in Bloomfield, CT, where he still has a large and close knit extended family.

Over the years, as his relationship with God grew, his writing became more inspired by revelations from The Spirit, and his deep love for his family. Most of his work involves Godly encouragement, and many of his works were birthed in creating greeting cards and tributes for his family. He is the President of Goode God Greetings. (www.goodegodgreetings.com)

In 2011, he completed an epic novel, "Our Season in Grasmere". It has since been published as two novels: "Prepare for Us a Season" and "Our Season in Grasmere". Chuck formulated his publishing company, Goode God Publishing, and published his first book, "Whispers Just Before Dawn", an anthology of poems, essays, and letters, in 2013.